in on the action

SEDUCING STEEL CITY
BOOK 2

ELLE DIAZ

Copyright © 2024 by Elle Diaz

All rights reserved.

No part of this book may be reproduced in any form or by any electronic or mechanical means, including information storage and retrieval systems, without written permission from the author, except for the use of brief quotations in a book review.

This is a work of fiction. Names, characters, businesses, places, events and incidents are either the products of the author's imagination or used in a fictitious manner. Any resemblance to actual persons, living or dead, or actual events is purely coincidental.

Cover design by Elle Diaz

For Meg, Deanna and Molly –
The real Witches and Bitches.
And for Brittany, my favorite jock.

before you start reading

This book contains:

- Mentions of disordered eating (orthorexia and extreme dieting) and related health issues, with character in recovery
- Specific mentions of body composition related to fitness and bikini competitions
- Depictions of a character dealing with an anxiety disorder
- Sexual harassment/catcalling
- Brief mentions of physical violence against a harasser
- Brief mentions of homophobia and transphobia
- Brief mentions of drug use

Heat Level: Open door with descriptive, explicit imagery

Disclaimer: All stunts described (including any involving yoga swings) are done by fictional trained professionals and not meant to be instructional.

one

I vy Lowell knew how to take a punch. She could roll out of a burning car after a high-speed chase, duel with a sword, and land in a perfect crouch from a wired backflip above a green-screen set.

She was used to taking calculated risks during her decade-long career as a Hollywood stunt performer. She'd made her name that way. Then she made her money in personal training, working with celebrities willing to suffer and pay for a superhero film physique. Ivy had a big break when a film she'd worked on became a surprise hit. Four *Aurora Dagger* films and some lucky investments later, she pointed her new luxury sedan east and headed home to Pittsburgh to open a gym.

That was five years ago. Every calculated risk had paid off and she was thriving in her second act as a business owner. Nothing scared her.

Except for Analeigh.

Analeigh Fonseca, the luscious owner of Besos Bakery who Ivy had been crushing on for more than a year. Analeigh, whose apple pie haunted her dreams and who made a Kouign-Amann worth killing for. Analeigh, who had the most adorable smile and an absolutely criminal ass, who stood at 5-foot-nothing and had no right to be so damn terrifying.

Analeigh, who was walking toward her table with a coffee pot.

"Top you off?" Ana asked, bright as a bell.

Ivy held out her mug, careful to keep her hand steady as Ana poured. Since she'd started coming here, she noticed Ana would leave the kitchen every day at 8:45 a.m., grab the coffee pot, and go around making small talk with the regulars. Ivy started coming almost every day for breakfast — it was close to the gym. Then she started coming for lunch, or right before closing. The small talk during coffee refills turned into longer chats when the bakery was empty, while Ana polished stand mixers and disinfected counters.

She'd once done the type of stunts that would make The Most Interesting Man In the World promptly close his bar tab, bowing to the superior adventurer. Now she got her thrills from Analeigh acknowledging her. Valentino gowns worn while rappelling down a building were sexy, sure, but not nearly as hot as Ana's chef whites.

Ivy's crush was persistent, but it was something she'd never pursue seriously. She was just a customer who Ana happened to be more chatty with sometimes. That was all. Did Ana flirt with everyone? Maybe. Maybe she couldn't help but be bubbly and charming.

"Nice ears," Ivy said.

Ana's chocolate eyes sparkled. "This is the most I'm willing to dress up for the holiday," she said, adjusting the black sequined cat ear headband. "At least at work. But that reminds me." She reached into her apron pocket and pulled out a cellophane-wrapped cookie, the package embellished with Besos's signature kiss-print white and red ribbon. "I saved this one for you."

Ivy took the treat. It was a rectangular sugar cookie that fit in her palm. The cookie was iced to look like a comic book panel, with a minimalist cityscape in the background and a tiny heroine in the foreground. The green and blue emblem and matching cape were unmistakable — Ivy had worn the real thing countless times, when she was the stunt double behind the beloved superheroine Aurora Dagger.

"How," Ivy started, trying to find her words, "do you expect me to eat this? I want to frame it. Analeigh!"

"You're welcome. And you're better off taking a picture. My cookies are too good not to eat."

Just like you, Ivy thought. "Thank you. How much do I owe you?"

"Don't even think about it," Analeigh said. "It's a Halloween present."

"You don't give presents for Halloween."

"Then what's the 'treat' part in trick or treat?"

"Good point," Ivy conceded. "So, you got any plans?" Halloween fell on a weekday, so every bar in town had declared the Saturday before as the night to dress up and party down.

"Eh, I don't know. I did get invited out by some friends, but I'm pretty worn out, and I'd have to whip up a costume. How about you?"

"I'll be bar-hopping on the South Side."

Ana put a teasing hand on Ivy's shoulder. Her nails were bare and neatly trimmed. Ivy loved to watch them as Ana quickly arranged and rearranged trays in the display cases, her movements elegant and confident. "To sign autographs?"

"Oh my god, stop!" Ivy knew she was blushing her freckles right off her face, even though Ana was just teasing. She was used to being peppered with questions about her time in the entertainment industry. It was fine talking about it with her close friends, who she knew liked her for Ivy, not for her Hollywood bona fides. But it was exhausting to talk about it with every single person she met. There was a glamorous side to it, of course, but stunts were just another job. There were bad bosses and gossipy coworkers, and cool people you'd go out to drinks with sometimes, just like with any job.

But in the conversations they'd had at the bakery, Ana didn't ask many questions about the celebrities. She asked which projects had been her favorites to work on (ones involving wire work), or which stunts had made her nervous (anything involving fire or driving). One night, when they were the last two people at the bakery, Ana asked her what the best dessert she'd ever had was.

"Aside from everything here?" Ivy asked.

Ana blushed. "Yes, aside from that."

"The honey buns at craft services on the first movie I was an extra in. I could barely afford canned soup back then, so it was the most decadent thing I'd eaten in a while."

The next day, there had been a row of glistening, thick honey buns prominently displayed in the pastry case. If Ivy kept a diary, she would have written a lot of exclamation points for that day.

"Thank you for this," Ivy said now, admiring the cookie again. "This is really sweet."

"You're welcome." She leaned ever so slightly forward — not quite within the personal space bubble, but right on the edge of popping it — and whispered, "Something special for my favorite regular."

Ana flipped her thick brown ponytail off her shoulder, and Ivy wished she could ball it up in her fist.

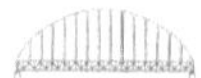

The Fool — *A new beginning. There's no telling where you'll land. The only guarantee is that you'll fall.*

Ingredient — *This card makes me think of mint, good for making that money and for new things growing. Also, lust, apparently? At least that's what* Cunningham's Encyclopedia of Magical Herbs *says. I guess money does make me horny.*

If you asked her, Analeigh would say she didn't perform love spells. But if you looked closer, you could make the argument that so much of her witchcraft practice revolved around the thing she loved most — baking. So perhaps, really, everything she baked was a love spell. Her pure happiness at bringing joy to people who ate her food went into every loaf of bread and perfectly piped icing flower. It was the unseen ingredient in every batch of meringues she made, meringues she'd perfected because she loved the ones she'd get with her grandfather when she was a kid.

Intention was powerful in spellwork. That's why whenever Ana baked something that she knew she was setting aside for the tall, muscular blonde who frequented her bakery, she tried to keep her mind totally blank. No stirring her longing into the buttercream. No charging the cinnamon in the crumb topping of Ivy's favorite blueberry muffin with her lust. No love spells for her.

Though she could not give herself too much credit for witchy ethics. She knew the way Ivy looked at her, saw the glint in her blue eyes when she walked her way and felt that gaze on her when she watched her leave. She didn't need a love spell.

What she needed was some courage to make a move.

Scratch that. What she really needed was a life with even an hour she could devote to a date.

She'd worked late at the bakery again. How often could she call it "working late" when it was what she did every day for the past two years that she'd been running the place?

It was hard tearing herself away. Besos was her baby. Even though she'd hired excellent staff and trusted them to do things the right way, she still worried that if she wasn't there involved in every step, someone would fuck up and burn down the dream she'd sunk all her savings into.

She felt bereft every time she left her baby in someone else's care.

Ana walked into her small apartment and tossed her purse onto the bench that wrapped around her corner dining table. A shelf in the kitchen served as her ancestor altar. She liked to think her dead were watching over her as she cooked.

She lit the candle on the shelf and fixed up a plate with the guava thumbprint cookies she'd sprinkled powdered sugar on just before leaving work.

"Te extraño tanto, abuelito," she said as she reverently arranged the cookies in front of the black and white photos of her known relatives who had passed, including her beloved grandfather.

"What are you going to do when the dead talk back?" her sister's voice said.

Ana was used to her baby sister trying to startle her. That was the only reason she didn't scream in terror.

"They're welcome to," Ana said, rounding the corner into the living room. "I've invited them in. They wouldn't just be dropping by unannounced."

Ari ignored the dig. "If they do, tell them I said hi."

Ana heard the washing machine. "I hope you brought some detergent, Aracely, because I'm almost out." Ari was 19, six years younger than Ana, and Ana always called her by her full first name when she exploited their age difference to mom her.

"Yeah, I've got you. And don't worry, I made sure to get the fragrance-free stuff this time," Ari said. "Did you bring any snacks?"

"Did you bring any homework?" Ana retorted.

"I finished an essay while I waited for you," Ari said. She stretched luxuriously on Ana's couch. Ana shoved her feet aside to make room. "I really thought things would get more challenging once I was into my major coursework, but college is still so much easier than high school," Ari continued, putting her feet on Analeigh's lap.

"I wouldn't know," Ana said. She'd been working in food service since she was 16. After high school, she'd gone right into working full-time in kitchens — as a server, a prep cook, a line cook, any job she could get. She saved as much as she could as she worked her way up from humble diners to being mentored by a legendary pastry chef at a five-star hotel. The hours had been inhuman, but the exhaustion and sleeplessness had been worth it when she could finally afford to open her own place. "How do empanadas sound?" she said as she searched through the fridge.

"Actually," Ari said, "I can't stay long. Can I borrow your red jacket? You're not wearing it tonight, are you?"

"Sure, you can borrow it. I'm not going out."

"What?" Ari looked affronted. "Isn't Halloween, like, your high holy day or whatever?"

Analeigh wasn't bothered that her culturally Catholic family (that celebrated Mass only at Easter) considered her paganism to be a novel little hobby. She did wish that she had planned something special for Samhain. The previous year, she and her witchy friends had taken advantage of Halloween and the thinning veil between the worlds to perform a ritual. To remember their dead, each person made something in honor of an ancestor and presented it as an offering to gain that ancestor's blessing. They told stories about their family members and friends who had passed, and Ana left feeling deeply connected to something bigger than her.

That was what she loved about witchcraft. It didn't matter to her if she was actually influencing the energies around her, bending them to do her will. She liked thinking about how things were interwoven. That's how she saw people, community. She liked influencing what she could and believing it would have some net positive effect on the whole.

This year, the coven was just going to go bar-hopping, and wait until the New Moon for their next magical meetup. Even though it wouldn't be the same sort of magical energy, Ana still wished she felt excited about going. It was a testament that she was only getting busier at work, not getting better at balancing things.

"I mean, yeah, I got invited out, but I don't have a costume. And I'm so exhausted. I was honestly just going to shower then scroll on TikTok until I pass out."

She couldn't remember the last time she wasn't exhausted. She'd been running on fumes for years, it seemed, but things were especially bad now, when people were starting to put in holiday orders. She was too tired for most things these days, working the hours that she did.

"No, sorry, that's just not acceptable. For one thing, your fairy godstylist is here," Ari said. "Plus, I put on a pot of coffee. And I made it strong, so being tired is not going to be a problem."

Ana realized that she wasn't going to win this. Her sister had always been the more outgoing of the two, the one who managed to work just as hard in her studies as Ana did in her career without ever stressing.

She surveyed her sister's outfit for the first time. "And what are you going as?"

"Raven Reyes!" Ari said. "You know, from *The 100?*"

Ana had watched the first couple of seasons and knew about the clever mechanic who refurbished a spaceship and flew down to Earth in the dystopian teen drama. "That's cute. No one's going to get it, though."

"Cool people will. Now come on. Let's figure out a costume so you can go out with your little coven tonight."

The red faux leather gloves their mom had gotten Analeigh for Christmas were enough inspiration for Ari. They were wrist-length, not elbow-length, "But you're going to wear long sleeves anyway." Ana's plush white bathrobe, which thankfully was in the clean hamper, would have to do for the fur coat. Dry shampoo plus flour hadn't worked the way they'd hoped for the hair, so they ended up making a quick detour at the party store for white hair paint and a faux cigarette holder.

Ana's own black dress, red heels and red lipstick completed the look.

"OK, but I love dogs!" Ana moaned for the fifth time. "People are going to think I'm a monster."

"It's just a costume," Ari said. "Do you know how many dudes you're going to see tonight dressed like Jason?"

"And they're probably serial killers!"

Ari grimaced, considering it. "Come on. That's … statistically unlikely. Very few people meet the psychological profile. Plus, you look hot. You're going to have bitches crawling all over you."

"That's the cringiest thing you've ever said." Ana sighed. "OK. I do look hot, at least."

"There you go! My work here is done. Now," Ari said, grabbing her backpack, "if we run into each other and you see me doing a row of shots, no you didn't."

Ana wasn't worried about that. The South Side was always so crowded that even if they did end up at the same bar, they probably would miss each other.

"Just don't leave your drinks unattended and make sure the car you get into is actually your Lyft, OK? Ask them who they're picking up and double check the license plate. And send me a link to your trip."

"Don't worry about me so much!" Ari said. She grabbed her sister by the shoulders. "Try to have fun tonight. You work your ass off. You deserve a break."

Her sister hugged her before leaving. Ana realized Aracely had never put her clothes in the dryer. The brat. That meant Ana was stuck doing it when she got back if she didn't want her washer getting mildewy.

She really did deserve a break.

She texted one of her friends after she ordered her ride.

two

I want someone who knows how to have a good time, but doesn't go overboard.

"I hate you guys so much right now."

"Leave me out of this," said Zach, his arms around the waist of Ivy's friend Camila. His voice was muffled under his Kylo Ren helmet. "I tried to talk them out of it."

"Not me, I encouraged it," said Seth, who was married to their friend Era. He had one arm around his wife, and the other around the plush baby Grogu that completed his Mandalorian costume.

While the two men had surprisingly not coordinated their costumes, the other three people across from her at the bar had.

"Come on, Ivy," Camila said. "It's an homage!"

"People are going to think I put you up to this," Ivy whined. "It's so … cheugy! Ugh, at least Rahul's costume is generic enough to be related to something else."

"Excuse you, there's nothing 'generic' about me in this tux,"

Rahul, her friend and employee, said. "And no one says cheugy anymore, gran."

Era, Camila and Rahul had dressed as Aurora Dagger — whose delicious likeness Ivy had consumed that day — her sidekick, Hyperbole, and their technical support, Mr. Thorn, respectively. It was the cutest and most obnoxious thing her friends had ever done, and she was equal parts delighted and mortified.

"Your costume is incredible. No one is even going to recognize you and put those pieces together," Era said.

And it was true that Ivy's Evil Queen costume was spectacular. Ivy may have called in a favor and borrowed one of the original costumes from the actress who played Snow White's wicked stepmonster on TV. A good push-up bra, some dramatic fake lashes and a perfectly laid lace front wig, and boom. She pulled a black cat hair from her grouchy little Sigourney off her sleeve. The cat seemed to enjoy her better when she was dressed as a villainess than in her usual athleisure, as if a corset and leather were cuddlier than cotton leggings and sweat-wicking half-zips. Maybe the ancient witch who had likely been cursed into her cat's form liked this getup for herself.

"Fine, you're right," she conceded. "OK, let's take a picture, since I know you're dying to."

"Allow me," said Zach. He pulled an attachment out from under his robe and added it to his lightsaber.

"Dude, is your lightsaber a selfie stick?" Seth asked in awe.

"Jesus," Rahul said. "You two are too much. I can't imagine the type of role playing you all get up to," he said, nodding toward both couples.

Era hissed, "Babe, that's supposed to be private" to Seth. Camila cackled.

"I don't know about Era and Seth, but let's just say Zach has made me a Reylo shipper through and through," Camila said.

"Can we please take the damn picture?" Ivy asked.

She wasn't really angry, of course. She loved these people an unreasonable amount. When she'd first moved to Los Angeles what felt like a lifetime ago, she'd found a community. Everyone she knew had been struggling — Ivy at times more than others, before she got her "big break" — but they all helped each other. Those days were defined by friends taking turns cooking dinner for the group, chipping in when someone was short on rent, or doing someone's hair so they looked good for a self-tape. That stayed with Ivy.

When her career took off, she spent a lot more time traveling and lost that sense of community.

That was part of why she'd moved back to Pittsburgh when she retired from stunt work. She'd hoped she could find that sense of community again.

She was so grateful that she did.

On the other side of the bar and unaware of the Star Wars/*Once Upon A Time*/Aurora Dagger crossover, Analeigh was knocking back the yellow shooter in her row of rainbow shots. She wanted to pace herself, but the yellow had a gross artificial pineapple flavor that she needed to wash away with green immediately.

She should have known it would be madness on the South Side tonight, but it was so much worse than she'd anticipated and her anxiety immediately made her want to take the edge off. She'd started to spiral because she couldn't remember whether she'd taken her meds today, but she was now too tipsy to worry about it.

"Holy shit, Analeigh! I've never seen you drink more than a glass of wine," Stacy said.

Ana took off a glove and wiped her mouth with the back of her hand after drinking the blue. She rubbed the lipstick smear in like it was lotion. "Do you think I'm boring?" she yelled back at her friend at a volume that was too much even for the loud club.

"No way, I think you're so fun. I mean, you work a lot, but you're just ambitious," Stacy said.

Ana pouted. "You're ambitious *and* you're fun. You work a lot *and* you go out." She waved her hand in the general direction of Stacy's getup, which wasn't a costume so much as an assortment of latex that she was sure had already been in Stacy's closet. She had on a corseted catsuit with a scandalously plunging neckline, and a hooded harness that covered her asymmetrical pixie cut.

"Yeah, but I'm a graphic designer who makes her own hours. You're running a fledgling pastry empire." She snatched the indigo shooter out of Ana's hand and downed it herself.

They'd gotten separated from the rest of their group. They weren't really a coven like Ari had called them. When Ana first started dabbling in witchcraft, she went to a pagan meetup where she hit it off with Stacy. Stacy had been brought up by a single mom who was a practitioner. She learned how to read a natal chart and which herbs were good in prosperity workings right around the time she read her first chapter book. Ana was the babiest of baby witches when they met, but they still bonded over fiction and music, and a deep appreciation for cake. Before Ana knew it, she had been adopted into Stacy's weird and wonderful friend group of occultists and tarot readers and devotees of ancient gods.

There was Jane, who wore preppy suits to work at the mayor's office and had a full-back tattoo of the Norse god Odin; Maggie, a bar owner who settled all their arguments over where to have dinner with her pendulum; and Harper, who practiced planetary magick and whose Leo new moon spell doubled Besos's social media following overnight.

Ana hadn't spent much time with any of them recently. She kept moving the goalposts for the bakery. Things will be less crazy after our soft opening, she said. Things will settle down after the holidays, she said. Things will calm down once I hire another part-timer, she said.

She'd swear she just had to get through the week, and she'd been swearing that every week for years.

"OK, let's get you to the bathroom and touch up that lipstick, yeah?" Stacy said, pulling Ana by the hand.

"But I didn't finish ROY G BIV!"

Stacy downed the violet shot for her and put $20 on the counter. "You see her?" she asked the bartender as she dragged Ana by her sleeve. "Soda water the rest of the night. Got it?"

"Boo! Boooooo!" Ana bellowed.

"I'm so happy you're actually out, but I don't want you puking all over yourself. So don't make me drag you to your house and put you in your jammies. Because then that'll just end my night, because I really want to hang out with you, and not while watching reruns of *The Office*. But I will do it if I have to."

Ana tightened her bathrobe belt in a huff and followed Stacy.

Once she'd peed, reapplied her lipstick and let cold water run on her wrists, Ana felt — well, definitely not sober, but a little bit more on this earth than she had out in the bar.

She was fixing the corners of her mouth when a familiar Black woman, wearing a familiar costume, walked in.

"Era?"

The woman she'd baked a wedding cake for over the summer pushed a braid away from her eye. Her hair was tinted in the signature blue of Aurora Dagger's wig.

It took a few moments for recognition to arrive. "Analeigh?"

They exchanged what Analeigh had come to consider a "business casual hug." She introduced Era and Stacy, and they moved aside for another patron to wash her hands.

"Did Ivy put you up to dressing like her?"

Era scoffed. "Oh no, she's pissed. What about you? What are you supposed to be?"

Ana hummed a few bars from the animated movie.

"Cruella! Nice! That's so funny — you have to see Ivy's costume now. You kinda match."

"Is she — is she here?"

"Yeah, come on, we're here with a few people."

Ana suddenly felt sickeningly sober.

Her legs felt as fragile as pulled sugar ribbons as Era led them through the crowd. She was a creature of routine. She had never seen Ivy outside of a work context. She'd caught a glimpse of her during Era's wedding, when Analeigh was setting up the cake, but Ivy had been talking to one of the groomsmen and had her back to her. She hadn't even known Ana was there.

"Look who I found," Era said to the group.

Ivy turned. Her eyes glistened with the shine of tipsiness. Her lips were glossy and red as fresh blood. And that dress showed a delectable slice of cleavage and collarbone iced with body shimmer Ana wanted to get all over her.

She looked Ana up and down through long lashes tipped in tiny rhinestones.

"You make one hell of a villain," Ivy said.

"Likewise." And here was her opportunity. She might not get another chance to shoot her shot, when they weren't in Ana's place of work as customer and proprietor, and when Ana was drunk enough to not care regardless.

"You wanna dance?"

Ivy finished the drink in her hand and set it down. "I very much do."

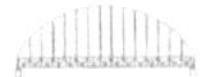

Ivy knew that two bodies moving together always involved choreography. It didn't matter if all the steps are planned in advance like when Ivy coordinated stunts, or negotiated in real time on a dance floor. There was a longer than usual length of eye contact that invited Ivy two steps forward, a precise tilt of the chin that urged a change of angle.

Each time the strobing lights sliced through the darkness, Ivy and Analeigh were closer, as if using each other's bodies to avoid stumbling. They were a flip book animation of two planets orbiting each other, making the circle smaller and smaller until they were one point of light in the sky.

Ivy danced across from Ana for one song, then wrapped an arm around her waist on the second. By the third, she had her nose and chin and the barest whisper of her lips under the collar of that ridiculously fluffy bathrobe. In her wildest dreams, Ana's collarbone would smell like caramel and cinnamon sugar.

Surely she was dreaming.

"I need water," Ana panted, lifting onto the balls of her feet to talk — well, yell — into her ear.

Ivy nodded and squeezed tighter when Ana grabbed her hand and pulled her toward the bar. Oh, this was bad of her. Ivy was at least a decade Ana's senior. She was too young, too pretty, too ambitious. Too much like every model and actress Ivy had given her heart to only to have it stabbed clean through with Louboutin heels.

She was two seconds away from shoving an ice cube into her cleavage. It was a trick Camila, who was a therapist, had taught her for anxiety. Surely it would cool her down enough to prevent her from doing something stupid.

"What are you drinking?" Ana shouted.

"Scotch on the rocks," Ivy told the bartender. "Put whatever she's drinking on my tab."

"No way, I can get this."

"Don't worry, I've got it," Ivy said. She winked at the bartender. Somehow, flirting with the bartender who was dressed like a cheerleader from hell made her less nervous. Ivy may have been an old-ass millennial, but she still had it.

"Scotch — so fancy," Ana said. "It's like a rich white grandpa drink."

Aaaaand there went Ivy's confidence.

"What did you get?" Ivy asked.

In answer, the bartender slid two shot glasses across the bar. They were topped with whipped cream.

Ana giggled as she handed Ivy one of them. "It's a blowjob," she said. "It's funny because I've never given one."

Ivy cringed. "I have, unfortunately."

Ana's big brown eyes got even wider. Ivy shrugged.

"I had to be sure, I guess," she said. "Cheers."

They clinked shot glasses and Ivy downed the creamy coffee liqueur. Ana met her eyes when she wiped a bit of whipped cream off the corner of her lips.

"Did I get it all?" she asked.

"Unfortunately," Ivy said.

"You've got a lot of unfortunatelys tonight," Ana said. She didn't say it so much as slurred it. Now that Ivy got a good look, she was looking a little wobbly on those heels.

"I see a booth that just vacated. Run."

They beat a mermaid and a pirate to the table, their voluminous costumes somehow not slowing them down much. Clearly emboldened by the booze, Ana sat next to Ivy instead of across from her. Ivy felt much like she did after a jump — giddy, like she could do the stunt in reverse and levitate back up.

"Can I taste your scotch?" Ana asked.

Ivy slid the glass over.

"That's not what I meant," Ana said, pouting.

Ivy slid over a glass of water. "This too," she said.

There was so much going through Ivy's mind right now. This all felt too impossibly good to be real. At any moment someone was going to yell "Cut!"

Glazed eyes fixed on her, Ana first took a big gulp of the water, then a torturous, slow slip of the scotch. She licked her full bottom lip, taking more of the faded red lipstick with her. Ivy wanted to finish the job. But she was sober enough to play the tape all the way through, to consider the possibility of rejection, or how awkward their next interaction outside this liminal space would be if she made a move. As tough as Ivy was on the outside, her feelings had been hurt by girl after girl after girl over the years.

Ana leaned in close. "That was tasty. Can I have a little more?"

Well. Ivy was no longer responsible for her actions, not when Analeigh's lips were, if you were being charitable, two inches away from hers. She wrapped her hand around her hair, like she'd wanted to so many times.

But hold on. It wasn't like Ivy was the only one who could be hurt in this situation. If they were to, say, start making out at this table, and then if Ivy were to feel her up a little in the bathroom, and then take her home to wear her pussy on her hand like Ana was wearing those red gloves, would she see it as a one-time thing, or would she get attached? And then there was the matter of how much she'd had to drink. She wasn't doing anything until Ana sobered up.

She didn't get a chance to wait that out.

"Daaaaaaamn."

A *man* had infiltrated their moment, sliding into the seat across from them. "I didn't know there'd be a show tonight, I didn't even get a wristband."

"Do you mind?" Ivy asked.

"Not at all," the dude said, chugging from his beer. He was dressed — quite tastelessly and cheaply, she'd say — as the zombie version of a recently deceased celebrity, and he was leering at them in a way that made her stomach turn.

"Can you please fuck off?" Analeigh said.

"Relax, baby," he said. Then, looking her up and down and no doubt clocking her features, said, "*Chica*," and laughed like he was watching the headliner of a Netflix comedy special.

"OK, you need to leave right now," Ivy said. She didn't even feel threatened or uncomfortable, just annoyed. Not only was this guy cuntblocking her, but she despised when men treated queer women just existing as their entertainment. It immediately put her on high alert.

"Come on, don't be so uptight." He gave Ana another lewd look. "Cruella! I'd let you drag me by a leash." And then he — hand on the Bible — *panted* like a dog.

Ivy had enough. "Come on, let's go find our friends," Ivy said, pushing Ana away from the table. Ana looked like she was about to lose it on the guy, so she hurried her along.

Walking forward a bit, Ivy spotted Era across the club. "Come on, everyone's over there," she said. She tried to keep hold of Ana's hand as they walked through the crowd, but Ana wriggled away. She waited a second too long to turn around and make sure she was still following her, and discovered that Analeigh was gone.

She swore.

Had the crowd doubled in the last minute? She pushed past people, lapping the perimeter trying to spot Ana. She tried the bathroom. No Ana to be found. It wasn't like she had her phone number or anything. Panicking, she did another turn around the room before heading outside.

Her relief to see Ana there on the sidewalk vanished when she saw the gross dude who had cornered them confronting her.

"Stay away," she heard Ana said. She was clearly distressed, but the few people smoking outside the nightclub weren't intervening.

"Come on, chica, you just need a real man." He grabbed Ana's arms. Ana tried to push him away, but he pulled her closer.

Ivy leapt into action. Coming up behind the gross bastard, she wrapped her arms across the front of his chest, using downward momentum to pry his arms from Ana. Then with some effort — the Evil Queen favored leggings under a high-low gown, but there was still quite a bit of fabric to avoid getting tangled in — she wound one leg around him (ew ew ew) and used her body weight to spin him onto the ground.

Ana took a stumbling step back to watch the scene. Ivy had the guy pinned down by his shoulders. Her intention wasn't to hurt him, just get him off Ana and give him reason to stay away. So much of her stunt training had been around safety, and her self-defense training emphasized the least use of force possible against an assailant.

She was vaguely aware of people busting out their phones to take video. "Would have been nice if one of you had helped her," she snarled. "Put those phones away or I'll do to them worse than I did to him."

The phones were quickly pocketed.

"As for you," she said to the dickhead zombie, who she was restraining by the shoulders without obstructing anything vital, "the next time you think of touching a woman without her consent, know that the people you least expect would happily step in and break every one of your fingers." It was an empty threat, but she grabbed his hand and pushed his thumb back just enough to get the message across. "Got it?"

"I've got it!" he whimpered. "Let me go!"

She obliged. She walked up to Ana and gingerly touched her arms. "Are you OK?"

The jerk had stumbled onto his feet and regained just enough nerve to hurl a slur at them.

So Ivy punched him in the mouth.

Ana gasped. Her hands flew to her mouth.

Ivy watched as a latex-clad woman walked out of the bar, frantically looking around until she spotted Analeigh.

"Shit! There you are," she said. She looked at the guy holding his jaw and at Ivy rubbing her knuckles. "Um, what the fuck happened?"

Ana tugged the woman to her side, teetering on her heels.

"Stacy, this is my friend Ivy. I mean, we're friends now, right?" she asked Ivy. "Since you did, you know, just. Oh god. Where did the side-walk go?"

"Come on," Stacy said to Ana. "I'll get us an Uber home."

three

Five of Cups — *No use crying over spilled milk (or sidewalk puke).*
Ingredient — *Ginger for power (and as a headache remedy).*

Somehow, Ana had managed to remove her dress while keeping on the bathrobe and one glove. Truly a feat.

With her alarm screaming at her at 4 a.m., each patchy resurfaced memory from the night before hit her right in her throbbing temples.

Had she really sat down on the sidewalk, waiting for the Uber that Stacy had ordered them while both she and Ivy pityingly stroked her back? Yup. Had she exited the Uber and promptly puked on the sidewalk in front of her apartment building? Uh huh. Was she now nursing a monster headache that was exacerbated by the chills and nausea she was experiencing? Oh yeah.

Of course, none of these thoughts were quite so coherent yet, and instead presented themselves in grunts and moans.

If she had just stayed with Ivy after they left the table, she might have had a very different end to the evening. Ivy was a lady, so

21

certainly she wasn't going to try anything with Ana being one sentient thought away from a blackout. But maybe she would have taken Ana back to her place, tucked her in, woken her up with some coffee and some good-natured ribbing about how drunk she'd been. And then Ana would do a little Debbie Ryan hair tuck behind the ear/lip bite combo and say, "I do remember one thing about last night." And then they could do smoochies and it would have been perfect.

But no. She'd had an anxiety attack after that guy talked to them, and her skin felt clammy and like it fit wrong under her costume. So she'd booked it out of the crowd to go get some air instead of just asking Ivy to go with her.

Well, that's why Ana didn't drink coffee in the evening — her nervous system became too susceptible to attack. Ana dragged herself out of bed and cinched the bathrobe tightly around her. She immediately regretted the pressure on her midsection and loosened it.

She would text Ivy and apologize, if she had her phone number. Stupid stupid stupid.

The only thing to do was to go into work mode. First, hydrate. She filled a water bottle and chugged it.

Next, grease up her internal organs. She fried three eggs and hoovered them down with a side of sausage and baked beans.

Finally, a sip of her homemade fire cider. She thanked every god in every pantheon that she'd bottled this batch a month ago and it was ready to go. The horseradish in the tonic made her eyes water, but the way it warmed up her insides felt heavenly.

By then, it was 5 a.m. and she was feeling a little more on the side of the living than having one foot in the ancestral plane. She showered, braided her wet hair, and drove to the bakery to do some damage control.

Even though parts of the night were lost to her semi-blackout, she remembered dancing with Ivy, the way the corset strings of Ivy's costume felt under her gloved fingers, the way she felt too hot for the bathrobe when she thought about unlacing it. She couldn't remember a thing she'd said to her, and that stressed her out. Surely she would have babbled and said something incredibly stupid, right? But maybe not? She remembered Ivy smiling and laughing, and not in a way that made Ana think she was laughing at her. And she remembered asking Ivy for a taste of her Scotch, how she'd told Ivy that wasn't what she meant after she'd slid the glass toward her. And how she didn't pull away when Ana said she wanted more, and Ivy's lips had been so close, so close that she could smell how the smoky Scotch mixed with Ivy's lipstick, that creamy violet scent…

Apology pastries. They were better than flowers and impossible to just dump into the trash. It took a lot of deep breathing to avoid putting her panic into every ingredient as she mixed.

Before last night, Ivy had been a cute but slightly intimidating fixture in her daily routine. Any nerves she felt around the woman because of her beauty and status were alleviated by her obviously reciprocated attraction. But now, Ivy had seen her make a complete damn fool of herself. She'd never gotten that sloppy before. She rarely even drank or went out, and the one time she took her stupid sister's stupid advice to let loose, she let loose all over an Uber driver's passenger door. Ivy would think her childish and embarrassing and would be right to. So she had to try to save some face. Not to try to pick back up where they'd left off before their almost-kiss was interrupted.

No, that ship had sailed and crashed into an iceberg. It had been such an enticing idea — letting go of her inhibitions just a little bit, crossing that boundary she and Ivy had silently set between them before vodka and bustiers and close proximity made that barrier between them seem laughably permeable. She'd been having so much fun with her, and then she took it too far.

There wasn't going to be any salvaging that heady moment, no. The most she could expect was to prevent a person out in the world thinking poorly of her.

The ovens were preheated before Ana even arrived. Bakers worked on unholy schedules. While Ana started bright and early at 6 a.m., that was actually pretty late. Nino and Haley started their shift at 3 a.m. most days, during which they'd bake dough that had been left to rise by the night crew, use the industrial dough sheeter to prepare the thin layers they'd need for croissants, and prep pie crusts, fruit fillings and vegetables.

"Morning, Haley. Nino," Ana said, tying on an apron and doing her first inventory and menu check of the day.

"Woah, you look rough," Haley said. "Your cheeks are all splotchy."

"Yeah, I know I look like shit, thanks," Ana said, laughing. Nino was feeding the sourdough starter and trying not to laugh. Haley was a fantastic teammate and a damn good baker, but she had zero tact. Working the early shift so she could avoid customer interactions was everyone's preference, including hers. "I went on a Halloween bar crawl last night."

"You went outside?" Nino said. "Like, outside of business hours? You socialized."

"There's no way," Haley said. "She must look like shit because someone died. Did someone die, hon? I'm so sorry for your loss."

"I'm about to throw you both out of my kitchen," Ana said. Her threat was toothless. "OK. Nino, can we spare enough puff pastry for six danishes and six turnovers? Special super late order."

Nino and Haley looked at each other and said in unison, "Apology pastries."

"Who'd you puke on?" Haley asked.

"And cookies," Ana said to herself, ignoring her, then asking, "Which cookie recipe would you make for someone really hot who you'd made a fool of yourself in front of?"

A little over an hour later, Ana had a hot basket of goodies to walk a couple of blocks over to Double Dare Fitness.

The mean part of her brain thought about how funny it would be if she dropped the entire basket of pastries upon walking into the gym.

She walked into the gym, which was brightly lit and full of people. It was on the same street as the bakery, a few blocks down, and even though she drove by it every day, she'd only been inside once, during the grand opening, to drop off "welcome to the neighborhood" muffins.

It was nothing like the steely and uninviting atmosphere in other gyms. There were no gaudy colors. Everything was in a gradient of soft blue and purple, the deepest, boldest shades of cobalt and violet reserved for the front desk and the corner that held a boxing ring.

Instead of a big floor full of machines that were close together, there were small spaces with benches and weights, like semi-private mini gyms. The high ceilings allowed for a tall contraption that looked like a grown up, extreme sports version of a playground, with monkey bars and climbing ropes. But the most obvious difference was all the groups of women sparring. Women with visible six packs, and women with soft, rounded bellies and generous thighs. Women of different ethnicities and races, and people who looked more masculine in build but feminine in their presentation. All of them looked strong and confident, like Amazons training for battle.

As she approached the reception desk, a short, buff man with deep brown skin who she noticed the night before with Ivy's group walked up. He dropped off some paperwork behind the desk, then turned and looked at Ana. Recognition bloomed in his expression, and Ana could feel her cheeks getting hot.

"Oh hi!" he said. "Ana, right? Are you looking for Ivy?"

"Um, yeah, I am," Ana said. "Is she around? I probably should've called."

The man, who had a name badge on a lanyard that said his name was Rahul, nodded and directed Ana to follow him. They walked toward the back of the gym, and Ana spotted Ivy immediately. The blonde was currently flipping another woman onto her back, and the two were laughing as she helped her get back up.

"You almost had me there," Ivy told the woman. The full-figured brunette blushed at the praise. "Let's pick this up on Wednesday as usual?" They briefly conversed before she noticed Ana, her eyes going so wide.

"Hi Ana!" Ivy said. "How are you feeling?"

Ana did not even know how to begin to answer that question so she just used the truth. "Humiliated," she said.

Ivy laughed — not at her, she could tell, just a good-natured laugh to decrease the tension. "You don't need to be humiliated. Who among us has not had a Halloween like that in our 20s?"

Of course Ivy would think that. She was a sophisticated, mature woman, and she was letting Ana know that she had acted like a college girl out on the town right after a breakup. "I promise I don't actually have a lot of nights like that," Ana said, though she was certain the woman wouldn't believe her. "But regardless of the frequency, I'm so sorry for how I behaved last night, and I am so grateful for you rescuing me from that douchebag. These are for you," she said, handing over the basket.

Ivy pulled back the cover, curious. She lit up when she looked inside. "Oh my God," she said. "This all looks … this is just too much. Thank you!"

"It's nothing," Ana said, now blushing over the effusive praise. She had the feeling Ivy's praise had that effect on everyone. It was earnest. Her enthusiasm was so easy to latch on to.

She walked Ivy through everything that she had prepared. There were cheese danishes, snickerdoodles, and guava and cream cheese turnovers. She had also packed some croissants that she had brought home before the nightclub debacle, and some flavored butters and jams to serve along with them. It was a pretty good spread considering how little time she had to prepare it, and the fact that she was on death's door. As it was, she was only standing because she had consumed an irresponsible amount of coffee.

Ivy squeezed her arm. "Thank you. You didn't have to go to all this trouble."

"And you didn't have to Black Widow that dude on my behalf, but you did."

"It was no big thing," Ivy said.

"The false modesty is not cute," Ana said, although everything Ivy did was cute. "Look at all these people. You're turning the women of Pittsburgh into action heroes."

"Pittsburgh is just where it starts, darling. First Pittsburgh, then the world."

Ana laughed and took her shot at an arm squeeze. Gods damn, this woman's bicep was hard enough to crack an egg.

She looked around her. She had so many questions. What were those sticks called that the women were fighting with? How long had they been taking classes? Did the maneuver Ivy used last night have a name? How about the one that girl just did to knock down someone a foot taller than her?

Feeling Ivy's gaze on her broke Ana's reverie. "Well, I'll get out of your hair. I'm sure you have classes to teach."

Ivy gave her a sly look. "I actually have an opening for the next hour. Things start to slow down a lot during the fall until everyone's New Year's resolutions. Do you want to learn some moves?"

"Oh, I couldn't," Ana said quickly, feeling nervous around Ivy in a way she never had on her own turf. "I mean, I can't because I have to go to work. But I also couldn't because the only exercise I ever do involves kneading bread dough." She didn't need to add "looking like a weak little bitch in front of an Amazon" to her list of humiliations.

"You know I wasn't always the lethal weapon I am now, right?" She gave Ana what she could only describe as "fuckboy face" and she had to laugh. "But I'm serious. Everyone starts somewhere. If you ever want to try, the first intro to MMA class is on the house."

"Maybe after the holiday rush," Ana said.

She said a hurried goodbye and turned to walk away. "Hey," Ivy called back to her.

"Hey?"

"Gimme your number," Ivy said. Not a question, and spoken in such an offhanded way that Ana almost missed the authority behind it. She was facing Ivy with her phone out before she could even think. Ivy grabbed her iPhone, turned it to face Ana so it would unlock, and shot herself a text. Ana just stood there, trying to not look foolish.

Handing Ana's phone back to her with a smile, Ivy said, "Now we can just talk whenever. Pastries or not."

"Oh, yeah," Ana said, her laugh sounding foreign to herself. "Totally."

"Text me if you want to take me up on that MMA class, OK?"

"I will, yeah. I'll think about it. I, uh, have to get to work."

Ivy gave her a nod and a wave, and Ana booked it out of there and powerwalked to the bakery. Her head was pounding again, and she didn't think it was the hangover resurging.

She'd just forgotten to breathe around that woman.

ANA

Hey, future Ivy. Here's Ana's number.

IVY

Hey, past me. Ana, this is Ivy. Also these
cheese danishes? I want to stage an opera
about them. Incredible

ANA

Thanks! *shrugging face emoji*

Shit. I meant *smiley face emoji*

IVY

winky face emoji

four

The Tower — *Everything falls apart like a shoddily built house of cards. Hold on to your butt. And then get ready to rebuild.*
Ingredient — *Barley's good for protection (let's diminish whatever the fuck that card is hinting at), and so are blueberries. Barley toast plus blueberry jam, and then my crumb-topping blueberry muffins to be extra safe (and because I'm craving them).*

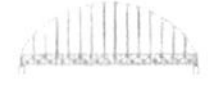

On Monday, Ana's part-timer for the mid-morning shift no-call-no-showed. It was pretty standard in the industry to fire someone for that, but Ana had let her get away with it twice before. The first time, she had claimed that she looked at the wrong schedule. The second time, she had called the next day, burst into tears, and claimed that she was too stressed out from her college classes and had fallen asleep and not woken up until the next day, when she realized that she missed her shift. Ana tried to be compassionate with her employees, because she dealt with way too much dehumanizing crap when she was the employee. But it seemed like this time, she was going to have to fire her.

So Ana's 6 a.m. to 4 p.m. shift turned into a 6 a.m. to 10 p.m. shift. She was lucky that her other staff members were capable and ready to close the shop on their own and urged her to go home.

On Tuesday, her lead baker, Sharon, went into labor two weeks early. Ana paid her employees three months of family leave, so she had been looking for help to fill in for Sharon, but hadn't found anyone just yet. She'd have to white knuckle it for the foreseeable future.

Then on Wednesday, one of her vendors called to let her know there was a supply chain issue that would delay flour delivery by two days. She burst into hysterical laughter for a solid minute, and the vendor awkwardly asked if she was OK.

"Oh, I'm dandy," she replied. Luckily she had enough inventory redundancy that she could make it probably one of the two days without more flour, but she'd have to call around town to commercial food suppliers to see where she could stock up.

When the afternoon rush ended and her bladder demanded she deal with the potentially explosive situation at hand, she took her phone into the staff bathroom and opened the group text.

Witches and Bitches

ANA

I need an astrology bitch.

STACY

I have been summoned!

Heath Ledger as Joker saying "Hit me!" GIF

ANA

What the hell is happening in the sky right now? Mercury isn't retrograde but something ducky is happening.

*Ducky

FUCKY fuck fuck fuck

STACY

Gimme a few minutes. I'm going to look at
your transits.

MAGGIE

How many people's natal charts do you have
saved?

STACY

Yes.

HARPER

Ooh, look at mine, too. I have a date tonight.

STACY

OK so Mars is currently squaring your natal
Saturn, which is like hitting a brick wall every
time you try to do something, and there's some
nasty shit in your sixth house of day to day
stuff, but those transits aren't going to linger.

Ooh there's some interesting conjunctions
happening in your eighth house of sex.

JANE

Ha ha conjunction

Because that's when the thingies are on top of
each other, right? And it's in the sex house?
That's funny, right?

MAGGIE

It's very funny, sweetie. Good job.

ANA

The Mars stuff sounds about right but the
other stuff?

Rihanna looking skeptical GIF

STACY

Listen, I'm just the weather girl. You're the one
who has to make the magic happen. As it
were.

HARPER

What's in my sex house today?

Ana tapped out of the group chat. She sent Harper some good getting-it-on vibes, but she didn't need further reminders of her abysmally nonexistent love life and severe bag fumbling with Ivy.

Thursday was chaos.

First, she found out that what would have been a very lucrative wedding had been canceled. So while she did get to keep the nonrefundable deposit, she was going to miss out on a decent payday. Next, the health inspector had arrived. She was meticulous about the cleaning of her facility, but it still put everyone on edge.

Around the middle of the day, when it was getting pretty chilly outside, she realized that the heater wasn't pumping out as much air as it should. She called her go-to HVAC guy, but he wouldn't be available to come and service the unit until the next week. So she was hoping that her bakery would not become inhospitably cold in the meantime. She was going to pray to every god in every pantheon that the unit hadn't finally crapped out forever, because she did not think that she could stomach the cost of replacing it and closing down the bakery for as long as it took for the work to be completed.

The final straw was when she had an incredibly awkward interview trying to find a replacement, even a part-time one, for Sharon during her maternity leave. After spending an hour trying to coax more than single word answers out of the interviewee, and poking some holes into her supposed kitchen experience, she thanked her for her time and told her that she would be in touch.

She would not be in touch.

When there was a lull in customers, Ana put up a "back in 15 minutes!" sign on the door and told her employees that she was going to be in the freezer for a bit, and to please not enter the freezer or be concerned about any of the sounds that would come out of it. Once the heavy metal door was shut behind her, she started screaming. She screamed, and she screamed, and she screamed. She took a deep belly breath, and then she screamed some more. It was satisfying to watch the stress of this week manifest into clouds in the cold freezer, and then dissipate before her eyes. She was going to need some tea with lots of honey, perhaps with a shot of something stronger.

Remembering the previous weekend's shenanigans and her promise to never drink again, Ana thought better of it.

Perhaps it would be good for her to take up some kind of hobby. Something to let out her frustrations on a more regular basis.

When she got home, she queued up some Colbert clips on her TV and went onto the website for Ivy's gym. She looked at the class descriptions and schedule, and spent just a tiny, insignificant amount of time ogling the photos of Ivy that were throughout the website. The time she spent on the instructor page was particularly negligible.

The intro to MMA classes were taught in a rotation among Ivy and Rahul. They fell within times that she was at the bakery. Yes, she was the owner. Yes, she made the schedule. But she had to be there.

She looked at the cost of the personal training sessions, which were also within the gym's normal hours of business, and they might be a little bit more than she could justify for her budget right now.

Still, she kept browsing the schedule. There was an eight-week Train Like A Superhero program. The classes were named after comics characters and focused on exercises inspired by their on-screen moves, and the entire program was for beginners. Then there was the intermediate 12-week program: The Superhero Sequel. There were workshops and demonstrations on different stunts, boxing, using bo staffs — which was apparently what those sticks were called. You could also just use the gym facilities and do your own thing at the stations Analeigh noticed when she dropped off her apology basket.

Remembering those strong women at the gym, Ana was filled with a longing that surprised her. She thought about the way Ivy had subdued that jerk, the power and confidence she had. She wanted to be that strong and capable. She wanted to not fall apart when deliveries were delayed and when she had to fire broke college students. She wanted Ivy to pin *her* down on the ground.

Ivy could jump through windows and fly on wires and beat up creeps on the street. She was *powerful*. She wanted that. Classic case of both wanting the girl and wanting to be the girl.

Sinking back onto the couch pillows, promising herself that tonight she would not fall asleep there, she wondered how she could possibly add one more thing to her life.

At 3 a.m. Ana rolled off the couch, showered, and wrapped her hair into a tight bun. She had a plan, and like most of her plans, this one involved pastry.

The hours between starting her day at the bakery and the gym opening felt interminable. Ana started baking the day's bread then tried to throw herself into the tedium of running her business — putting in orders, invoicing clients, checking and re-checking her schedule so she knew when she had deliveries, when she had to crumb coat and chill cakes and when she would need to devote long stretches to intricate designs. Today she'd have to finish decorating a cake for a wedding that happened on Saturday, and that would take most of her shift.

When the gym opened at 7 a.m. on Friday, Ana power-walked over with a container full of spanakopita. She knew that was one of Ivy's favorites.

To her delight, Ivy was the one at the reception desk this morning.

Clearly surprised to see her, Ivy said, "Hey! You're not bringing me more treats, are you?"

Ana waved the spanakopita under Ivy's nose. "Sorry, I did. But this time it's a bribe."

"A bribe, huh? How can I be of service?"

A million ways Ana could think of, but she probably should stick to the one.

"I'd love to train with you, but your business hours and mine overlap. So that's where the bribe comes in."

"I'm listening," Ivy said, mouth full of spinach pastry.

"Would you consider staying open one hour later twice a week, in exchange for your personal training fee plus baked goods?"

"Huh."

Ana's stomach dropped. "Uh oh. Huh, what?"

Ivy took another bite and took her time chewing and swallowing. "I think you're getting a raw deal. Just twice a week? I get to kick your ass and I get carbs?"

"OK, three times a week."

"Now there's a smart businesswoman. You've got yourself a deal."

"Really?!" Ana was embarrassed about the girlish squeal she emitted.

They shook hands. "Can we start tonight?" Ana asked.

Frowning, Ivy said, "I actually have, um, a standing karaoke thing."

It was delightful to know that Ivy did dorky things like karaoke and wasn't just a perfect Amazonian war goddess.

"But how about tomorrow?" Ivy offered.

Damn. "Late delivery for an evening wedding. Want to just plan for Monday?"

"You've got it."

Ana floated halfway to the bakery.

The other half of the walk, the anxiety attack took hold.

Oh no. Oh no. Oh no.

How was she going to survive three hours a week *sweating* in Ivy's presence?

The cakes in the freezer were going to need earplugs. She felt a whole lungful of screams rising up.

$$five$$

I want someone willing to try new things. All SORTS of new things.

"Are you sure you don't want me to stay and help? I don't want you to have to do all the closing duties by yourself."

It had been a busy Monday, and Rahul was helping Ivy stack mats during their last official hour of business. "This is plenty of help — I know you just want to stay for the pastries," Ivy said. "Those are mine."

"Fine, don't share," Rahul said, spraying down a rack of dumbbells with disinfectant. "Plus I wouldn't want to interrupt your date."

Ivy leveled him with an icy look, her arms crossed and her hip cocked. "Watch it. You know I'm your boss, right?"

"Yeah, OK," Rahul snorted. Ivy sprayed him in the leg with the bottle of clean water she used on the benches after the industrial cleaners.

Rahul was one of her favorite people. They'd met when she first moved back to Pittsburgh. She met him through Camila, who had met him through Era's then-boyfriend, now-husband, Seth, who had met him at a networking event. Rahul had at the time just started T, and when he found out Ivy was a personal trainer, he mentioned that he wanted to bulk up his shoulders. He'd been uncomfortable around other men at his gym, not knowing if they'd be cool or lose their shit if they clocked him as trans. Ivy understood — in her experience, cis men at the gym already tended to be loud and wrong about pretty much everything, when they should have been focusing on their atrocious bench press form.

Pretty soon, Ivy had gone from training him to befriending him, then finally hiring him. He was only part time because he was a full-time lawyer, but he made the absolute best of the hours he put in at Double Dare. He was the most knowledgeable and charismatic trainer on her staff, but the one with the least availability because of his real job. She constantly heard about how comfortable clients felt working with him, even the most nervous newcomers who had never picked up a weight. And even though he could only devote a few hours a week to training clients, he was very involved in brainstorming classes, vetting equipment and filling in on admin tasks that could be done remotely.

She'd been working with her lawyer to draft up partnership agreements to give him a stake in the company, but she didn't think he'd ever sign them. He talked often about how one should never, ever, ever go into business with friends or family, because he'd seen it go catastrophically wrong over and over in his legal practice.

"But I'm your friend and we work together," Ivy had said.

"Pfft," Rahul responded. "I don't work with or for you. I'm just helping out." And he'd winked.

It was with that same good-natured snark that he teased her now.

"That girl has a huge crush on you," he said.

"'Girl' is the operative word," Ivy said. "She's so young. A baby. A zygote."

"And you're a withered old crone," he deadpanned, nodding.

She sprayed him again.

"I wear my crone status proudly," Ivy said. She was about to turn 40. She had thoroughly enjoyed her thirties after her disastrous twenties. Even though she'd racked up the professional successes, she'd felt like a runaway truck in her personal life. Now that she was older, she felt the most confident and secure with her place in the world that she ever had.

That was part of why she loved teaching. She knew how to come home to her body, to trust and empower and protect it, and when she could pass a little of that knowledge along to someone else, it made her feel truly invincible.

"So if she asks you out or makes a move on you, are you going to let her down easily, or?" Rahul asked.

"Oh, she's not going to make a move on me," Ivy said.

"Really? Because you two looked pretty damn cozy at the bar."

"She probably doesn't remember any of that," Ivy said. "She was hammered. I don't think she gets out much."

"You did say you didn't want a party girl, so, point in her favor?"

"Again, you keep saying the word 'girl' so let's focus on that. She's 25. Her brain just finished developing. I remember what I was like at that age, and if I was going after older women, it definitely wasn't for more than indulging my praise kink."

Rahul was staring at her in a way that made her want to crack another joke. She didn't like how much he saw her, sometimes. Sometimes she wondered why she'd ever wanted to be an actress, when she had so much difficulty with being perceived. Maybe it was different when you were pretending to be someone else.

"I'm just saying, I know what you say you want, but I also saw how you were looking at each other the other night. It might get a little messy if you're not careful."

"I'll be careful, don't worry," she said, waving him off.

Rahul left with a few more suggestive comments tossed over his shoulder, and Ivy watched the clock. It was five minutes past the time she'd set with Ana. Would she bail on her? She wouldn't do that, would she?

At eight minutes past, a blur that solidified into Ana streaked across the front door. The apologies were all over her face even before she said them.

While Ivy tried to appear gracious as Ana explained the chaos she'd just had to deal with at the bakery, she appraised her workout gear … you know, to make sure it was suitable for the activities they'd be doing.

She wore her hair in two French braids tucked into a low bun at the nape of her neck. Her black leggings hugged her plump thighs and full ass just right. She wore a faded, baggy T-shirt knotted to one side.

"I'm so sorry I'm late," Ana said. "Stupid cooler wasn't keeping temp, and I had to wait for my technician, who has never been on time a day in his life, I'm sure, and I promise I am usually a lot more together than the last few times I've seen you might suggest," she continued.

Ivy feigned seriousness and brushed past everything Ana said. "You bring the goods?"

Confused for a second, Ana quickly caught on. She looked over her left shoulder, then her right, and lifted a Besos bag before clutching it to her chest. "You have to hold up your end of the bargain first," she said, pulling the bag away from Ivy's grabby hands.

"Fair enough. Do you need to refrigerate it?"

After Ana confirmed it could stay at room temp, Ivy had her set down her bags and meet her on the main floor. She ran Ana through the plan: they'd start out with a joint-freeing series to loosen up, then learn basic punches and combinations.

She could tell Ana was nervous, but then again a lot of people were the first time they started training, especially if they didn't have a fitness background or hadn't trained in a while.

They each pulled up a yoga mat and started running through the series, gentle movements loosening up the neck and shoulders all the way down to ankles. Ana hesitated with even these simple movements, watching Ivy's demonstration closely for a few seconds before following along. The close observation made for immediate good form, though Ivy asked her to slow her movement for the head half circles.

Ana sighed with pleasure when they ran through wrist exercises. Ivy could hear the little pops.

"You have no idea," she said when Ivy looked at her curiously. "Piping work on a five-tier wedding cake is a recipe for carpal tunnel. Worse than any office job, I'd bet."

"I believe it," Ivy said. "Feeling good?" she asked once they'd finished the series, which she told Ana she learned during a yoga teacher training in college.

"So you always wanted to do something in fitness?" Ana asked in response.

"In a way," Ivy said. "I was always athletic. I was pretty serious about gymnastics as a kid and into high school, but eventually the pressure was just too much trying to balance training with academics and having some semblance of a high school experience. So then I just switched to sports. Played basketball, took dance lessons. Dance was where I got bit by the performance bug, and I moved to LA after college to try to act."

"Did you book any parts?" Ana asked.

"Mostly I got a lot of background parts and did some dancing in music videos, and I did personal training to make ends meet. Then I got to talking with a stunt coordinator on a set I was an extra on, and one thing led to another, and I fell in love with stunts."

Ana was hanging on her every word, and Ivy suddenly felt self-conscious. The story of her failures as an actress, how she drifted from thing to thing trying to find something that fit, didn't usually make her feel inadequate, but Ana was sort of intimidating. She was so much younger than Ivy yet seemed to know exactly where she was going with her career.

But then again, Ivy saw firsthand that Ana had her share of hot-mess-twenties behavior. There really was no escaping that, was there?

"What made you fall in love with them?"

Ivy thought about it. "Well. I guess ... I was always watching the behind-the-scenes and listening to the director's commentary on every movie I loved. I liked knowing how everything came together. The special effects, the deleted or extended scenes versus what ended up in the movie, how the costumes were decided. When I got into stunts, I was really nerdy about it. It was the physicality I loved plus another movie secret I could obsess over and learn everything about. Anyway. Enough of me yapping. You ready to do some shadowboxing?"

She got off the mat and extended her hand to Ana, pulling her to stand. Ana's hand was warm in hers, slightly rough in places. She thought she felt a squeeze back, the gentlest of pressure, but she had to have imagined it. Or maybe Ana was one of those easily affectionate people, the kind of girl who held all her friends' hands. She already knew Ana was a lesbian, but she still had that deep rooted gay girl insecurity about whether a girl was just being friendly or actually flirting.

Once they got to learning jabs and crosses and uppercuts, Ivy realized the real issue with training Ana would be working on her coordination. She had two left feet and kept shifting out of the proper stance, forgetting which punch came next.

Knowing Ana was getting flustered, Ivy said, "You're doing great. Let's slow it down a little. Here's that jab again. Mirror what I'm doing." Ana followed instruction and extended her right arm in a too-forceful move.

"You're hitting too much from your shoulder," Ivy said. "That's how you get injured, and without much payoff because you aren't putting the power into the punch. You really want to be punching from your core. Try to keep this whole part of your body still," Ivy said, waving over her own torso.

Ana thought about it and tried again. Still too much in the shoulder.

"That's closer. Is it OK if I touch your shoulder?"

"Sure," Ana said. "Go ahead."

"All right." She walked closer and slightly to the left of Ana and extended her left hand in a "stop" gesture. Placing the heel of her hand on Ana's front shoulder, she said, "Punch without pushing my hand from this spot."

She heard Ana take a slow, deep breath. She could smell mint on her breath, feel the warmth of her shoulder through her sleeve.

"Whenever?"

"Yup, go for it."

Ana punched, and Ivy's palm stayed in place.

"So much better!" Ivy said. She broke the contact between them and saw Ana deflate. Ooh, she did not need another reason to want to keep touching her. "Again. Good. Now that uppercut. OK, you need to lean away from yourself more with that, because too much momentum the way you're doing it and you're going to break your own nose."

The thing was, Ivy's job required her to watch her clients' bodies closely. She had the knowledge about technique and anatomy that they needed to prevent injury and actually get better. And she was giving Ana that same professional attention, regardless of her attraction.

But she had to admit to herself that watching Ana this closely, without being able to hide behind her phone or a cup of coffee, made her feel exposed. She wished she could have taken an acting class to prepare for this. Then maybe she would have been able to get into the headspace of someone who wasn't struggling to not look at how Ana's chest rose and fell, or how her ass looked mid-lunge. Or how the sound of her heavy breathing made her imagine that sound in a deeply unprofessional context.

They kept at the shadowboxing for 20 minutes before Ivy brought out the small punching bag. "I'll call out combinations and you just do everything you just learned but while making contact."

Ana quickly got flustered again. "I hit like a bitch, don't I?" she asked.

Ivy burst into laughter. She couldn't help it. "When I'm done with you, no one is going to be able to say you hit like a bitch." She looked at the time, amazed at how quickly it had passed and how she'd forgotten to keep track. That was not like her.

"I think that's our time. Now show me this dessert."

They got back to Ana's bags and she pulled out and opened the Pyrex container, revealing two dozen doughy balls that smelled rich and cinnamony.

"These are buñuelos," Ana said, beaming. "I make mine with cassava flour and serve them in a spiced syrup." She pulled a container of a dark amber liquid out of the bag, plus two disposable bowls and utensils. "I thought maybe we could share them?" she asked, a little unsure.

Ivy's stomach did a backflip. "Of course," she said. "Not that I couldn't inhale these by myself in three seconds."

"Same," Ana said with a laugh. "Especially after all that. I haven't had a workout like that in ... um, ever? I'm sweating in places I didn't know I could."

"I love nothing more than good food after physical exertion," Ivy said. Ana blushed. Maybe Ivy had been imagining the hand squeeze earlier, but she wasn't imagining the charge that was between them at the phrase "physical exertion."

"At the gym, I mean," Ivy said in an attempt to cut the awkwardness. If anything, drawing attention to the possible double entendre made things worse. She hastily dipped a fritter into the syrup and stuffed it in her stupid mouth. "Holy hell," she said, swooning. "This is incredible."

Ana grinned and it was like someone hard turned up the lumens on the studio lights. Her teeth were so damn straight and white. She knew actors who spent a fortune on whitening treatments that didn't give them as stellar a smile as Ana's. "If you like," Ana said, "I can make a savory version with cheese next time."

"I would very much like," Ivy said. "You're going to need the nourishment," she added. "I'm not going to take it easy on you next class."

Ana gulped. "Guess I'll have to throw in some extra pastries for us, then."

Catching the "us," Ivy decided not to get her hopes up these post-workout snacks would keep being a partnered activity.

"Guess you will," she said.

Ana licked her fingers clean. Ivy wanted to die.

"How do you feel about coconut?" Ana asked.

six

I want someone who actually wants to be in a long-term relationship. No more situationships.

Food was such a big part of Ivy's life now that it was hard to imagine a time when it had been a constant preoccupation in a different way. Now she was focused on who she ate food with, on the ambiance, on the taste and the memories made preparing and eating food. But just a few years ago, it had been a different story.

One month, she'd be obsessed with tracking every macro, down to even a bite of someone's dessert she couldn't resist trying. Another month, it would be intermittent fasting that caught her attention. She'd done paleo and keto, she'd devoured peer-reviewed papers trying to find the absolute healthiest combination of food to be the leanest, fastest, most impervious version of herself. She'd never been diagnosed, but she thought the pattern bordered on orthorexia. Her parents had always been health nuts, and that perception of what "good" foods were had become a fixation when she started working in the entertainment industry.

Her low point had been when Ivy really messed up her health by competing in a bikini contest. It was before she landed Aurora Dagger, so she was paying her rent mostly through personal training. She'd just gotten dumped by a waitress she'd been dating for three months, and needed something to consume her focus. One of her clients was a bodybuilder and training for a competition, and Ivy was intrigued. So she thought she'd give it a go.

To achieve that kind of physique required a brutal, punishingly restrictive diet and overtraining. It made her sick to think about it now. She'd gotten down to a very low 12 percent body fat. Before, she'd been closer to 20 percent, which was typical of female athletes. She stopped getting her period, and her hair got really thin. The second she was done (she'd placed fourth), she celebrated with a feast: burgers, fried chicken, cheesecake, all her favorites that she'd restricted when she got serious about fitness, and cut out completely for the competition.

Afterward, she felt terrible. She was too poorly nourished to logically think it through, to reason that it was just too much food all at once when her body had become so deprived. Instead, she started a new food obsession. She would regain her period, her higher body fat, her thick mane, by eating super "healthy."

It took years of working with a doctor who taught her how to eat intuitively to get Ivy to a place where she wasn't assigning morality to food. Her friends made fun of her for still counting macros sometimes when she was trying to put on muscle, but she'd been able to stop obsessing about food labels and pesticides and additives. Now she was nourished enough to lift heavier weights and go harder on her workouts, and take on more personal training clients.

And she realized that she'd missed out on a world of delicious flavors and cuisines. There was so much more to life than dry chicken breast and limp broccoli. There were steamed pork buns with pickled onions and hoisin sauce from her favorite ramen place; Venezuelan arepas stuffed with carnitas and topped with corn aioli; spicy shrimp tempura rolls; hearty layered Palestinian maqluba topped with fresh parsley; and the most rich slice of chocolate cake she'd ever had in her life, served with a cup of coffee poured by an adorable baker.

Now she was able to enjoy the beautiful sushi she was sharing with Era and Camila. Ivy ordered the dragon roll, because she loved eel, and it freaked out Camila, the least adventurous eater in their group. She was still hesitant to try a lot of foods even though her boyfriend, Zach, was helping her expand her culinary repertoire.

The three women shared gyoza and vegetable tempura and pots of green tea. Era was celebrating the release of the demo version of her indie gaming company's next project, which was part dating sim and part task manager about a magical bookstore. The game was focused heavily on relationship themes, and Camila, who was a therapist, had been a consultant on some of the dialogue.

"So what happens next?" Ivy asked.

Dipping her Philadelphia roll in spicy mayo, Era said, "First we track the high-profile feedback from streamers playing the demo, and see what the reaction is in the comments. From there we start zooming in on feedback from average consumers. We do some more fine-tuning, and then work our way to a closed beta version we can refine even more."

"That sounds like a lot," Ivy said. "So when would the game be fully released?"

"Oh, by spring," Era said. Ivy knew her eyes were popping out of her head.

"Do you sleep?" she asked. The team at Era's company wasn't that big. It was incredible how much they could get done during the four-day workweek Era insisted on for everyone but herself. She seemed to always be on call, much to the dismay of her husband, Seth, with whom she had yet to go on a proper honeymoon.

"How about you, Ivy? What have you got going on?"

"Oh, you know. Not a whole lot. The swordplay class is going awesome. There's a waitlist every night for spots. I'm thinking of making it permanent instead of seasonal, but I'll have to hire more trainers to make the schedule work without cutting something else. Then I started training a few new clients one-on-one. Including Ana," she said, adding that part after a pause. She knew her friends were going to ask her a million questions and tease her relentlessly. They knew all about her crush on Ana, after Ivy had introduced them all and Era hired Ana to do her wedding cake.

"Oh?" Camila asked, failing to sound casual. "Did this start after Halloween?"

"Yeah," Ivy said, fascinated by a piece of battered sweet potato. "Though I can't say I want to pursue 'the ability to subdue drunk douchebags' as a marketing strategy. Could be a liability issue."

"Yeah, and there aren't a lot of opportunities to swoop in and rescue cute bakers you're obsessed with," Camila said.

"I am not obsessed with her," Ivy said. "That's ridiculous."

"How many times a week do you go to the bakery?" Camila asked.

"Just, you know, two or three. Or four. But they have really good breakfast and it's so close to work. You know I'm not a morning person, I'm always in a rush."

"Uh huh," Era said. "Follow-up question. How many times a week are you in there twice in one day?"

Ivy glared at her.

"How about three times in one day?" Camila said, two seconds away from pointing and laughing by the look of glee on her face.

"You know, I wasn't this mean to you when you started seeing Zach," Ivy grumbled.

"Oh my GOD, yes you were!" Camila said, a bit louder than was appropriate for the restaurant. She struggled with volume control.

OK, so Ivy had teased Camila quite a bit when she started dating Zach and tried to convince herself they weren't actually dating.

"Maybe I am a little obsessed," she conceded. "But the training is all business, really. And yes, she is very pretty, but as you know, I have very specific things I'm looking for in whoever I date next, and I don't think getting distracted with a 25-year-old is conducive to my plans."

"Oh yes," Era said. "The hallowed Wife List."

"Don't call it that," Ivy said, even though in her mind she'd also started calling it the Wife List. One night at karaoke, Ivy had vented about a situationship that just ended, knocked back a few tequila shots, and opened her notes app. "I'm done with these girls who don't know what they want," Ivy said. "I know what I want! And it's different from whatever that whole disaster was!"

And so the Wife List was born. It became a document Ivy expanded and revised often, as much a journal of things she learned about herself as it was a wishlist for a potential partner.

"At any rate, you'd have a checklist, too, if you'd had as many bad girlfriends as I have," she said now.

"So would you say," Camila started, "that you need a Wife To-Do List because of your Girlfriend Done List?"

Era and Camila laughed hysterically at this.

Her list was nothing compared to what other people she knew did. One of the students in Ivy's Dance Battle class — which combined interpretive dance with fight choreo — had met their husband on a dating app, but not before keeping records of every person they talked to or went out with from the app. They tracked their interests, where they had gone on their date, what they did for work.

"For one, it helped keep them all straight," they said with a giggle. "And it helped me take it seriously, treat it as a goal. Might sound cold, but it worked for me to take some of the romance out of it and make it practical. Plus," they'd said, shrugging, "I like data."

If Ivy were to start her own similar spreadsheet, it would be deeply depressing. What patterns would emerge from her data? One incredibly boring dinner with a paramedic — which she thought surely would be a job for an interesting person — led to her temporarily adding "must have seen two Channing Tatum movies" to her list.

There had been some good dates, with prospects that ultimately fizzled out. Rahul had set her up with a gorgeous lawyer from his firm. They had excellent conversations and shared one pretty good kiss, but by the third date they'd run out of things to talk about. Then there had been the reporter who was side-splittingly funny but ghosted Ivy as soon as she got too busy at work. A sex, drugs and embezzlement scandal in local government would do that to a journalist.

"Online dating is rough. It's basically a full-time job. I've got three first dates just this week. Not everyone just meets their person, you know, in person. Out in the world when you're not looking."

"I definitely got lucky," Camila said, getting that far away misty look she got whenever she talked about Zach, who she'd met at an arts festival over the summer and fallen fast and hard for.

"Same here," Era said. "And I definitely wasn't looking. And if I had been, Seth wouldn't have been on my radar. He's so far from what I thought was my type, but somehow, it just works."

Camila nodded emphatically. "I get that you want to be clear about what you'd value in a partner, and that's awesome," she said, slipping on her therapist hat. "Just don't be so rigid with your expectations that you miss out on interesting women who you might actually hit it off with."

Ivy knew where Camila was coming from, and while she got it, she didn't think anything on her list was that huge or specific a demand.

She was tired of relationships that burned hot with passion and excitement before inevitably burning out. She wanted something that would last.

Like her parents' marriage. They were closing in on 50 years, and although they weren't perfectly happy all the time, they were adequately happy most of the time. Ivy wasn't a hopeless romantic. She was a pragmatist.

Her crush on Ana? It was the exact thing she was trying to get away from. She was about to turn 40. It was time to get serious.

seven

Two of Cups — *Partnership, connection. Coming to an agreement.*
Eight of Swords — *Anxiety. Being your own worst enemy. The solution is close, you just can't see it.*
Eight of Pentacles — *On that grind.*
Ingredients — *That Two of Cups with the Eight of Pentacles makes me think I need a lot of coffee today, but that Eight of Swords is making me question how smart that is. Maybe hot chocolate? With chili pepper to put some pep in my step.*

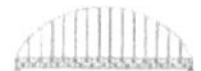

Ana started every day at 4 a.m. It was an ungodly hour, a phrase Ana found pretty funny considering it was the time she communed with her gods and the ancestors. She made espresso in her stainless steel greca — moka pot to her gringo friends — and set out three cups. One was for her, which she poured milk into and sweetened heavily. One was for the gods. The other was for the ancestors, which she set on their altar along with fresh water and a lit candle.

As she sipped her latte in front of the flickering light at the altar, she pulled out her tarot cards and shuffled. Every morning she pulled at least one card for guidance about how the day would go or what she should keep in mind as the moved through the day. And often, she would jot down notes about her readings in a notebook she called her tarot/recipe grimoire. It was basically a journal with her daily interpretations of the cards and what ingredients and recipes they made her think about. While she admired the intricacy of astrology and the reverence and mythology tied to serious deity worship, those were more of her friends' things than hers. She liked tarot because it was like a story she was telling herself about her own life, and as such, it was easier for her to tie to something she loved, like food. Everything sort of followed from there: studying tarot and linking the cards' messages to ingredients led her to further study on those ingredients and their magical correspondences. She could then pick out the right ingredients for a candle spell, or channel the ingredient's energy into her recipes.

As she shuffled, two cards fell out of the deck, so she turned them both to face her.

The first was the Two of Cups. Two figures toasting together, signaling a beneficial partnership. Or, if you listened to every tarot video on her TikTok For You Page, "a soulmate connection." Certainly people weren't meeting soulmates left and right the way these videos suggested.

The second card was the Eight of Swords. Ana hated this card. It showed a person who was blindfolded and alone surrounded by swords, as if caged. But the swords are spread out enough that, if the person chose to, they could just walk in between them and escape. It was a card about fear and feeling trapped when the prison is actually within your power to escape.

As an anxious person who second-guessed everything, Ana pulled this card a lot. She really resented the spirits for that.

Just for funsies, she pulled a third card. Laughing, she set the Eight of Pentacles next to the other two. It was the card of the daily grind.

"Nothing new there," Analeigh said to herself. Looking at the picture of her grandfather on the ancestor altar, she added, "It's our lot in life, I guess."

Analeigh had worked since the moment she was legally able to. Her first job had been at a fast food chain, which was the most miserable experience of her life. The way people were willing to scream and curse at a teenager over their chicken nuggets being served with the wrong sauce made Ana lose quite a bit of hope in humanity early on.

Her senior year of high school, she'd worked at a trendy clothing store, feigning intense cheer and helpfulness to customers and making sure all the overpriced flannels were facing the same way on the rack, the hangers forming question marks. She had nightmares about the denim wall, in which she failed to perfectly fold and align them in size order, and they turned into a million gaping mouths with supernatural suction powers, trying to drag her into the pits of hell as she clung desperately to the earring carousel.

She realized then that she should probably cut back on the Red Bulls she chugged all day.

Once she finished her daily spiritual practice, the rest of her day moved at a decidedly more hectic pace. The car ride to work would be the longest she'd be sitting from now until late in the evening.

Besos Bakery was the most beautiful place Ana had ever seen in person, and she had made it so. When she first leased the storefront, it was barren and blank, just white walls and hardwood floors that needed some love, and a kitchen with outdated appliances.

So she and her family got to work making the space what Ana envisioned for as cheap as possible. Ana's dad and younger brother had restored the floors with rented equipment and YouTube tutorials. When Ana was panicking about how she could never afford the wallpaper she wanted, her mother staked out local secondhand stores every day until she found a $300 vinyl sticker machine for $30 and used it to cut stencils they then used to paint the black damask pattern onto the walls. Ari and Ana had bought a shelf worth of drugstore lipstick, kissed pieces of paper, scanned them into a computer, and printed them at FedEx into three long, narrow prints they framed behind the pastry cases.

Ana bought a set of five battered bar stools and reupholstered them in magenta fabric, then worked with her dad to build the bars themselves facing out into the street. She bargain hunted and haggled for kitchen equipment. The booths, the tables, the diner chairs were all secondhand and painstakingly restored, costing her a thousand splinters plus calluses she could never lotion away.

She loved every inch of this place, loved the way people oohed and ahhed at the girlie luxury of it all, at the way the pastel macarons with the edible gold dust looked against the backdrop of pattern and color and light. Everyone took pictures under the neon "!Besos, amores!" sign. They glowed, happy and full and content, under the warm pink light.

It was her dream, on the surface. Here's the thing that should be made more clear when people tell you to follow your passions. What they really mean is "monetize the things you love," which leads to you mostly doing things you don't love under the veneer of it being your passion. Ana was passionate about buttercream, not renovations and balance sheets. But she spent more time on the business side of Besos than she wanted to.

Now that she was in it, though, and had come this far, she thought she should keep expanding as much as she could. The idea of opening a second location was a fevered one. She felt energized by the delusion of it. She'd done it once. Why couldn't she do it again? Why couldn't she get it done in six months instead of eight? Hell, why not three months? Why not a bigger location, with a full drink menu and a cookie conveyor belt? That would get her featured on some travel blogs for sure. Blow up on TikTok. Become an international destination. Rule the world with turnovers and cubanos on house-made bread.

It was a lovely delusion, one too far off for now. But someday.

For now, she was intent on Besos being profitable, even if it meant she had to stay up all night reading accounting books and all day posting content, ordering and doing inventory.

She'd rather spend all her time in the alchemy of baking. No one in her life would ever geek out like she did at how the most nuanced change in technique could make the difference between picture perfect macarons and ones you'd be embarrassed to feed to your dog. She could spend days, weeks, perfecting a recipe, trying different balances of acidity and sweetness, changing ingredients by incremental measurements and logging the differences.

She knew the secrets for perfectly flaky croissants and biscuits that melted in your mouth. Her buttercream was unmatched. Her lemon filling could topple kingdoms if she wanted to use her powers for evil instead of for filling people's bellies.

But she didn't have the luxury of focusing only on the fun parts of the job. Too many people depended on her, and not just her employees. Ari depended on her, too.

That part was a stressful secret she was keeping from her parents. They were a tight-knit family — dinners together once a week, constant phone calls, a hopping family group text she had to mute often if she wanted to get any work done. Aracely had racked up scholarships, but they didn't cover the entirety of her tuition or other expenses. Ana saw how much Ari would have to take out in loans to make up the difference, and she stepped in to fill in some gaps. It took her finances from stable to precarious very quickly.

That was a recurring theme for the Fonseca family. Just when it seemed like they'd gotten their heads above water, here came the deluge.

All it took was for the family car to need its spark plugs replaced, and suddenly they were behind on rent, and catching up on rent meant falling behind on utilities, and borrowing money from relatives to pay off the power company meant the tax return they were going to use to buy a slightly less crappy used car was already spent. Ana, Ari, and their little brother Antonio, who was still in high school, had never gone hungry, but the sense of lack and instability permeated every other resource in their lives. It was why Ana lay awake at night thinking about rising ingredient prices and how to budget to meet her first priority of paying her employees a salary they could actually live off. Ana would be good and gods damned if she ever perpetuated the type of capitalist bullshit that made it so hard for her own family to get ahead.

She'd hoped today she could focus on decorating a five-tier wedding cake that needed to be delivered in a few days. But of course, everything had to go wrong instead. The cooler was supposedly fixed, but it was still about a degree warmer than ideal. One of the outlets shorted out, so she'd had to move several stand mixers to the other side of the kitchen until she could get the electrician out there. And the church group that they catered for once a week told her at the last minute that they'd have an extra 20 people attending the event.

None of the regulars would have guessed by her friendly demeanor that she was about to yank out her ponytail.

By the end of the day, she was ready to punch whatever Ivy put in front of her.

Despite being totally out of her element during their first class, Ana had enjoyed the hell out of herself. Working in a kitchen required running around a lot, but it was a different level of exertion from the gym.

For today's offering, she was bringing croquetas de jamon, potato balls, and chewy coconut cookies drizzled in dark chocolate and pineapple syrup. Ivy looked like she might faint when she took a bite of a cookie.

"I am so tempted to cancel class so I can eat this now," Ivy said.

"That would be in direct violation of the terms of our deal," Ana said. "Plus, I am so sore, and I read that means I have to keep at it or the soreness will just get worse."

"That's true," Ivy said. "That's DOMS — delayed onset muscle soreness," she added at Ana's quizzical look. "Right now, you're tearing muscle fibers and when they rebuild, that's how you get definition. It's your muscles repairing themselves as you get stronger."

Ana patted her belly. "I'm not looking to get swole." She gave the softness an affectionate squeeze.

Maybe she should have felt self-conscious at the too-long glance Ivy gave her midsection, except what she saw there wasn't anywhere near judgment.

They ran through the same warm-up as the previous session, then practiced combos and footwork, adding kicks into their repertoire. Ivy held padding over her arm and directed Ana to kick as Ivy changed heights. She was so scared of kicking Ivy in that adorable little nose. Her faith in Ana was sorely misplaced, because Ana kept getting distracted by the curve of Ivy's lips, and the honeyed lowlights of her expensive-looking balayage slipping out at the nape of her ponytail.

It was exhausting and invigorating, being in Ivy's presence. She was Red Bull and vodka. Or maybe more like gentle lullabies blared on a subwoofer.

Post-training, when Ana returned from the locker room after splashing water on her face and wiping the sweat off her chest, she caught a glimpse of Ivy's phone from over her shoulder and saw the distinctive pink and orange of everyone's favorite sapphic dating app at the moment. How could Ana ignore the way her stomach soured at the realization, how her vision seemed to enhance and play in slow motion Ivy's clear gesture of swiping right?

Maybe she should dust off that old profile. Was that what she needed to do to get Ivy to admit her attraction to her, to clear the way for Ana to admit her crush in return? She knew the dating pool wasn't the biggest in Pittsburgh. Surely they'd match. An app would be a great middleman for admitting you were crushing on someone. If they rejected you, at least it wouldn't be face to face. Easy to pretend nothing had ever happened.

Except it wouldn't be easy, would it? Imagine if she swiped right on Ivy and then waited and waited and realized she'd rejected her. How could she face her? She wouldn't be able to keep working out at this gym. She may not be able to keep working in this city. Or the state. She'd have to move. Underground, probably. She'd have to dig a hole deep enough to hide her shame, lay some foundation, build up some walls, and figure out some sort of plumbing. How much would that set her back? Were there already bunkers you could rent in the apocalyptic event you swiped right on your crush and they saw and ignored it?

That was an untapped market if she'd ever heard of one.

eight

"So how did you hear about this, anyway?" Camila asked Era as they waited in line to get their headphones for the silent disco.

"I hear about things," Era said, a little defensive. "I'm cool. I'm hip." There was a pause. "Jason's sister's roommate is the DJ." Jason was Era's executive assistant at the game development company she founded. "But still, I heard a cool thing, I shared it. Therefore I get the clout."

"You definitely get the clout, babe," Ivy said, putting a reassuring hand on Era's shoulder. "I'm excited about this."

"Me too," Camila said. "Who all is coming? Nat said she might make an appearance." Nat was one of the therapists Camila was opening a new practice with.

"Rahul just texted that he's in the Uber," Ivy said.

They'd reached the front of the line. There, the woman who scanned their tickets showed them how to use the special headphones for the event. There were three different stations the DJ would be streaming music to, and you could switch between them on the headphones. Each station lit up the headphones in a color — red, blue, or green — designated to the station, so you could tell if the person across the dance floor was listening to the same song as you.

"This is my ambivert fantasy," Camila said, as she flipped from red to green and back to red. "Going out but being able to literally tune everything out when I want to."

Ivy liked the concept. The theme of the evening was pop divas, and on the blue station, Ivy found a remix of a song off Carly Rae Jepsen's latest album.

They got their drinks then made their way outside, where it seemed most of the revelers were dancing. A few songs in, Ivy was already glad she'd gone for her comfy sneakers despite them clashing with the gold fringe minidress she'd picked out. Camila said she was already regretting her shoe choice, though she was toughing it out and dropping it down.

Rahul showed up once Ivy switched to green and a Beyoncé song that was burning through the crowd. She took her headphones off for a bit to greet him.

"This is cool," he said. "I haven't been to one of these in a while."

"This is my first time!"

"There was a boy band one a few months ago," he said, dancing to the sound of one headphone so he could hear her. "I went with that girl, the Twitch streamer. Remember her?"

"Oh yeah, she was cool."

"She really appreciated my historically accurate boy band choreography."

They went to the bar, and Ivy got to appreciate what a good concept this was. It was like watching something go viral in real time — she'd observe a person in a group switch to a new color, point excitedly at their headphones, and soon half the dancefloor had tuned in, not wanting to miss out on a superior bop. She'd have to get the vendor's contact info. This would be really fun to host at the gym.

The crowd was about evenly divided now, half elated and voguing to Britney Spears's "Oops...I Did It Again" and half getting lost to an

EDM remix of a Dua Lipa track. A few adventurers were holding down the fort on green, belting out a Kelsea Ballerini breakup ballad.

It was wild, being in a space with so many people having wildly different experiences, singing different songs off tune but not even noticing, just dancing to their own beat as if there was no one watching. If she stepped back from it and just observed, it was like looking around a crowded movie theater before the lights went down, spotting the big groups, the families, the awkward first dates reaching tentatively across an arm rest.

Here, she watched a girl in a pleather bodycon dress dancing by herself, emoting with every inch of her body like she was one of Taylor Swift's backup dancers and it was the final stop of the tour. She watched a couple slow dancing, eyes on each other like they were having a conversation without speaking. The voyeur in Ivy couldn't help it, and she switched her headphones to green to find they were listening to "Snow Angel" by Renee Rapp, and she almost wept. She switched to red, embarrassed to have intruded, even unnoticed, on the intimate moment.

Across the dancefloor, Ivy saw the DJ, headphones also in red, and they made eye contact as Ivy sang a Lizzo song to herself and tried to work out her feelings through twerking. The DJ pointed at her and winked, starting to mirror her dance moves. She was cute, with a pink moneypiece against her bleach blonde hair, and wearing a black dress that looked drawn on her. Her lips were so shiny with gloss they caught the strobe lights.

Ivy knew all her lines in the script of picking up a cute girl. It was the same way you befriended a girl, with compliments and shared interests. And then, you were direct, so there was no confusion that a request to hang out sometime was anything but platonic.

She knew what song to request, where to hit her mark if she wanted to dance in her line of sight all night. She knew how to place the dominoes so innocent touches cascaded into kisses on cheeks, on lips, on stomachs, on inner thighs. There was nothing like seducing someone. But the kind of girls she used to seduce, the ones who would seduce her ... well, they weren't good for her. Not her liver, not her wallet, not her heart. This wouldn't be her first cute DJ. She had so few firsts left.

She thought back to when she first moved to LA and took up with an aspiring model. For the three months they hooked up, they'd end up drinking too much on empty stomachs because they subsisted on kale and energy drinks, or indulge in too much nose candy and end up screaming at each other outside a nightclub. Then they'd pass out in one of their beds, make up, eat more kale, go to the gym and push each other too hard, body checking, running miles going nowhere until they collapsed.

Ivy had grown up, leveled out. Anyone she'd be interested in dating seriously would be similar, right? But on a cellular level, Ivy feared every relationship was a clash with a winner and a loser — or two losers. The dramatics had been left behind as she got older, but if anything, relationships just got more complicated. And Ivy was prone to getting carried away by her feelings and the idea of what someone could be, more than who they were.

But she couldn't let that stop her from trying. She wanted to find love. She just wanted to find it with someone who was a good match for her. She had so much to offer a partner — she was hot, stylish and successful, and super charming while making a first impression. When she met someone, she knew how to make them feel instantly included and comfortable. She was a great friend, always down for a good time, but she was also dependable — the kind of friend who would be there for you when you were in crisis, who could be your emergency contact.

And she was fucking fantastic in bed. She could have a woman swinging from the chandeliers with her tongue. The girls who said they'd never enjoyed being fucked with a strap-on? They changed their minds when her rubber met their road.

So why was she having such a hard time? She had no problem getting women to swipe right. What she struggled with was wishing they'd swiped the other way after meeting them and becoming demoralized by the complete lack of chemistry. Was there something wrong with her that she wasn't finding these women appealing who had been perfectly suitable on paper? Was she the problem?

No, she wasn't. Ivy wanted to settle down, but she would stay the course on not settling. She walked up to the DJ, who lowered her headphones when she saw Ivy.

"Hey, can you play 'Super Graphic Ultra Modern Girl' by Chappell Roan?" she asked her.

The DJ gave her a perfectly straight-toothed grin. "Yeah, babe. Switch to blue for me and I'll hook you up."

"Thanks," Ivy said. When the DJ winked, she thought again about making a move.

Instead, she walked back to her friends and pointed to her headphones so they'd join her on blue. Era and Camila both lifted their drinks — Camila's nonalcoholic, Era's alcoholic and caffeinated — and cheered at the first words of Chappell's sultry, sardonic delivery recounting a terrible first date. By the middle of the first verse, the crowd was bathed in blue light and moving like each person had become possessed by their most fabulous, ass-shaking selves. Rahul had befriended a girl giving away glowstick necklaces, and was hula-hooping his around as he danced.

Ivy twirled, free and optimistic, choosing to see her romantic future through her own glittery lashes. Screaming the chorus, she asked the universe or whoever was out there listening — the dating app algorithms, maybe? — to bring her a hot, fun, ambitious, sexy woman like her.

nine

On the New Moon in Scorpio, taking place in the middle of November, the coven was finally getting together for an actual ritual. It had been a hot minute. Either they got together for non-witchy things, or someone always had to work late (Ana) or had vacation plans or family obligations that got in the way of them all being together. Even though this was the busiest time of the year for Ana, she was desperate for the energy boost she got from her witchy women, so she made it a priority to free up this evening to make some magic.

Jane was hosting the ritual tonight, and she had a flair for the dramatic. It was as if her split personae were her performance art — buttoned up political operative by day, dark witch queen by night.

She'd told them all in the group text to wear all black, and Ana realized to her dismay that the one cute black dress she owned was in the dirty hamper. She must have not taken it to the dry cleaners (read: treated it with Dryel) when she last wore it, to a funeral for her mom's cousin's stepmom who Ana's mom swore Ana had been so close with when she was little. Ana had no recollection of this woman — had no idea why she would want to go to her funeral. But, even though Ana had gotten better at disagreeing with her mother on smaller matters, she still couldn't bear it when she turned on the waterworks. Watching someone cry in Spanish just hit different, she supposed.

Sighing, Ana looked through her closet for something suitable. The best she could do was a black chef's jacket that she only wore for fancy catered events. She checked it for any stains or streaks of flour, and hoped that with black jeans, beaded jewelry and dark lipstick, she'd look sufficiently occult.

An hour later, Ana rang the smart doorbell with a Pyrex container of pomegranate salsa in hand. Footsteps approached, followed by Jane's deep, clear voice. "Who seeks passage over this threshold under cover of darkest night?"

Stifling a giggle — she was trying really hard to be reverent, damn it — Ana cleared her throat and answered, "I, Analeigh, seek passage, and I bring my own light."

The porch light turned on and the door opened. Jane wasn't there, and even though Ana knew she was just behind the door, she still gasped when Jane jumped out and yelled "HI ANA!"

"Are you trying to use me as a sacrifice?" Ana joked, holding her chest and catching her breath.

"I'm sorry, I shouldn't have," Jane said, wrapping Ana into a hug. "Everyone's in the kitchen. Can I get you a drink?"

"Just white wine if you've got it, or water's fine." She was remembering her last liquor experience.

"I've got you. Grab a black candle from the basket over there," Jane said, gesturing to the mantle above the fireplace, "and a pen to carve it with, and we'll start the ritual right at 9."

Ana felt underdressed, predictably. Jane was draped in flowy black lace; Stacy had a black brocade trench over a black spandex bodysuit; and even Harper looked more done up than she did, in her understated black turtleneck and flowing skirt. Ana knew she was the only one who would care that she wasn't styled to the gods. But even if her friends loved her in a burlap sack, Ana still wrestled with that feeling of inadequacy nurtured during the years she'd spent on celebrity gossip Twitter and outfit-of-the-day blogs, convincing herself she needed luxury streetwear to go to her Pittsburgh public school. Back then, she would spend a week's pay from her after school job on square cubic zirconia earrings she thought would look classy, only to fixate to the point of panic about how they were never facing the same way on both ears and maybe her earrings could never be symmetrical because one piercing was half a millimeter closer to the edge of her ear than the other, and she hated her parents for piercing her ears while she was a baby and unable to scrutinize the placement or argue about how her ears were going to grow and might affect the look.

She got her anxiety diagnosis pretty early in life.

After catching up with everyone, they settled into a companionable quiet to carve their individual black pillar candles. The theme of today's gathering was about dark desires, hidden truths and intense passions. Jane had asked them all to think about the most secret wishes of their hearts and seek the courage to bring them to the light. They'd use pens to write affirmations or sigils onto the candles, then anoint them with herbs and oil and burn them to manifest their intentions. The candles were too big to burn in one night — Ana would have to remember to light hers at home over the next few nights to finish working the spell.

They sat in a circle in Jane's living room, ignoring the snores of her golden retriever on the couch. Jane gave them each a piece of kindling and explained the ritual. They would light their individual candles, use their flames to light the fireplace, and Jane would lead them through a guided meditation as the fire burned.

"We'll put our own candles out, and I'll have my eyes open to watch the fireplace," Jane said. Even though she didn't look at Ana when she said it, she still knew the explanation of safety measures was for her benefit, and she appreciated it.

Harper called the corners — Earth in the North, Air in the East, Fire in the South, and Water in the West — casting a circle to protect their working. This was Ana's favorite part of a ritual. In some ways it felt like being a child playing pretend. But when she really got into it, she just felt like the magic worked, like she was in this safe bubble, a forcefield that hummed around her and filled with power with every breath. She could feel the ground under her feet, the ocean in her veins, the wind in her hair even in an air-conditioned room. She focused her mind on the fire of life, warming her skin from within.

The circle cast, Jane directed them each to add their flame to the fireplace.

"Stacy, will you lend your light to our fire?" Jane asked. Stacy stepped forward with her pillar, lit the kindling stick and tossed it into the fireplace. A puff of blue smoke rose, and Ana almost clapped her hands. She'd have to ask Jane where she got whatever powder caused that effect.

"Harper, will you lend your light to our fire?" Harper rose and went through the same motions as Stacy.

"Ana, will you lend your light to our fire?" Ana walked the few feet to the fireplace very slowly, gripping her candle tight. She placed her lit kindling gingerly on the flame, and was greeted with blue fire then green smoke.

"And I, Jane, keeper of the flame, add my light to our fire." When she added her kindling, she added a pinch of the powder sitting in the small cast iron cauldron (a tiny Dutch oven from Target — she knew this because she'd made the recommendation) and tossed it into the flame, turning it a vivid magenta.

"Witches, close your eyes and turn your gaze to your inner fire. Feel the power of this circle grow as you follow my words, and let that energy flow and grow through you, a bright, steady blaze illuminating your dark desires."

Ana's body was humming with peaceful energy as she slowed her breath. Guided meditations merged perfectly with the anti-anxiety techniques that most worked for her, like body awareness and deep breathing. She could feel a pleasant tingling in her legs and arms, and a comforting warmth in her belly from the wine and the heat of the flame.

"Place your hands on your chest and feel your fire warm them, and on the next exhale, let a spark from that fire enter your grasp. Let this small ember in your hands light your path as you find yourself in a dark and ancient forest. You can smell the pine and the scent of recent rain. Sure-footed, you walk to the tallest tree in the forest and press your palm to its bark. How does it feel? Does it feel cold under your warm skin? Do you feel the roughness of the bark? Is it dry or moist?"

Ana heard Stacy snort and Jane shush her, stifling her own giggle.

"I couldn't think of another word, OK?" she said. Resuming her deeper intonation, she continued, "As you commune with the tree, your flame ignites the tree's own spirit, and it begins to glow with an otherworldly energy. As you look up, you see more trees illuminate in the same way one after the other, as if they're lighting a path for you.

"Following the path so kindly revealed by the trees, you find a door in the middle of the forest. Picture this door. Picture its height, its color, the type of doorknob."

The image that came into Ana's mind wasn't what she would have expected. Instead of some ornate carved oak door with an antique brass knob or whatever, all she could picture was the door of the walk-in freezer at her bakery. Well, she had to go with that, or else she'd stress herself right out of the ritual mood.

"Behind this solitary door," Jane continued after giving them a few moments to ponder, "is everything you want, even the things you might not admit to yourself you want. The things you keep secret from even your sisters. As you picture these desires, what it would be like to live them, how it would feel to embody that version of yourself, you see the sigils you carved on your candle appear as flaming marks on the door."

Ana tried to picture the symbols and words she'd carved on her candle on the door of the walk-in and what they meant to her. If she could sum up her desires in one sentence, it would be, "I want to feel energized." She meant it in the physical sense — she would love to be able to cut back to two cups of coffee from her current three or four, because even though it helped her get through her workday, its jittery effects ran counter to the goal of her anxiety meds. But she also meant it in the inspired, excited, optimistic, turned-on sense. She was only 25, but she felt 125 sometimes, like she had nothing to look forward to but toil and struggle and sore feet. She missed the passion she had when she'd first set out to open her own business, before the realities of accounting and annoying customers drained it right out of her. In her dream life, she would be able to work fewer hours and spend more time developing recipes. She'd have more of a social life and time to explore other hobbies. She'd be less stressed about money — no. She was going to think big — she'd be financially secure and money would be an afterthought, a tool readily at hand instead of a prize to grind for.

When she thought of who she wanted to be on the other side of that door, she saw her own face free of the dark circles she hadn't found the right concealer to cover, her lips the bright red of her store's kiss-print wallpaper instead of the clear Chapstick she used most days. She was wearing ... a gown? One with a high slit and that hugged every curve, glowing in the moonlight. She was laughing, dancing, excited and free.

This vision was so clear. She felt like she could reach out and touch herself.

So she did. In her mind's eye, she reached for the door, and her mystical daydream self looked up from whatever she was laughing at and looked right at her, tilting her head. Like a mirror image, she reached for the door, and Ana could feel her there, lining up her palm with hers.

As she smiled at herself, pale arms wrapped themselves around her alternate's waist and a face buried itself in Daydream Ana's neck. Ivy's face.

Oh. She wasn't expecting that. She wondered if she should redirect this little visualization back to the topic at hand. But as she heard the crackling fire, the daydream carried on without her prompting and she watched it like a voyeur — watched Ivy kissing her daydream self's neck, bringing her hands to the straps of her gown, tugging them down and letting it drape to the floor, exposing her to herself, as her fingers trailed down and covered what she'd exposed, revealing only what that hand was doing as it toyed with her, as her dream self's breaths quickened and Ana in the here and now struggled to keep her own breaths steady.

With Jane's voice interrupting her voyeurism, the vision faded like smoke waved away by a hand. "Everything you want is on the other side of the door. Now, open it."

In the vision, Ana kicked the walk-in open with all her might, and it opened to a blinding light.

After they finished the ritual and snuffed out their candles for transport back to their homes, the women gathered in Jane's kitchen again for snacks and chatter. Everyone was buzzing with the good vibes of the ritual. Ana certainly felt a rush of energy afterward, just not the kind she'd anticipated.

There wasn't a ton of hidden symbolism to parse or anything. Plenty about why Ivy had shown up while Ana was in a relaxed, trance state wasn't surprising, since she'd, ahem, appeared when Ana was in similarly relaxed states in the privacy of her own bedroom. But Ana knew there was something there other than unabashed horniness. If Ivy represented her dark desires in more than a sexual way, what were those?

Ivy carried herself with strength and confidence that Ana admired. She never seemed very stressed or rushed despite being a successful business owner who seemed as busy as Ana was. And when she was around, Ana just felt this fun energy, like she didn't have to take herself or anything around her so seriously.

She laughed to herself as her friends chatted and snacked around her. The eternal lesbian dilemma — do I want to be her, or be with her? Apparently, when it came to Ivy, it was both.

ten

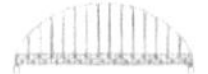

Training Ana, it was easy to understand how she'd started a successful business by 25. She couldn't stand being less than excellent at something. Ana took Ivy's instruction as seriously as if she had a six-movie deal riding on her ability to perfect a roundhouse kick.

After another night of professionally whooping Ana's ass (Ana's words), Ivy was on that knife's edge of exhaustion and kinetic, excessive energy. Ana must have felt the same, because she was fidgeting a lot, bouncing her leg up and down as she sat on a weight bench rebraiding her hair.

"Hey," she asked, her hands still in her hair, "do you have to head home right away?"

"I mean, I don't have to. It's just my cat waiting for me. Why?"

"Do you want to go get a drink or something?" she said.

Ivy felt surprised, then conflicted. That boundary she was trying to set would be a lot more permeable if she hung out with Ana outside of either of their workplaces, especially if there was alcohol involved. Still, she found herself saying, "Sure! Do you have a place in mind?"

"I do, actually," Ana said. "There's this cute bar not too far from here. My friend and her wife co-own it. It's called Lost Marbles. They make cool craft cocktails."

"Sounds great. Let me finish cleaning up here and we can go. I'll drive."

Twenty minutes later, they were walking into a small, ornate space with soothing peach lighting. "This place is beautiful," Ivy said. "How did I not know this was here?"

"They haven't been open long," Ana said. "Maggie and her wife both have other jobs, so it took them a while to finish renovations."

"I can see why," Ivy said, looking around at the cozy space with its wing back brown leather chairs, its green and gold Victorian floral wallpaper and the wooden bar, covered in a layer of resin inlaid with gold flakes and vibrant wildflowers.

"Ana!" a woman who'd walked behind the bar called out. "I can't believe I'm seeing you out twice in the last month."

"Hey Maggie," Ana said with a grimace. "I know, I've been promising I was going to come for so long. But you can't even talk! You weren't at Jane's this week." Ivy wondered who Jane was and what Maggie had missed, finding herself once again more curious than she'd prefer to be about Ana.

"You're right," Maggie said. "Running a business is some bullshit, huh? And I'm on opposite hours from you so we're like ships passing in the night. Hi, I'm Maggie," she said, nodding at Ivy.

They introduced themselves and made pleasantries. "Whatcha drinking?" Maggie asked.

"Hmm," Ana said, glancing at the cocktail menu. "Got anything on the secret menu?"

"Secret menu?" Ivy echoed.

"My experimental drinks. My idea is to rotate specialty cocktails seasonally, but I've gotta test out the recipes on some willing victims. Do you both like rum?"

"Love it," Ana said.

"I never mind a mojito."

"This is better than a mojito," Maggie said, winking. She got to work mixing rum and a smoky purple syrup in a shaker, then adding lime juice and bitters. She poured the contents in two sugar-rimmed martini glasses.

"This has my house-made lavender bitters and elderflower simple syrup," Maggie said, spearing dark cherries with skewers fashioned to look like arrows and placing them in the glasses. "I haven't come up with a name for it yet," she said.

Ivy took a sip and swooned. "This is like candy," she said. "Is that cinnamon I'm tasting?"

Maggie nodded. "In the elderflower syrup. It's infused with cinnamon and clove."

"The flavors play nice together, but I still taste the rum. Which I like," Ana said. She took another delicate sip, paused, then took a deeper swig.

"Glad you like them. Let me know if you need anything else," Maggie said, moving to the other end of the bar to take an order.

"Maggie is in my coven," Ana said, like she was telling Ivy a saucy secret.

"Your coven? Like witches?"

"Yeah, it's just me and a few other women who have varying levels of pagan interests. I don't see them as much as I'd like because I'm always in the weeds at the bakery. But our group text is kind of the only thing keeping me sane sometimes."

"I have one of those," Ivy said. "So do you actually believe in that stuff? Like, spells and astrology?"

Ana took a long sip of her drink. "I do, actually," she said carefully.

Shit. That came out sounding judgmental, hadn't it? It wasn't that she was judging it, really. She just wondered how serious her interest in it was, the same way she'd want to know if someone was casually into something or "writing fanfiction and attending cons" into something. "That's totally cool," she said, cringing at the implication that Ana would need her to validate what she believed. "It's just, I know a lot of people into stuff like astrology or getting tarot readings, but I've never met someone who called themselves a witch. I hear a lot of people on social media call witchcraft 'spicy psychology.' So I wondered if it's that for you, or something more serious, or something in between. I just am interested … in you."

She felt like she was bungling this, and it made her feel guilty about some of her dates and how she'd judged them based on similar conversational fumbles.

Ana smiled. "It's all of the above. The spicy psychology idea makes sense to me, sure, but I don't really care why something works so much as it does, and my practice makes me feel really intentional and in control when things feel out of control. So yeah, I do believe it, earnestly. It's not all TikTok tarot readings and hexes. Take this cocktail," Ana said, rotating the glass. "This could be a spell."

Ivy was intrigued. "How so?"

"Well, the thing that immediately comes to mind is the lavender. It's known to promote peace and harmony. Think of how every pillow spray has lavender in it. Then there's the cinnamon, which helps speed a spell up and promotes prosperity."

"I've seen people blowing cinnamon on their front doors."

"On the first of the month, yup. To bring the money in. And then the cloves, those are good for protection. Lime is purifying and energizing. And the rum itself, well, sugar sweetens someone's disposition, or sweetens a situation so it works in your favor. Sugarcane is associated with Venus, the goddess of love, so you could say this is good for invoking lust."

"Doesn't all alcohol do that?" Ivy asked.

"I don't know, I never feel lusty after drinking a heavy porter," Ana said.

"Fair point. I think I've got a name for this," Ivy said.

"Yeah? What have you got?"

"Light As A Feather," Ivy said. "It's witchy, but it can also represent how the drink makes you feel. Floaty and relaxed."

"Mm hmm," Ana said. "I like that."

"So speaking of likes," Ivy said, feeling like there was something to this idea of lust-inducing potions, "are you dating at all? I'm on the apps, and it's a nightmare."

She wasn't sure if it was the cocktail clouding her judgment, but she thought she could see Ana deflate. "Too depressing," Ana said. "It feels cold-blooded, you know? Just making a split-second decision on someone based on nothing. I mean, I don't even know what I would write on my profile. 'Works 70 hours a week, will probably ghost you over a bread emergency.' I don't think I'd get many suitors."

If fucking only. If Ana showed up on Ivy's dating app matches, she would swipe right hard enough to dislocate her thumb. The whole damn wrist, actually. And then she'd immediately regret it. She didn't think Ana was like her reckless, hot-tempered, toxic girlboss exes, but she was still at a different life stage than Ivy was. Ivy had already done the whole "working 70 hours a week" thing. She wanted to enjoy life now, to make her job secondary to her friendships, to traveling, to indulging in her hobbies. Ana probably wasn't there yet, and that was OK. But it would be unfair to both of them to try to ignore all that.

"I kind of bristle at the idea it's cold-blooded," Ivy said, thinking of her lists and her records of the dates she'd been on. "I wouldn't say I base my swiping decisions on nothing. Women get really in depth in their profiles. You can get an idea of what someone's beliefs are, what they do for work, and obviously whether you find them attractive. Just like what we do in person all the time. What's the difference with doing it on your phone?"

"I guess you've got a point," Ana said. "I didn't mean to take something general and make it specific to you, though. I can tell you're someone who would put a lot of thought into this."

There was an awkward silence then. Ana broke it, continuing, "So, what is it you're looking for? On the apps, I mean."

"Um, let me think." She had such a clear picture of this until this very conversation. "I think probably someone in her 30s or 40s, established in her career but not a workaholic. Likes the outdoors, active. Good relationship with her family. Someone open to having kids or with kids of her own. Stuff like that. Shit, I have a whole list."

Ana took a long sip of her drink. "I could see you as someone's stepmommy."

"I don't know how to take that," Ivy said with a laugh.

"A compliment, I guess? I think I was trying to make a 'step on me, mommy' joke but it didn't land. But seriously, do you really have an actual list?"

Blushing, Ivy said, "Yeah, I do. Is that terrible?"

"I guess it depends on what's on it. I want to see!" Ana said, bouncing up and down in her stool.

"It's embarrassing."

"No, listen," Ana said, putting her hand over Ivy's. She wanted to put her other hand on top and trap hers, tug her back to her lair. "It's good to know what you want. Women are called every fucking name from now to next Tuesday for wanting things. You should want things, Ivy."

"Oh my god," she said. "You're a lightweight."

"In the ring and with rum," she said, giggling. "The list. Hand it over."

"How about I just summarize the highlights," she said, finding the note on her phone.

"Ugh, fine," Ana said.

"So, the first thing is financial security. I don't want to be someone's sugarmommy. But I also don't want someone who is married to their work and I can't reliably make plans with."

"Makes sense," Ana said. "What else?"

Ivy's heart sped up. She had a full paragraph on her list about needing a partner who could keep up with her sexually, and she wasn't about to tell Ana that. She settled for saying she wanted someone fun and open-minded, who was willing to try new things.

"In bed, you mean?" Ana asked, raising an eyebrow suggestively.

"Moving on," Ivy said. "Someone with her own life. Hobbies, friends, interests that differ from mine so we can learn from each other."

"This all sounds pretty reasonable so far."

"Someone who isn't, like, unhealthily enmeshed with their family."

"You say unhealthily enmeshed, I say, don't talk about my mother that way," Ana joked.

"I do have some hyper specific stuff on here. Like, no cocaine. I had an ex who had a big coke problem. It was awful." She flipped her phone screen-side down on the bar. "You don't do coke, do you? To keep up with your work schedule?"

"Of course not. I drink a pot of coffee before 8 a.m. I can't also do cocaine, I would have a heart attack."

"You should maybe tell your doctor about the caffeine thing, maybe," Ivy said. Ana waved her off.

"I don't have a primary care doctor. Are you kidding me?"

"You should have a primary care doctor, you know."

Ana waved her off. "So your ex who had the problem. What happened with her?"

"She went to rehab a few times, both before and after we broke up. I think it was easy to convince herself, to convince both of us, really, that she didn't have a problem, but that was because everyone around us had a problem." Watching Ana draw circles along the rim of her cocktail glass, she continued, "When I first got to LA, I spent a lot of time on the party scene. Watched so many people waste away in front of me. My ex is in recovery and doing really well, but I don't think I've fully recovered from her. Having to smuggle your coked-out girlfriend out of a club and to the hospital before paps get a shot of her with blood pouring out of her nose … that kind of thing stays with you."

"I'm really sorry you went through that," Ana said quietly. "I'm glad she's doing better now. And that you didn't end up in the same place."

"Me too," Ivy said, "on both points. But I guess what my list boils down to is, I want someone I don't have to rescue."

"Someone you don't have to rescue," Ana said, nodding. She took a big gulp of her drink. Ivy wondered if she was thinking about Halloween, how Ivy had helped her with the guy who was harassing her. She wanted to say something to exclude that situation, to say it was different, but doing that was too explicit a link between Ana and the list. Ana might wonder where else Ivy was comparing her to her bullet points.

"Online dating is like a second full time job," Ivy said, and regretted it. Damn, why had she said it that way? And with the eye roll to boot? She'd made herself sound like a player, like every queer woman in Pittsburgh was throwing herself at her.

Visibly uncomfortable, Ana tried to laugh. "See, that's why I don't do it. And back to what you were saying about phones, I mean, I suppose our phones are such an extension of us. Some witches use them for spellwork, too. Like with wallpapers with sigils — like, magical symbols that stand in for a phrase — on them, so they're 'activated' whenever you wake your screen. Or," she paused to show Ivy the black glass, "as a scrying mirror."

Ivy laughed, happy for the subject change. "Doesn't it scare you, thinking you could divine your future?"

Ana shrugged. "I rather be prepared. I don't anticipate 90% of the shit that goes wrong in my life. It would be nice to get a heads up on even 10% of it so I could adequately adjust my anxiety meds."

Ivy snorted. "I'll drink to that. Thank God for SSRIs." It made a lot of sense to her when Ana put it like that. She knew from her own life and career that you could anticipate and prevent some danger, but no situation was ever completely under control. Existing in a human body around other human bodies at any given moment had so many variables. So you might as well prepare for what you could.

"Store-bought serotonin is just as good as from scratch," Ana said. "I'm an authority on 'from scratch' so I know what I'm talking about."

They drank and chatted more, ordering another round. She asked Ana more questions about witchery, and she felt really warm and fuzzy watching her be so excited about something. Of course, she'd already gotten the sense that Ana was a passionate person by observing her at the bakery and now at the gym, but having this new interest revealed made her yet again want to know every single thing about her. This wasn't a date, but it was more interesting than any first date she'd been on recently, because she wanted to continue the conversation. Have a second date. And a third. And a fourth.

Ivy wouldn't mind being able to divine the future. Would she ever find someone more appropriate for her, more likely to be ready for the kind of commitment she was looking for, but who could make her feel this way? Charmed, curious, giddy, turned on, impressed?

She finished her drink and ordered another, though she no longer felt Light As A Feather.

eleven

I vy made it home, turning on her air purifier to drown out the downtown noise outside her place. Sigourney was snoozing on the rope bridge that connected the two abstract trees of her cat condo. She often picked the oddest spots of the overpriced structure to sleep on. Instead of choosing one of the fuzzy padded limbs or the nook shaped like a little house, she'd sleep on the wooden bridge or one of the hexagon shelves that acted as a kitty staircase. She scratched behind the snoozing cat's ear, and Sigourney opened one eye, meowed, and went back to sleep.

"You've got the right idea there," Ivy murmured, and stretched her arms wide overhead.

She got ready for bed then poured herself a glass of merlot. As tired as her body felt, her brain was wide awake. She thought of putting on a comfort movie, but whenever she started watching something she had to finish it. There were a couple of novels she was working her way through, slowly. She bought too many books and didn't read fast enough to keep up with her bookish spending, and her attention wandered enough that she could only read a few chapters before switching to a different story. None of the ones she was currently working through appealed to her.

She went to her shelf and looked at the section that held scripts from her stunting days. Ivy had given up the idea of acting long ago. Being a stunt performer had been a fun and rewarding career, but she still wondered, sometimes, what would have happened if she'd pursued the more visible side of entertainment. What if she'd been the one delivering the lines, not the one delivering the punches and having her face CGI-replaced with the real star's? Even though she never delivered lines, she still read all the scripts of projects she worked on, even memorizing the lines of the characters whose stunts she performed. It made her feel more connected to them. Maybe she didn't need to understand the pathos of a character just so she could drive their car between two skyscrapers, but she still wanted to. It made it more meaningful, made her feel connected to her work as a mental craft and not just a physical one.

Reaching for a blue hardbound volume and flipping to a random page, Ivy started to read a few pages of the script for the second Aurora Dagger film she had worked on, just to reminisce. The first film had made Delilah Collins an overnight star, and Ivy had been contracted to be her double for the next three films in the franchise. Her pay went from a pittance to something she could actually thrive on, and a few well-timed interviews about Delilah's training regimen turned her into not just an in-demand performer, but also a sought-after personal trainer.

Those movies changed Ivy's life, but that wasn't the only reason she loved remembering her part in the franchise. Aurora Dagger was a queer superhero, a risky bet for a studio even as they'd been criticized for a never-ending roster of white cis men headlining its films.

Because of the first film's unprecedented success, more studios started to realize they didn't have to figuratively bury their gays in B-plots and innuendos that could easily be cut for foreign markets. They still did all of those things, of course, and the action genre was still very male and very white and very straight (well … allegedly). But slowly, more types of stories were making their way onto the screen. Ivy remembered the first time she saw a little girl dressed as Aurora Dagger. She'd had a break from filming and been visiting her parents in Santa Fe, where they had retired. It was Halloween, and they'd had a steady stream of trick-or-treaters. There had been a family with four little boys and one girl, and while the boys had all dressed to the same theme, as superheroes of another franchise, the girl stood out in her cape and blue wig, beaming with her jack-o-lantern basket.

Ivy remembered choking up. "You know, I know Aurora Dagger," she stage-whispered.

"Really?!" The little girl gasped.

"She would love your costume. I can't wait to tell her about it."

Smiling at the memory, Ivy flipped to a random page in the script.

EXT. BLACKLEAF CITY - NIGHT

AURORA DAGGER scans the city from atop the Cobalt Building. Her unease is apparent even behind her mask as she looks at the glittering metropolis, its lights hiding a writhing darkness. She shows little reaction to the gentle landing behind her, but every nerve ending has sparked to life.

AURORA

You took your time getting here.

CHARMER

Busy day at the office. Meetings, robberies, water cooler gossip, poisonings.

Aurora spins to face her sometimes-nemesis and current ally.

At this point in the movie, Aurora's tech support, Mr. Thorn, had run an analysis of the high-tech fabric of Charmer's costume after she'd used one of her special diamond-cutting daggers to snag fibers during one of their melees. The tactical mesh was impervious to most weapons and absorbed light to help her blend into her surroundings, but it did nothing to hide the villain's alluring curves. That was one of the notes the director gave Delilah, to give subtle cues with her eyes at the lust hiding under her stoic façade.

AURORA

We had a deal, Charmer. No more killing, not if you want my help taking down King Schnauzer.

CHARMER

Relax, princess. By the time the poor sap in question even realizes he's been poisoned, his bedraggled maid will have found the antidote and the note I left her with instructions. And maybe I managed to slip her a check that should more than cover her leaving his employ.

AURORA

I don't have all night. Did you get the data?

Charmer grins behind her cowl and starts to unzip her jumpsuit, slowly dragging the hidden zipper past her throat and collarbone, revealing a bra made of the same tactical material as her costume. She reaches between her breasts and pulls out a medallion.

On her original shooting script, Ivy had annotated this section. As written, it felt like it was for the male gaze. But if Ivy had been writing this, with a queer audience in mind, she would have had Charmer unzip enough to pull the medallion from a pocket at her collarbone.

A character like Charmer already used her sexuality overtly to further her agenda. Her cleavage being on display wouldn't be a sign of intimacy between her and Aurora.

But a collarbone? That's for a lover to behold, obsess over, kiss.

CHARMER

This might look like a mere trinket, but take a look at the ridges at the edge.

AURORA

The markings ... it's a code.

CHARMER

It's a back door passkey to Reddeck's intranet. Once inside, Mr. Thorn can do the rest.

AURORA

I'm impressed, Charmer. We might get you on the straight and narrow yet.

CHARMER

Darling, I will always be crooked. It's more fun. As for narrow ... what do you bench these days? What's the margin of error for your super strength? Your shoulders look sensationally wide.

. . .

Charmer moves closer. Aurora caresses the cheek
of her cowl, and Charmer sighs into the touch.
She practically purrs.

AURORA

We have to stop this, Kaia. We're on different
paths.

Charmer leans in, and the trap is set. Aurora
realizes it when her arms enclose her. A nanotech
harness materializes around them, binding them.

CHARMER

Oh, we're going to the same place, Ms. Dagger.

AURORA

Charmer, what are you doing?

Ivy liked this detail of Aurora saying Charmer's real name in a
vulnerable moment, then switching back once she'd betrayed her.

CHARMER

Hold on tight, sugar.

Charmer shoots a grappling hook in the air across
to the fire escape of the adjacent building as
Aurora tries to no avail to undo her restraints.

. . .

82

Both Ivy and Delilah had to do wire work for this scene, but Delilah was only lifted a few feet off the ground so they could get her closeup. Ivy had to go much higher. She didn't dangle from an actual helicopter, though. The movie didn't have that kind of budget.

83

She's never seen this technology, not at this level. She sees the helicopter materialize above them, hears the roar of the propeller, and feels the wind rush past her as Charmer shoots the hook at the aircraft and pulls them both into it, destination unknown, her best laid plans foiled.

twelve

Ten of Wands — *Heavy burdens. Too much to do. Put your back into it.*
Ingredient — *I don't know, man. I had half a protein bar for breakfast. Ivy says I need protein to build muscle, but what does she want me to do? Buy a cow? I'm not made of money.*

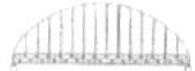

Ana was dying.

Her feet and lower back had never been this sore. She'd been training with Ivy for a couple of weeks, and apparently the soreness of exercise never went away, it just got a bit more precise. She was discovering muscles she didn't know she had. And on top of that, she was really getting into gear ahead of Thanksgiving. Over the past week, she'd been working nonstop, partly out of necessity to catch up on invoicing and pre-baking and freezing pie crusts for the Thanksgiving orders, and partly because throwing herself into work distracted her from what she was feeling.

Had she been wrong about Ivy having a crush on her? Since she was apparently dating every woman in Pittsburgh and judging them based on a rubric, she seemed to have her hands full.

It was fine. She'd get over it, eventually. Ivy was older, and wealthier, and more successful. She shouldn't have been surprised to hear that Ivy was actively on the dating scene, and she assumed the fact she mentioned it meant she wasn't considering dating her. You didn't tell someone you were interested in that they'd have a whole lot of competition if they went after you, right? Unless you were an asshole. Or was that how you wooed someone, by making them jealous? She really should have paid more attention to the cooks she'd worked with during what would have been her college years, because truly, she didn't know what the hell she was doing when it came to dating. It sucked, because she really liked her and had a good time with her, but she was fine just being friends and training with her, she supposed.

The stupid irony was, she was working so much to distract herself from her crush that she was even more stressed and anxious than usual, which made her want to take her frustrations out at the gym even more. She made the self-sabotaging decision to squeeze in another gym trip on Sunday, the one day of the week the bakery was closed. Usually, she used that day to go in and catch up on paperwork or schedule social media posts, but the overworking had, for once, put her on track.

When she walked in, Ivy saw her right away and gave her a confused look. She told the woman she was holding the heavy bag for a "just a sec" gesture and walked over to Ana.

"Hey! What's up? We didn't schedule a daytime session I forgot about, did we?"

"No," Ana said. "I just, you know, had some time today, for once, and thought I'd come in and use the weight machines. Maybe the stationary bike. That's OK, right?"

"Yes, of course!" Ivy said. "You're welcome to come in any time." She bit her lip, as if thinking, but then said, "Let me know if you need anything" and walked away.

All right, then. Ana walked to the stretch cage and loosened up her arms before heading to the assisted pull-up machine. She was making slow progress on this. She needed to offset a lot of weight to be able to do even one push-up, but today she was able to adjust the assistance to five pounds fewer than she had been, meaning she was lifting more of her body weight. It was more difficult, but not unbearable. She appreciated the small changes in ability she noticed.

She didn't have much prior gym experience to compare this place to, but she could guess most gyms didn't have so many women, or so many visibly queer people at that. The idea of "visibly queer" was difficult for Ana, because she'd always felt invisibly queer. She'd figured out she was a lesbian pretty much as soon as she had a concept that there were "boys" and there were "girls." She was only interested in the latter. When she first started dating, she had this issue of hitting on girls who were then taken aback because they'd assumed she was straight. The out gay girls often made the same assumption about her. More than once she'd Googled "how to dress gay" and she just couldn't find a plaid flannel that really spoke to her.

But because she had also been really bad at telling who else was queer, her Googling did lead her to learn about queer flagging. Looking at a woman's manicure or clocking the carabiner wasn't foolproof, and Ana worried she was stereotyping, but it did help.

In this space? The vibe, the energy? It was queer as hell. It was the eye contact and head nods, the enamel pins and ironed-on patches on gym bags, the casual displays of affection of women working out together. And it felt so welcoming. There was one woman attempting the salmon ladder who had a whole cheering squad encouraging her. There were women in ratty sweats and others in expensive designer leggings, women completely covered up and others in tiny shorts and crop tops. There were Black women, brown women, fat femmes, and no one looked uncomfortable or out of place. No one looked like they were worried about getting harassed or covertly filmed and posted on someone's Reels, or getting a dick Airdropped to their phone.

Gods damn. Ana might actually become a gym rat, for real.

She finished her set of pull-ups and moved to the free weights to do some shoulder exercises. She was debating whether she should hit legs, too, when Ivy walked up to her.

"Looking good, Analeigh," she said. "Are you closing up shop Thursday for Thanksgiving?"

"I am, actually," Ana said. "I have some pie orders to deliver the day before, but after that I have a few days off. Are you doing anything?"

"Nope," Ivy said. "The last couple of years, I've done Friendsgiving. But our usual dinner isn't happening this year."

"Oh?" Ana asked. "Why not?"

"Well, Camila and Zach are spending the holiday in California with Zach's dad. Era and Seth are hosting their families for their first married Thanksgiving. Rahul decided to visit his sister in New York for the holiday. And Liam, Camila's ex-husband, is kind of doing a hermit thing right now? So, I'm probably just going to put a frozen pizza in the oven and call it a day."

"You should come to my place. We don't do Thanksgiving, exactly, or at least I don't. It used to be my favorite because of the food, but I can't get on board with its origins. So instead I have my family over and cook for them when I'm ready to put up my Christmas tree, and we're doing that on Saturday."

"Really? You really want to invite me to your not-Thanksgiving tree trimming party?"

"Yes, really!"

"I don't want to intrude on family time."

"Please. Please intrude. I always end up having too much food, because even if I say 'don't bring anything,' everyone decides to anyway." Ana's brain was just now catching up to her mouth. Was this a terrible idea? It was, wasn't it?

"OK, I'm in! So since everyone breaks the 'don't bring anything' rule, what can I bring?"

Maybe a trough of lavender essential oil to huff for her nerves.

Actually, that wasn't such a bad idea. She put a pin in that for later, mentally combing through her pantry for ingredients for an anti-anxiety ritual.

"Why don't you bring a six-pack?" Ana asked. "I'm not a beer girl, but my dad and uncle are, and they like trying craft brews."

"Local variety six-pack. Got it," Ivy said. "I'll see you then!"

Soon after she got home that evening, Ana got to work. She had lavender in essential oil and dried form. She could make a topical with the oil, or use it to anoint a candle, or she could use the lavender flowers in a tea and speak intentions into it.

What else did she have? Rosemary was for healing and protection and could chase away nightmares, and what were nightmares if not a form of anxiety? Mint was good to eat for tummy troubles, and when she was anxious, that was the part of the body in which she felt it.

Oh, and cloves. She loved working with cloves. They looked like barb wire and added bite to any protection working. She loved the way they looked guarding a tall black candle that was carved with sigils, anointed with olive oil, and rolled in herbs.

She decided she was going to make a simmer pot. She'd throw lavender, rosemary, mint and cloves into a pot of water, bring it to a boil and lower the temperature to keep it going for hours.

First, she scrubbed down her kitchen, imagining any stagnant or negative energy disappearing with every wipe of the rag. Thumbing through her well-worn copy of *Cunningham's Encyclopedia of Magical Herbs*, she looked up the elements associated with each ingredient. Lavender and mint both were related to air. Rosemary and clove were related to fire. Obviously there was the water element with the simmer pot itself, but she was missing an earth element. For something meant to make her feel more grounded, earth was crucial. The back of the book included a table of elements and herbs that went with them. She skimmed the earth section until she found oats, which she'd just restocked. So she tossed a handful of oats into the pot.

She put on a Spotify playlist of artists like Celia Cruz and Gloria Estefan, some of her abuelito's favorites, and hummed and danced as she worked. While the herbs simmered, she grabbed a blue chime candle for calm and a porcupine quill she'd bought at a metaphysical shop in town for this specific purpose. On the notepad she kept in the kitchen to take notes while she created recipes, she wrote the phrase, "I am calm and clear headed."

Then she crossed out every vowel and duplicate consonant, until she ended up with: M CL ND R HD.

She drew the shapes of each letter and doodled them in different combinations, until she came up with an abstract symbol that seemed like a good visual representation of her intention. There were several semicircles resting on straight lines, enveloping smaller shapes.

To her, it looked like being hugged in safety, with a solid foundation, while juggling the responsibilities of her life. It was pretty good for a quick sigil. She took her porcupine quill and started carving the candle, visualizing herself feeling calm and centered, capable of handling whatever life threw at her. When she was done, she wiped off the excess wax and blew on the sigil, then rubbed a drop of lavender essential oil on it. She placed it in a holder and lit it.

The kitchen was filled with a beautiful, cozy fragrance as she cooked dinner, keeping an eye on the candle to make sure it was still burning clean and safely.

By the time she finished eating the roasted vegetables and apple butter pork loin she'd made for dinner, and the candle had burned out, she felt solid. That was the only way to explain it. When she was anxious, she felt like a wisp blowing in the wind, like the sooty smoke from a candle when she hadn't trimmed the wick. Everything about her felt wobbly — her weak knees, her gurgling stomach, her chattering teeth and goosebumpy flesh and throbbing temples. But right now, she felt as rooted and unmoving as an ancient tree.

thirteen

I wouldn't judge anyone by their family of origin, but it would be a nice bonus if their family was cool. Also, I would hope they were out to the people who mattered to them. That Kristen Stewart holiday movie where she's visiting her still-closeted girlfriend's family sent me into a spiral.

One thing Ivy hadn't missed about Pennsylvania? The alcohol laws. When she first moved back, she'd forgotten that liquor was sold only at state stores, and that beer was sold elsewhere. Not being a huge beer drinker herself, she rarely entered that separate area of the grocery store, and had no strong opinions about craft brews. She picked out a six pack of an IPA with a cool vaporwave logo, and a variety pack from the same brand.

At the checkout, the woman in front of her was having a terrible time with the point of sale. "I really need to call my bank," she mumbled, looking at the cashier apologetically. "The chip doesn't always work."

Ivy watched her try again and be greeted by angry beeping.

Worried about being late and hating to see someone in that predicament, she said, "Here, I've got it," leaned over, and waved her phone at the tap-to-pay symbol.

"Oh, thanks," the woman said. "I can go to an ATM and pay you back."

"Nah," Ivy said, waving her off. "My treat."

She made it to Ana's with time to spare, which eased her nerves. When Ana opened the door, Ivy felt the ground fall away from her feet. It was like she forgot how beautiful Ana was each time they parted, only to be shocked by it the next time she saw her. Her makeup was done up, but her hair was in a messy topknot and she wore a baggy t-shirt and bike shorts.

"Am I extremely early?"

Ivy looked around at Ana's pristine kitchen and became alarmed she'd gotten the time wrong. This didn't look like any pre-party kitchen she'd seen before. She set down the beer she'd brought, feeling anxious.

"You're on time," Ana said. "I'm just a procrastinator. Time got away from me. Plus my family tends to run at least an hour late. I thought it would be nice to ease you into them instead of you being the last one to show up."

That had been really sweet of her, and Ivy smiled. She got the sense that because of her own anxiety, Analeigh was very aware of what might make other people feel anxious.

"Do you need help?" Ivy asked.

Ana considered. "I don't need it, but I wouldn't mind it. I did do some prep, so it's not going to be a total crunch. I've got marinade ready, vegetables cut up, pie crusts prepared. Want to be my sous chef?"

Nothing would have made Ivy more excited or terrified. She wasn't a slouch in the kitchen — perhaps the one positive result of her food-obsessed early fitness days, when she cooked everything because she didn't trust anyone else to. But she was no Analeigh.

"Just tell me what to do," Ivy said.

Soon Ivy was boiling pasta and preparing the cheese mixture for Ana's spaghetti torte, while Ana tossed apples in fragrant spices that made the whole kitchen smell like a storybook. Awkward at first, as she moved around Ana in an unfamiliar kitchen, preparing unfamiliar recipes, Ivy soon got into the flow of working alongside her.

"Do you have a turkey?" Ivy asked.

"No turkey," Ana said. "Well, not 'no' turkey. I have a few drumsticks for anyone who wants turkey. But it's too dry for my taste. For meat, we're making herb roasted chicken and a chipotle honey glazed ham. On the side, we're having sweet potato stuffing, ricotta and sweet corn stuffed squash blossoms, the spaghetti torte, and whatever my family brings."

"Marry me," Ivy said, and wished immediately she could take the joke back because it didn't feel like a joke. Ana gaped then recovered.

"See, you think marrying me would mean home cooked meals every day, but most nights I come home and eat ramen and Ben & Jerry's."

"You're kidding," Ivy said.

Ana shook her head. "I wish I was. I get too tired to cook and honestly sick of looking at food all day. You know what isn't food? Twizzlers."

"I get it," Ivy said. "It's not like I go home and work on my bench press. Want me to knock out some of these dishes we made so far?" Ivy asked.

"You sure?" Ana asked. "I guess I should change."

Soon the kitchen was back in, if not pristine condition, at least presentable. Ana returned dressed for dinner, and she was a sight. She'd put on a dark floral dress splashed with peonies and violets against deep greenery. It showed off her soft arms and plump legs, the dip of her collarbone and her long neck. Her hair was piled on top of her head in a neater bun, and she'd wrapped it in a beaded string that made it look like she was wearing fairy lights. Her lips were shiny with plum gloss that Ivy longed to taste, and she'd touched up the copper shimmer that decorated her eyelids above her impossibly long, dark eyelashes.

"I feel underdressed," Ivy said.

"Is it too much?" Ana asked. She started smoothing out her skirt and fussing with her hair. "My family always teases me because I never wear the right thing. I'm always either too fancy or too casual, never in the middle."

Ivy frowned. "No, I didn't mean that. You look perfect. Your family teases you?"

Ana looked chagrined. "Just a little," she said.

"Want me to fight them?" Ivy offered. Ana laughed.

"No. Thanks though. And you're not underdressed, by the way. You look … very chic. Like a moneyed and well-traveled tia who will nurse merlot all night. Speaking of." Ana went into the fridge and returned with two Dos Equis beers. "You're going to want to be at least two deep before my family gets here."

The doorbell rang, followed immediately by pounding at the door. Ana gave her a dire look. "Chug."

Ana's family burst into her apartment, their boisterous presence filling every corner of the small apartment. Ivy was an only child and didn't have many cousins, so she wasn't used to big family gatherings. Ana's family dinner included her parents and her younger sister and brother, which she expected. She hadn't expected Ana's uncle with his much younger wife and their young twins, and her uncle's grown daughter and her baby. Ana's parents both wrapped her in bear hugs when she reached out for a handshake, air-kissing her cheek as they did. Her sister, Aracely, went straight to the kitchen and returned with the Dos Equis. Ana's brother, Tony, plopped down in an armchair in the corner to play his Nintendo Switch, and his mom yelled at him to stop. He rolled his eyes and put it away, but took it back out as soon as Ana's mom went to the kitchen to unload the stack of dishes she'd brought.

"Mami, I told you that you didn't have to bring anything," Ana said, winking at Ivy.

"Mira," Judi said to her daughter, stern, "you can't have too much food because the boys eat horses, and you can always have leftovers. I brought Tupperware."

"It's 'eat *like* horses,' Mami. And of course you did," Ana said. She swatted her mom away as she started opening the oven and moving dishes around. "Mami! Go into the living room," she said. She poured a glass of chardonnay and placed it in Judi's hand. "Go relax. Or start fluffing out the tree. I've got this."

"Fine," Judi said. She hooked her arm through Ivy's. "So, Ivy," she said. "How do you know my daughter? How long have you been 'friends'?" She wiggled her eyebrows at her. Ivy laughed despite herself. She knew Ana was out to her parents and that they were cool with it, but she didn't necessarily want to shoot down her mom's obvious suggestion they were dating.

"I've been going to Besos since it opened, and now Ana is training at my gym," she said.

"I need to get back in the gym," Ana's dad Roberto said. "I used to be a boxer, you know."

"Oh yeah?" Ivy said, lighting up.

"Yes. I worked for UPS."

It took Ivy a second to get the joke, and Roberto laughed uproariously at his own pun. Judi rolled her eyes, hiding her smile behind a sip of wine.

While she chatted with Ana's parents, opening the plastic branches of the artificial Christmas tree and unboxing ornaments, the twins sat in front of the TV to watch cartoons. Ari had picked up her cousin's baby and was bouncing the little girl on her lap, while the mom, Estela, cued up Ms. Rachel on an iPad and set it on the end table, immediately transfixing the child. Ana's uncle Vicente was watching Tony's game over his shoulder, heckling him on what sounded like a boss level. Tony was cursing at him and laughing, while Judi yelled at him to watch his language.

"Food is ready!" Ana yelled. She had to, to be heard over the cacophony. There was a pause in the noise for a split second before everyone lined up in Ana's small kitchen to pile food onto paper plates. Part of the group crowded around the round table off to the side of the kitchen, while the younger family members who weren't infants plopped onto the couch with their food, using the coffee table to hold their drinks.

The food was incredible. Along with what Ana had prepared, there was more chicken in a lemony marinade with crispy skin and tender, juicy meat served with savory yellow rice with vegetables;

sweet corn in a rich bechamel; and flan that glistened like a polished tiger's eye.

As soon as she was done eating, Ana's mom tried to do the dishes, and Ana had to physically get between her and the sink to get her to sit back down. Meanwhile, Roberto was trying to figure out how to stream music from the TV to Analeigh's Google speaker.

"Yes, please, papi, before Ana starts blaring Taylor Swift," Ari said.

Ana put her hand over her heart as if scandalized. "Wow, the casual homophobia in my home."

Ari rolled her eyes. She was staggering pink metallic ornaments on the tree, rearranging the silver ribbon that had been spiraled around it. "I cannot sit through another PowerPoint presentation about Taylor Swift's secret gay affairs. Why don't you play actual out queer artists? Like, Renee Rapp, Chappell Roan, Janelle Monae, Cherry Mercedes."

"I do, and I also play Taylor Swift," Ana said. "And as far as I'm concerned, Taylor is out. There is no way 'Dress' is about a man. 'Maroon'? There's no straight explanation for 'Maroon.' And have you heard 'Ivy'? 'Ivy' is pretty gay."

"It's true, I am," Ivy, the person not the song, said, eliciting a cackle from the entire group.

"Isn't it kinda messed up to speculate on if someone's gay?" Tony said, shocking everyone that he was even paying attention to the conversation.

"Only if you think it's a problem that someone's gay," Ana said. "She's a public figure. I'm talking about stuff that she's said in her lyrics and publicly known shit, not outing her. And what's she going to do? Send me a cease and desist letter for calling her a girl kisser in the privacy of my own home?"

"She might," Ivy said seriously.

"Basta ya," Ana's dad said. "Someone come show me how to use the maldito speaker."

"I better go help him," Ana whispered to Ivy. "Last time he messed with my TV, I ended up subscribed to Hulu and not realizing for three months."

Ivy put her hand to her chest in horror. "You could have been watching *Only Murders in the Building* that whole time."

"I know!" Ana said. "It's so good!"

Ivy watched Ana patiently show her father how to stream music, and Roberto picked a merengue song, grabbed Judi, and started dancing. The baby looked away from Ms. Rachel and started laughing and clapping, enthusiastic and off beat. Even Tony was tapping his toes. He reluctantly got to his feet when Ana dragged him up, but to Ivy's surprise, he was as good a dancer as his father was. The twins wanted to dance, too, so they grabbed Ari and started dancing with her, handles clasped in a circle and jumping around more than moving with the music. Ari jumped with them.

The song ended and everyone cheered and clapped. Roberto spotted Ivy watching from the wall, pointed at his eyes and then at her to say "I'm watching you," and went straight for her.

"Do you know how to dance merengue?" he asked.

Heat rising up her neck, Ivy nodded. "A little."

Knowing that Ivy was so present in her own body, because Ana had seen her in action at the gym, she would have expected her to be a decent dancer. She'd danced in music videos, after all. But that was choreography, all elbows and sliding across the floor, more acrobatic than dancing merengue or bachata or salsa. But apparently Ivy was good at anything involving her body, because she danced to Latin music like she'd been raised on it. Ana's dad had to show her the steps of the dances, but within a few bars Ivy had it down, hips fluid, feet confident, swishing her blonde hair and throwing her head back in laughter. At one point, Roberto spun her out, and Ana's uncle, Vicente, grabbed Ivy's free hand and twirled her into him.

Just great. Her male relatives were fighting over her lesbian crush in front of their wives and children. Ana shook her head.

"Hey! You want to sleep out in the front yard tonight?" Vic's second wife, Vero, shouted. She was smiling, and Vic bowed to Ivy and gave her a big kiss on the cheek before going over to his wife and kissing her neck like he was trying to gobble her up.

Ari had freed herself from the twins, who had finally gotten bored of dancing and gone back to the toys they'd brought. "Well," Ari said in a whisper, nodding toward her dad who was now dancing with their mother, "go dance with your girl."

"Aracely," Ana hissed. "Shh!"

But Ivy was dancing by herself, a bit awkward now, and she was looking at Ana like a girl locking eyes with her crush across the room at the homecoming dance, willing them to ask her to dance.

Her feet moved before her brain could catch up to stop her, before her anxiety could scream at her not to, that it was already too much that Ivy was here, in her home, cooking with her and meeting her family and dancing with her dad and laughing with her mom. It was too much that she'd asked Ari a million questions about school and listened to her complicated explanation of how she planned to change the world merging data and digital narratives. It was too much that she had gotten Tony's attention long enough to ask if he'd played a game Era had developed and gotten an enthusiastic confirmation.

But even if it was too much, here she was, pulling Ivy close and dancing with her in front of her whole family to Omega's "Estoy Enamorado." And as they moved their hips in sync, laughing quietly, looking around as if to remind themselves they weren't alone, Ana thanked every god in every pantheon that Ivy, as far as she knew, didn't speak Spanish. Because if she did, and she listened to the words and added those up with how Ana was lacing her fingers with hers, if she measured the distance between their chests and hips and determined it was one inch closer than was appropriate for dancing with "just a friend," then she would have pieced it together that the "I'm in love" was more than a translation.

After everyone left — not without a big argument between Ana and her mom, who had almost thrown hands in an attempt to do the dishes — Ivy tried to find excuses to stay. First, she helped with putting away the leftovers that Ana's family hadn't taken with them, as they exited with many hugs and kisses and lingering conversations in the open doorway. Then it was the aforementioned dishes. And then it was the realization there was one whole pie left. After Ivy asked if she could take home a piece, Ana said, "Actually, want to have it right now? We could start *Only Murders*. If you want."

Oh, Ivy wanted. She was one big vortex of want. Her want was going to devour the entire city like some kind of primordial kaiju if she didn't sate it or smother it. So they piled on scoops of ice cream onto their slices of apple pie, sat on the couch in the twinkling glow of the tree, and watched Selena Gomez flirt with Cara Delevigne.

"Want another slice?" Ana asked.

"Yes, please. No ice cream this time."

"How about whipped cream?"

"Oh, absolutely whipped cream," Ivy said.

Ana took her empty plate and returned it with more pie and a picturesque swirl of cream. Ivy dug in and got a glob of it on her chin. Trying and failing to be graceful, she tried to lick it off her lips and dab the excess with a napkin, only to get it on her fingers and have to lick it off there.

All the while, Ana had been watching her. Ivy hadn't noticed at first, but the way her gaze was so fixed on her, on her mouth, she knew it hadn't just gotten there.

She cleared her throat and set the plate down on the end table. "Ana, I —"

She didn't get to finish. Ana had closed the distance on the couch and made landfall on her lips, with speed that almost knocked the wind out of Ivy, she was so surprised. Her lips were cool from the ice in the drink she'd been sipping, and Ivy could feel them warming on hers. How could a kiss feel like this? Like a flower blooming in a time lapse and a tsunami hitting the shore, and the first taste of sweet, cinnamony apple pie filling on your tongue, all at once.

Trying to regain her balance, to keep herself from floating up to the ceiling, she grabbed at Ana's back, pulling their chests together. That wasn't enough for Analeigh, who crawled into Ivy's lap. And then it was Ivy's turn to escalate, because Ana sitting on her lap in that dress with her prim little knees together like a good girl would not do. She leaned back while grabbing Ana by the hips until she had no choice but to wrap her legs around Ivy's waist if she wanted to stay upright. And damn it all if she didn't almost pass out at the thought that only her trousers and whatever underwear Ana had on were separating them now, that she could just reach her hand in between them and slide right in.

Ana moaned, and Ivy had to check that she hadn't actually done what she'd been fantasizing about. But no, she was just relishing the kiss, luxuriating in it.

She was adorable. She was everything Ivy had imagined.

Everything Ivy had intended to confine to her imagination.

This wasn't right. What if she was right, and this could never be more than a casual hookup? Ivy wasn't sure her heart could take that. She couldn't fall for this girl — again, very strong emphasis on girl! Letting this kiss continue could only lead to bad things, to leading each other on and letting each other down. And then Ivy would have to find a new bakery to go to for breakfast.

Oh god. She was never going to be able to go back to the bakery. No more cubanos or eclairs for her. She might as well drop dead.

Ivy removed her hands from Ana's back and pressed them against her chest, a gentle push to separate them. Ana looked at her, expectant, hungry. With rising dread, Ivy realized she would interpret this as a signal they should change location. Like, go to her bedroom. Ivy had to picture tackling herself to keep from running with that assumption.

"Hey," she said, voice already hoarse from how long they'd been kissing, "I'm so sorry, but I've gotta go."

Clambering off her, looking a little dazed and hurt, Ana asked, "Is everything all right? Did I — did I do something wrong?"

"No, no, you're perfect. Absolutely fucking perfect," Ivy said. She wasn't helping matters, so she gathered herself. "I had so much fun. I just need to get going, OK?"

"OK," Ana said. Fuck, those liquid brown eyes looked extra watery right now. Oh no. Ivy had made this girl cry, or she would be responsible for tears coming very soon. She wanted to kick her own ass right now.

Ivy didn't know what to do. Did she kiss her goodbye? Maybe the cheek would be safe? Should she hug her? She just stood there, not knowing what to do with her hands, watching Ana straighten her pretty skirt and look embarrassed. Ivy zoned in on her purse and rushed to it.

"Thanks for having me over," Ivy said, as she practically ran out the door.

Fumble of all fumbles. Mistake of all mistakes. And she didn't even get to finish her damn pie.

fourteen

Queen of Cups reversed — *My emotions are all over the place.*

Chariot reversed — *Something has gotten derailed.*

Four of Cups — *Fuck this shit.*

Ingredient — *??? Chamomile to calm the fuck down.*

Ana's anger required a quarantine zone in the five mile radius around her. It made her sweat caustic, like it was burning her from the inside out before disintegrating everything she touched. But who or what was she really angry at?

At first sight, she was angry at Ivy for bailing the way she did, leaving her feeling like she'd done something terribly wrong. But she didn't want to be kissing anyone who didn't want to be kissing her. So that just left her. There were a few reasons Ana was on her own shit list. First, she was pissed at herself for crying after Ivy left. Then she dropped a cast iron pan on the floor and cracked a tile, which meant she'd never get that security deposit back.

But mostly she was angry at how she couldn't be chill about this.

She knew what someone mature and sophisticated would do, what the Ana she was trying to manifest into existence would do. She'd either show up and calmly discuss the situation, coming to a clear understanding of how they felt about each other. Or she'd vanish from Ivy's life. If Ivy couldn't respect her enough to not leave her panting with her skirt up by her hips and no explanation, then Ana didn't need to waste time with her.

But what if Ivy kept showing up at the bakery? Could she just ignore her? What if she wanted to talk to her? Ana would be cornered. She could only stay in the walk-in freezer for so long.

She paced from her office at the back of the bakery to the front door and back three times, pausing at the door handle each time, before deciding she was going to face her and be done with it. Maybe she wasn't sophisticated. But she could be direct. She could ask Ivy to talk about what happened and they could both say how they felt. At least she'd know where she stood. She'd probably look pathetic in the process, but her mother had always told her she'd never regret making a choice that was true to herself, even if it left her in a vulnerable position.

When she got to the gym for her usual session, she'd calmed herself down enough that she was actually eager to see Ivy. They would talk, like two adults, and everything would be fine. Or at least, everything would be out in the open.

She didn't expect Ivy to greet her with a distant, reserved smile rather than a sheepish grin or quip about their makeout session. She would have settled for a vague apology for bailing, or even a joke about whether Ana was up for doing the hundred burpee challenge today. Instead she told Ana to warm up on the jump rope to prepare for drills.

Ana glared at her between the rapid obstructions of the jump rope in her vision. As her heart rate increased, it was like the blood was pumping directly to her annoyance, as if rage were an organ inside her that Ivy was poking at, and it was about to hemorrhage everywhere.

She tossed the rope down like a gauntlet. "I don't want to do drills today," Ana announced. "I want to train on staff."

Ivy raised one arched taupe brow at her. "All right," she said. "Let me get the equipment."

They started warm-ups, going through range-of-motion and stretching exercises with the staffs.

"Let's go through a sequence slowly, then repeat it a few times. I'm going to up strike, and you'll block then cross strike and spin. I'll block then helicopter spin." She paused to demonstrate, spinning the staff overhead with two hands.

"And I'll side block," Ana said, infusing some sass into her voice as she met Ivy's move with the block before she'd announced it. Ivy smiled at her, and Ana felt like she'd been hit in the head.

"Right," Ivy said. "And then the sequence will start over."

"Got it," Ana said. "I'm ready."

"All right. Nice and slow the first few times."

The first time through the sequence, Ana got flustered and didn't grasp the staff correctly when blocking. "That would give me an advantage," Ivy said. "Let's do that part again. I strike, you block, we repeat."

They repeated that combination a handful of times before starting at the top of the sequence again. Ana's confidence surged, and with that, so did her anger. God, she loved watching Ivy with the staff, with the sheen of sweat on her freckled skin, and the measured ferocity of her stare. She put too much force into her next cross strike, and Ivy raised an eyebrow at her. It ticked Ana off, the fact Ivy could be surprised by the level of power behind her maneuvers. She hated low expectations of her.

After her next spin, she struck instead of preparing to block. Ivy looked at her curiously, as if perhaps Ana had just forgotten the next part of the sequence. But she hadn't. Ana knew what her next move should be, but instead she performed a down strike, followed by a cross, gaining on Ivy's space.

Ana could tell she'd taken her off guard. "Ana," she warned. "Fall back."

"What the fuck was that about last night?" Ana asked.

"Listen — " Ivy said.

"No, you listen!" Ana said, refusing to acknowledge how ridiculous it was to ask a question and then demand silence when the answer was about to be spoken. She was crowding Ivy now. She had her back against the ropes and had no room to do anything but block, trying to push Ana back toward the center of the ring so she could more freely maneuver. Their staffs were crossed, and all of Ivy's composure had fallen away. She was glaring down at Ana over the intersection of their weapons. "That was fucked up! You can't just leave like that without explaining and then act like nothing happened today!"

"I was waiting for the right moment to bring it up," Ivy said through gritted teeth. "Because I didn't want my bullshit to eat into your session. But if you want to talk about it right now, Ana, then let's talk." The words were glacier cold, but her eyes were wild. A dare, a challenge. Another gauntlet thrown. Having lost focus, Ana was easily outmaneuvered by her more skilled opponent, who was now pushing her back toward the ropes on the other side of the ring. "Let's talk about how I've wanted to fuck you since the moment I saw you, how I would have had you out of that Cruella costume and on your knees in my bed if I could have."

"Then what's stopping you now?" Ana said, letting her staff drop. She was shaking but trying not to show it, trying to retain whatever semblance of power she was putting on like a costume. "What's stopping you from putting me on my knees?"

"Because I'm closer in age to your parents than to you, and that makes me feel like a creep, Analeigh."

"Oh," Ana said, cringing. "You didn't have to say all that."

"See? I'm a dirty old woman."

"Maybe I want you dirty," Ana said. Feeling something come over her, Ana lifted Ivy's chin, quite bold to do to someone taller than you. But it was like Ana had shapeshifted, because somehow, she felt like a giantess. Ana was against the ropes, but it was Ivy who was diminishing, looking into Ana's eyes with hunger for something sweet. "Maybe I want to get filthy."

And Ana kissed her.

Of the thousands of times Ivy had imagined kissing Ana — millions, since her holiday party — Ivy never imagined herself angry. But she was furious. Why had they not been doing this since the second they met? Since the dawn of time? Why had she wasted so much time sleeping and eating and filing income taxes and kissing other women when she could have been kissing Ana? It wasn't fair, and she had some nerve to come in here and be angry at her, when clearly Ivy was the aggrieved party. No one could possibly have suffered as much as Ivy was suffering right now, wishing she could clone herself because it was bullshit she had to choose between kissing Ana's lips and kissing the rest of her. But if she broke the kiss, she was going to die. Dilemma. Catastrophe.

"Why did you leave?" Ana gasped out. She was holding onto Ivy's ponytail like it was a rope over a cliff, like she'd fall to her death if she didn't. "Why did you leave me?"

"I'm sorry," Ivy said, slouching so she could kiss the sweat off Ana's cleavage, so she could bury her face in her neck. "I'm stupid. It was stupid."

She'd tugged one side of Ana's sports bra up from under her tank top and was sucking her nipple.

"Oh god," Ana pleaded. "Please, I want you so bad."

Ivy tugged at the waistband of Ana's leggings and shoved her hand into Ana's lacy underwear, past the soft curls wet with longing, and Ana melted into her. God, she was beautiful like this, yielding to her touch while breathlessly issuing commands, rocking her hips into her hand and directing her, then rewarding her with the most gorgeous moans when Ivy did it just right.

"Yes, just like that. Oh god, Ivy." Her head was tilted back over the ropes, arms extended and holding onto them for dear life. Ivy watched her knuckles turn white and her cheeks flush as she gasped and cursed through an orgasm.

Ivy felt like she'd just run a marathon. She'd done that, put that goofy contented smile on Ana's face, gotten her soaked enough to warrant a wet floor sign.

"More," Ivy said, because apparently she'd forgotten every other word.

"Come to my place?" Ana asked, followed by a moan when Ivy nibbled the top of her breast then flicked the nipple with the tip of her tongue.

"Your place is like ten minutes away," Ivy said. "Fuck, that's too long."

"I know," Ana whimpered. "I know." She pushed Ivy away and set her bra to rights. "I'm going to go, OK? Wait five minutes and then come to my place. You're going to show up, right?"

Ivy understood, logically, why she was asking that question after the stunt she'd pulled. But right now that felt like the dumbest question she'd ever heard.

"Five minutes."

"That makes it fifteen!" Ivy said, pulling Ana back by her waist and claiming her lips again.

"Mujer del demonio, let me go!" Ana swore. "We're wasting time talking!"

fifteen

ANA

Hey, if you're at my house, you need to leave
right now.

ARI

What? I just got here. I have laundry.

ANA

I need you to leave. I'll do your laundry. Just
leave it.

ARI

What the hell, I have a Hot Pocket in the
microwave. Is everything OK?

ANA

ARACELY, TAKE YOUR HOT POCKET AND
LEAVE MY HOUSE!!!!!

Tearing through her apartment like a hurricane, Ana rushed into the shower, eager to scrub the sweat off herself. The water scalded her, the pressure pounding everywhere Ivy had kissed. She was so sensitized that it added to her painful desire. It was agony waiting for Ivy to come to her rescue.

She was still dripping wet when she heard the banging on her door. Nearly slipping on the wet floor, she wrapped a towel around herself — "wrapped" was, perhaps, a generous word, as was "around," because she wasn't too worried about modesty — and ran to answer the door.

"Ivy," she breathed, and quickly the breath was knocked out of her. Ivy was taking her oxygen for herself, kissing her, grabbing her, with a force that felt like more of a battle than their earlier tussle with the bo staffs.

The towel was where? Who knew. The next thing she was aware of, other than Ivy's mouth and hands and the unintelligible horny words bouncing around her brain like pinballs, was the outline of her shower-drenched body on Ivy's clothes. It was urgent that she take those clothes off, right away. They had to be thrown in the dryer. Her woman couldn't be walking around with wet clothes. It was unacceptable.

She opened her mouth to say so but she was too stunned by the speed at which Ivy had shoved her into her bedroom and onto her bed so that she could — and there was no other word for this — *feast* on her.

Ana didn't know what to do with her hands. She wanted to touch Ivy, and not just her hair — God, her hair was so pretty, like sunshine. But if she stopped her, if she pulled her up to strip her down, she would lose this feeling of being savored like ambrosia, worshiped like a goddess. Between licks and kisses, Ivy moaned. As close as she had been moments earlier, Ana was surprised at the way Ivy was edging her, tonguing her clit until she was on the verge and then pulling away to use her hands, to use her tongue to fill Ana. The next time Ivy let her pleasure dip into a valley, she ran her fingers through Ivy's hair and gently tilted her head up, so they were making eye contact.

"You look so beautiful between my thighs," Ana said.

Ivy smiled and licked her lips. "You look good from this angle, too."

"Come here," Ana whispered.

They broke apart long enough for Ana to kiss her and help her out of her clothes. They had both wanted this to happen so fast when they were at the gym, and as soon as Ivy walked through the door and attacked her with pleasure. But now, looking at Ivy — lips red from their fierce kisses, like she'd just spent an evening sipping merlot, her small breasts and strong arms and long, bare legs twining around hers — Ana wanted to slow time down. What god did you pray to when you wanted a night with a lover to last forever, when the feel of her pussy gripping your fingers and the taste of her felt like they were changing you on a cellular level, like you needed to give her time to rewrite your brain with every stroke of her tongue, and you needed to pay her in kind? Which deity would listen when it was Ivy's name, not theirs, that she cried out?

The first time Ana came, it was on Ivy's fingers. The second, it was against her thigh as she fingered her to her own release. The third, they lay on their sides and went down on each other, and only then, feeling Ivy's legs shake on either side of her head seconds before her own release, did Ana finally feel satisfied.

"Hey," Ivy said, after Ana came back with a bottle of water and two glasses of red wine.

"Hey," Ana said. She crawled back into bed and started kissing a trail down Ivy's body again. Ivy sighed.

"Do you want to stay the night?" Ana asked, terrified and hopeful.

"Yes," Ivy said. She straddled her for another kiss. Ana had to set her wine down blindly so she could reciprocate.

"Do you want to talk now?" Ivy asked. Ana's hand was between her legs again. She smirked, smug, when she made Ivy gasp and pull her hand away, clearly still too sensitive.

"We don't have to talk tonight," Ana said. That would be her offering to whatever god would listen, in exchange for this perfect night. "Tomorrow. I want to just keep enjoying ourselves. I feel like … I don't know, we should both sleep on things since everything's been so heated." She would suffer through the uncertainty of whether this was the only night they'd ever have together.

"Well," Ivy said. "We finished one thing we started. Do you want to finish the show we were watching?"

Ana laughed. "Sure. Come here," she said, patting the spot on the bed right next to her. When Ivy positioned herself, Ana tugged her so she was on her lap and could wrap her arms around her waist.

"OK," Ana said, kissing Ivy on the cheek and taking a sip of wine. "Let's restart that episode. I don't remember a thing about it."

A beautiful, ringing note woke Ivy the next morning.

She crawled out of Ana's bed, seeing that she had left her an oversized T-shirt. She put it on and helped herself to a cup of coffee then headed to Ana's living room, where the ringing had come from and where the scent of dragon's blood incense was emanating.

"Good morning," Ana said, looking at Ivy as she lit a candle.

"Good morning," Ivy said. She was a bit nervous to approach what was clearly an altar, with saint candles and black and white photos, and what she recognized as the likely source of her wake-up call, a tuning fork.

"Sit down," Ana said, patting the spot next to where she sat on the floor, cross-legged.

"What are you doing?" Ivy asked, hoping her curiosity wasn't rude.

Ana was quiet a moment, as if trying to figure out the best way to explain it. "This is my ancestor altar. Every morning, I take a few minutes to sit down, pour a cup of coffee for me and for my ancestors, and pull some tarot cards. It makes me feel like I'm honoring them and like they're guiding me. Like they're still here, through me."

"That's beautiful," Ivy said. She wondered, then asked, "What if some of them don't like coffee?"

"Well, this guy definitely did," Ana said, pulling a picture frame from the display and holding it out to Ivy. "This is my maternal grandfather, Jose. We were very close, but he died when I was in middle school. My earliest memories were of him sitting in a rocking chair at our house, drinking cup after cup of coffee and watching telenovelas. Also smoking a lot of cigarettes, but they're expensive so I don't buy those for the altar. Plus, I always hated that he smoked." She looked at the photo with a wistful smile before putting it back. "Sorry, abuelito. I don't like anything that hurt you."

"Do you want me to give you some privacy? While you pull the cards?"

"It's OK," Ana said. "It won't take long."

"Do you have to go to work today?"

"I do," Ana said. "But in the afternoon, just to do payroll. Maybe I'll actually hold myself to that." She started shuffling the cards.

"I just have to go in and sign. Do you not have an accountant? Or HR person?"

Without stopping her shuffle of the cards, Ana shook her head. "Nope, not in the business budget right now. Most of that stuff falls on me."

"Is it just your grandpa who you honor so specifically, like with things he likes?"

"I definitely give him more attention than my other ancestors," Analeigh whispered, like she didn't want them to hear her. "Because I was close to him and I know the most about him. But this is for all my ancestors, and I put things that I think they would have liked culturally, like Cuban foods and little trinkets from Puerto Rico."

"If you're cooking for all of them, then I'm sure they'll forgive you for giving your grandfather a little something extra," Ivy said.

A card fell out of the deck and Ana picked it up. "The Empress," Ana said. She held the card against Ivy's face. "You kind of look like her, actually." She pulled the next two cards in the pile and pondered them, while Ivy grabbed the Empress card.

"We're both just blonde," Ivy said with a laugh. "She's more voluptuous than I am. I actually feel more drawn to this card," she said, pointing at the masculine figure of the Chariot. "Even though I didn't really do stunt driving more than a couple of times. I was a pretty terrible driver. Still am." She pointed at the middle card. "This one looks scary."

Ana picked it up and glared at it. "Eight of Swords. You just love to follow me, huh?" she asked the card. "I get this one a lot. It's about being trapped in your own fear."

Ivy examined the blindfolded figure, surrounded by blades in the ground. "So nothing's stopping her from getting out, right? She could just take the blindfold off, walk between the knives?"

"Exactly," Ana said. "Good intuition."

"I don't know a ton about tarot, but I do know that it relies on archetypes, right? It tells a story like the hero's journey?"

"Yes," Ana said. She looked through the deck until she found the one of a young person about to absentmindedly walk off a cliff. "The journey of the Fool through everything that could happen to a person. Love, death, rebirth. Betrayal, addiction, success, joy. And like my friend the Eight of Swords, fear."

"What is it you're afraid of?" Ivy asked.

"Everything," Ana said. She set the Eight of Swords on a holder and shuffled the other cards back onto the deck. Strange to give something that felt so negative pride of place, Ivy thought. "I'm afraid of driving to work and walking to my car alone at night. I'm afraid of going bankrupt and how it would hurt everyone who relies on me for their income. I worry about whether I misread the expiration date on a food package or if I'm going to accidentally serve something with nuts to someone who is allergic, or if I'm going to suddenly develop an allergy myself and not realize it when anyone is around who could call 911 or stab me with an EpiPen, and then I'll die alone and the last thing anyone will say about me is that they were drawn in by the smell of my rotting corpse, and I'll always be remembered as the rotting corpse lady."

At first Ivy wanted to laugh, but she restrained herself. She realized Ana wasn't joking, and the last thing she wanted was to make Ana feel bad, like her fears were laughable.

"It sounds hard," Ivy said, "being afraid of so many things. There is a lot to be afraid of, but still. I get how uncomfortable fear is. To feel it chronically … that's terrible."

"Thanks," Ana said. "I do take anxiety medication. It helps, but it doesn't totally fix the problem."

"I get it," Ivy said. "But I'm glad it helps at least." She looked at the photo of Ivy's grandfather. "So. Any clue how they might feel about me? Am I making a good first impression?"

"Well, let's ask them," Ana said. She shuffled the deck again and a card fell out again. "The Ace of Wands," Ana said. "It's kind of the thumbs-up of the tarot. You see it?" It was a hand holding a staff, and it did remind Ivy of the gesture.

"So, that's a good thing?"

"Yeah, it's a good thing."

"I wish I could feel better about my ancestors, but they were probably terrible people."

"Probably," Ana said. She laughed at Ivy's expression. "But. The books I read about ancestor veneration talk about that. If you have ancestors who did bad things, it's even more important to work with them. To heal all those generational wounds, to understand what they did and how you can do better for the people who will come after you. Plus, I think, I mean I'm assuming, that going to the other side changes you somehow. That once you're not mortal, you're not bound by mortal folly."

"That's … that's a really lovely thought," Ivy said.

"So," Ana said. "About last night."

"And the other night."

"Yeah, that one, too. So … what's the deal? Why'd you bail on me? Is it just that you remembered you're closer in age to my mom than to me?"

"Ugh. I thought you said we didn't have to say all that."

"But you already did," Ana said. "So now we have to talk about it."

"Well, it's a fact. And it's also a fact that I'm at a phase of my life in which I'm looking for something serious."

"And you don't think I'm a serious person?" Ana said. "This feels very *Legally Blonde* coded. Are you calling me a Marilyn and not a Jackie?"

"No, Ana. If anything, I think you're too serious of a person. I'm worried about, I don't know, tying you down when you should be going out, going through a hoe phase or something." She looked cautiously at the altar. "I apologize if that was disrespectful."

"How do you know I didn't already have a hoe phase?" Ana asked, ignoring her last remark.

"Well, did you?"

"I mean, depends on who you ask. It's not like you deflowered me and have to make an honest woman out of me now."

"So your brother isn't going to challenge me to a duel?"

"Please. Not unless it's in *Mortal Kombat*. Look, I'm not worried about the age gap. I like you, and I'm a fucking adult, and I can date whoever I want. The question is whether you want to date me. Because you can't decide that for me. You can only decide it for yourself."

"You think I can fucking resist you?" Ivy said. "I'm trying to control myself because we're in the presence of your ancestors."

"Well, since they're here being nosy," Ana said, shuffling the cards. "Hey, grandpa," Ana said, "do you think Ivy should ask me on a date?"

Ivy stopped her mid-shuffle and pulled the top card from the pile.

"The Ace of Wands," Ana said. "Thumbs up."

"Cards don't lie," Ivy said.

sixteen

Honesty is so sexy. About the big things and the silly stuff.

Teenage Ivy would have loved to take a girl to the Row House Cinema for a horror double feature, but the theater opened long after Ivy moved away. Plus, it was nice to be able to enjoy it now as an adult, when she could get a craft beer at the Bierport to bring into the movie.

She didn't get to come here as much as she would have liked, being an overworked overscheduler whose friends preferred sitting and talking versus sitting and watching. The theater had frequent double feature events, and right between their Halloween offerings and their Santa slasher extravaganza, they were hosting a double feature they'd advertised as Beauty Rituals. First up on their double feature was *Spring*, followed by *Neon Demon*.

This was the secret Ivy would take to her grave. She often spoiled movies for herself. Sometimes it was on accident. She liked to look at early reviews and scour IMDB pages to see whether anyone she knew had worked on a film. But then she'd keep going until she was deep into a subreddit or a Discord channel discussing the film, and then she'd know every plot point.

It was more intentional with horror. Ivy knew so much about special effects and stunts that one might think nothing scared her anymore. She knew how the sausage was made, and knew the sausage was just corn syrup and prosthetics. But she was too good at getting into the movie, even after working on films had removed so much of the mystique.

So she had to keep removing that uncertainty. She was more fearful about performing stunts than anyone would have picked up on. It's just that by the time the cameras were rolling, she'd done so much practice and research, understood all the physical mechanics at play and everything that could go wrong, and she wasn't afraid anymore.

That wasn't something she was about to let Ana know. Ivy would just have advance notice of when any jump scares might happen, so she would know exactly how to time putting her arm around Ana.

Ana was going to Uber right after work to meet her there. When Ivy saw her, her heart was thudding out of her chest like a Looney Tunes character. She looked stunning. She was in a long sweater dress with an ikat print, pointy boots ("Very witchy," Ivy told her), and a navy trench, and her hair was in a high, bouncy ponytail.

While she was ogling her, she didn't realize Ana was doing the same.

"You look ... wow."

"Thanks," Ivy said. "I was feeling more masc today." She'd braided the sides of her hair back and slicked the top layers into a pompadour. Her clothes were monochrome forest green: a fitted T-shirt, tailored trousers, lug sole boots, and a trucker jacket. There was something about when she dressed like this that felt delicious. The way she spoke, the way she walked, her demeanor all changed, like she was playing a character she really liked and could step into their shoes.

"I like it!" Ana said. She cozied up to Ivy and grabbed her hand. Her lips were so glossy, and now that she knew how soft they were, she couldn't wait to taste them again. She turned them to look at their reflection in the window. "We look good together."

"Yeah we do," Ivy said. She loved that Ana could be so open about what she felt. She angled them out of view of anyone who could see her squeeze Ana's butt. Ana widened her eyes and smacked Ivy's ass in response.

"Ow! Wallet pocket!" She shook her hand around, and Ivy took it in hers and kissed the knuckles.

"There there," she said. Ana's brown eyes were boring holes in the back of her skull.

"We better get in there before I mount you in this lobby and get us both arrested," Ana said. "I don't think anyone I know would bail me out."

Ana insisted on buying the tickets. "Huh, I would have worn a costume if I knew I could get a dollar off," she said after she paid. They grabbed beers at the underground taproom — Ivy's was called Space Queen, and Ana's was the Cheesecake Sour — and traded swigs of each other's selections as they settled into their seats.

The first movie, *Spring*, was about a young man who fled to Italy after a very bad night. He falls for a beautiful woman who he soon discovers transforms into a series of eldritch horrors ahead of a final transformation, repeating a cycle she's lived for centuries. It ended up being more charming and romantic than scary, though there was one scene that made Ivy jump despite her earlier preparations.

In the intermission between flicks, they got fresh beers, both trying a chocolate porter, and popcorn to share.

The second movie was *Neon Demon*, starring Elle Fanning as a new model in Los Angeles. The film was equal parts stylized and grotesque. Ana put her hand on Ivy's thigh and squeezed during a particularly distressing scene involving an eyeball.

It was dark when they got out of the theater, past the dim light of the glowing paper lanterns in the hallway and into a perfect fall night. Pittsburgh could be unbearable, too humid in the summer and a frozen hellscape that made it impossible to drive safely in the winter. Spring just made her sneeze. But fall was crisp and just the right amount of gloomy. There wouldn't be many more days like this.

"So, what did you think?" Ivy asked Ana as they walked to Ivy's car.

"I liked the first one better, but I enjoyed both."

"I think I liked the second one the most."

"Oh yeah? What about it?"

Ivy laughed, realizing all at once the ways the movie had resonated. "Well, I'm about to turn 40 and I've worked in the entertainment industry, so I've been around those young women. I understand the obsession with youth and beauty, how for some people it's something you'd do anything for."

"Is that how you felt?" Ana asked. "Or ... feel?"

She had to think about that one. Though she still spent more money on skincare and beauty treatments than any of her friends in Pittsburgh, it was significantly less than she'd spent a few years ago, and worlds away from what she knew actresses her age and younger were spending to keep up their looks.

"I mean, I'm only 39, but I've been through so many beauty standard cycles already. Like, I know women who had fat taken out of their stomachs and put into their asses just to turn around and suck it back out a few years later. And then people started taking the fat out of the inside of their cheeks for that really chiseled, gaunt look. And I'm not immune to it. You know that vampire facial? I did that. Cryotherapy? Did that, too. I think it made my nipples permanently erect, not that I have a before photo I can compare them to."

Ana giggled. "Am I going to find an IV of B vitamins at your condo?"

"God, no. That freaks me the hell out."

"But being in a freezing cold metal tube or sticking needles all over your face is just chill?"

"None of this is rational," Ivy said with a laugh. "But for people in the entertainment industry, there is just so much pressure. Even if you are an adult who is playing an adult, if your character is meant to be 'mature,' it's still maturity by way of the ingenue. Just a hint of crinkle on the face. Lips full. Neck immaculate, though probably hidden by a turtleneck. Breasts up to your chin. And now it's seeping more into the mainstream than I've ever seen. You know I got an ad on TikTok for an anti-aging straw?"

"I literally got three ads for that back to back today. Like, can we not have the tiniest thing that isn't a stressor? I have to be stressed about how I drink water now? It's a win when I even remember water."

"It's awful and I hate it, but guess what? I still get the Botox. I still use the retinol and the eye patches and the tape that keeps me from scrunching my forehead when I sleep."

Frowning, Ana asked, "Wait, that's a thing?"

"Yup. I haven't worn it in a few nights," Ivy said. "And look." She pointed at her forehead. "Crinkle crinkle."

Ana got on her tiptoes and kissed Ivy between her eyebrows. "Beautiful."

They reached Ivy's car and drove quietly for a couple of minutes. While the aesthetics of aging caused Ivy anxiety, she appreciated the way that aging transformed her, honed her to the truest, sharpest form of herself. She'd known so many women who were terrified of turning 30, and she'd welcomed her thirties, feeling like she'd unlock some kind of superpower just by virtue of being out of her struggling twenties. She felt similarly about turning 40. She had accomplished so much and had wonderful people and a fulfilling vocation in her life.

"You know," she said, breaking into the silence, "I think originally I wasn't concerned with youth or beauty, exactly, so much as I was with perfection. With aesthetics as a symbol of what I was able to do, with how healthy I was." She shook her head. "I was deluded if I thought anything about how I was in the early days of my career was healthy. But I must have believed deep down that if I just ate as much celery as possible, I would never die."

To her surprise, Ana laughed. "I'm sorry. It's not funny, I just think about how much my twenties have wrecked me, and how every day feels so long, but I still stay awake thinking about how scared I am of death."

"I hate to think that everything painful in our lives goes back to fear of our own mortality."

"That might be why I'm so into the ancestor veneration," Ana said, thoughtfully. "Just making my peace with the idea of not being here. Slowly. And realizing that even when I'm gone, maybe some part of me will be left. As a memory, or even if no one remembers me, as just the idea of someone in the past who existed."

"This is ... a lot."

"Well, we did just spend six hours in a dark theater watching human bodies do incredibly disgusting things," Ana said. "Hey. Can I tell you a secret?"

"Sure," Ivy said.

"I looked up spoilers for both movies," Ana said. "I might be more of a coward than I let on when you asked if I liked horror, and, well, I didn't want to make a fool of myself by screaming or jumping out of my seat."

Ivy laughed. "Wow, Ana."

"I know, I'm lame. I'm sorry. I wasn't going to tell you, but I felt bad."

"No, I'm laughing because I do the same thing. Constantly, not just when I'm trying to act cool in front of a cute girl."

"You think I'm cute?" Ana asked.

"Come on, Analeigh."

"Oh, my government name and everything."

Ivy leaned over while they were stopped at the red light and kissed her. Both their lips were slick with balm, sweet and melting from the heat of their kiss.

seventeen

The Lovers — *Maybe I'll get lucky tonight.*
Ingredient — *Carrot for lust? If you say so, Cunningham. I'll get a carrot cupcake somewhere, though it won't be as good as making it myself.*

Downtown wasn't as stressful for Ana when she wasn't the one doing the driving, and when she didn't have somewhere to be by a specific time. She was excited to see Ivy's condo. She sort of imagined it as a very industrial, chic loft with expensive minimalist furnishings, a vintage record player, and one of those clear-door refrigerators that she was sure only people who had never worked in the food industry owned. Those were common in restaurants for displaying dessert and they were an absolute bitch to keep clean.

She was partly right. It was a loft, with the industrial exposed ceilings and brick walls that were straight out of Pinterest, but it was not minimalist at all. It was sort of ... chaos? Not messy, exactly, but lived in and full of cozy clutter. There was the vintage record player, yes, but it was adjacent to the TV on a console that looked like it had been decoupaged in miniature movie posters from hundreds of films, grouped by color to make a gradient of pink to red. That was the clear focal point of the room, but it was far from the only busy area. Ivy had a truly ostentatious cat tree, and a built-in bookcase that was half full of books, half full of DVDs. Ana knew that when you went into a home full of books, you needed to examine the selections and see if the person's tastes were trash or not.

Ivy's bookshelf had a lot of books about the film industry: *If It's Purple, Someone's Gonna Die: The Power of Color in Visual Storytelling; Dressed: A Century of Hollywood Costume Design; The Stuntwoman: The True Story of a Hollywood Heroine.* She had a lot of fitness books, too, ones about anatomy and training splits, and one called *Deconstructing the Fitness Industrial Complex.* There were some bestseller lit fic titles, and — here was something — historical romance novels.

"So, what's the verdict?" Ivy asked, watching Ana appraise her shelves. Ana blushed, feeling caught.

"I'm surprised that you read historical romance. This one was great," she said, picking out a title by Lisa Kleypas. "And this one," she said, grabbing a thick tome by Laura Kinsale called *Flowers from the Storm.* "So what's your favorite book?"

Ivy went to the shelf and grabbed *Circe* by Madeline Miller.

"I've seen people talk about this one so much, but I hate reading hyped books. I always think I'm going to be the only person who hates it," Ana said.

"Ooh. Oh my," Ivy said, and pressed the book to Ana's chest. "Trust me, there's no way you're going to hate this one. Please take it. I don't need it back any time soon, so take as long as you need."

"OK," Ana said, hesitating. "But I'm telling you, if this is your favorite book and I don't like it, you can't hold it against me."

"I promise I won't. But you'll love it. You're a badass woman and a witch to boot. It was basically written for you. In fact, you can hold it against *me* if you hate it."

Ana blushed at the compliment. "How would I do that?" Ana asked.

Ivy thought about it. "Hmm. How about 100 burpees? One of my favorite torments to inflict on someone else, so it would be righteous retribution."

"I'll keep your offer in mind," Ana said. "Ooh, hi, pretty kitty."

A black cat was rubbing itself against Ana's leg, purring loudly. She got down on one knee and offered the cat her hand, and the cat leapt into Ana's arms.

"Hello, little love!" Ana cooed. "What's your name?"

"That's Sigourney," Ivy said. "And I have never seen her jump on someone like that. She's usually very standoffish or hides from guests. Sig! I'm going to get jealous!"

"Sigourney," Ana said in a singsong voice, and was delighted when the cat purred at her name. "You like me? I like you!" Keeping the cat cuddled in her arms, Ana continued her tour around Ivy's place. "What's this?"

"This," Ivy said, stroking the bundle of fabric dangling from the ceiling, "is my aerial yoga silk." She unfurled the fabric to its full shape, revealing it was a U shape. She spread the fabric wide enough to take a seat, and swung around to face Ana. "I've been thinking of installing some at the gym, but the schedule is already so packed and I don't think I have the bandwidth to add a new discipline right now."

"How do you use it?"

"Lots of different ways," Ivy said. "You can hold it to support yourself in a forward fold," she said, demonstrating. Ana was a big fan of the view of Ivy hinged at the hips, melting her chest toward the ground. "You can use it to do a supported down dog." Here, she put the fabric on her hip flexors and put her hands on the ground. "Or," she said, resetting herself, "you can put the fabric along your tailbone, reach above you, and then —" she shifted her weight back and kicked off the ground, catching one ankle and then another with the fabric until she was suspended, head a foot off the ground, feet together, arms hugged to her chest.

"Oh my god," Ana said. "No, no way. I could never do that. That's terrifying. I don't have that kind of coordination or strength."

Faster than made any sense, Ivy righted her body and jumped out of the silk. "Yeah, you do. You could do this. But you don't have to,

you know. I would never make you do something you weren't
comfortable with."

"Thanks," Ana said, nevertheless touching the fabric with envy in
her heart. She wanted to be brave like Ivy. She wanted to be able to
toss herself upside down without fear that she would break her neck,
or anxiety attack herself into a cardiac episode. "Speaking of comfortable," Ana said, moving closer to Ivy, "you should show me your
bedroom."

"It is *very* comfortable," Ivy said, trailing her fingers from Ana's
shoulder down to her wrist before grabbing her hand. "But don't take
my word for it."

Ana followed her, blood pumping out of excitement now. What an
honor, what a decadent treat, to get to be in Ivy Lowell's bed.

Ivy woke up surprised that she'd remembered to set the coffeemaker
the night before. She had been a little preoccupied and, then, too tired
to go do her daily closing duties. She smiled, replaying the events of
the night before. If she could have, she would have counted every part
of her that Ana had kissed, every part of Ana that she had kissed. She
would pause and rewind, play back some frames in slow motion.

The happiness warming her own body chilled when she realized
she was in bed alone.

She wasn't sad for long. Ana called from the kitchen, "Hey, I made
coffee. You want it the same way as at the bakery?"

Ivy pulled the covers over her mouth to mute the squeal of giddiness threatening to come up. "Yup, just Splenda and cream."

"You don't have cream," Ana said, peeking her head into the
bedroom. "Oat milk?"

"Yes," Ivy said. "Thank you. And sorry, I know it's probably a really
depressing kitchen for you."

"You would be surprised how much I can do with what you have in
the fridge," Ana said. She could hear Ana stirring one mug, then the
other. "Can I use your pans?"

"Yeah," Ivy said as she accepted the coffee and rubbed her eyes. "They're under the —"

"I already found them," Ana said, winking. "The temptation to reorganize everything the correct way is heavy right now."

"Oh, the correct way?" Ivy teased.

"Yes, for efficiency."

"How long have you even been awake?" Ivy asked, looking at the clock. It was 7:30.

"Couple of hours?" Ana thought. "I think this is my third cup? Anyway, you want a croque madame?" Sigourney appeared in the kitchen and proceeded to rub up against Ana again. Ana picked her up and gave her little kisses on her forehead, then kept milling about her kitchen, with her cat, like she lived there.

It was making Ivy feel things. The kind of things that made you run to a jewelry store and ask someone's father for their blessing.

"I have eggs? I thought I was out."

"I ran to the store for a couple of things while you were asleep," Ana said. "Hey. After breakfast ..." there was a long pause, "think you can teach me that inversion on your yoga hammock thing?"

"I'd love to! But only if you want."

"I'm feeling brave," Ana said. "Just don't let me crack my head open."

"You won't," Ivy vowed. "I will protect your head as if it were my own."

"I've seen some of your movies," Ana said. "That's not as reassuring as you think."

"We should probably do this before breakfast, actually," Ivy said. "Don't want to, hmm, scramble our eggs."

"Har har," Ana said. She set Sig down, and the cat ran off to the bedroom, where she usually napped in the morning. She stretched her arms overhead and then paused to pick something off her shirt. "Aw! Sigourney! You gave me a whisker! I'm so honored." She walked over to her purse and tucked it inside. When Ivy gave her a funny look, she grinned. "Naturally shed cat whiskers are amazing for protection spellwork. OK. I'm ready to get on that yoga swing. I'm not scared. I'm a little scared."

"It's OK, let me show you again." Ivy leaned back into the hammock and narrated the steps. "When you get to this part," Ivy said, swinging one leg up, "I can put one hand on your back and one on your leg to help you flip. We'll lower the hammock first so it's at your hip height, because I'm taller, and then do a couple of stretches first so you can get comfortable with the silk."

"All right," Ana said. "I'm trusting you."

Ivy always felt a sense of pride in her training because of the trust her clients placed in her. But hearing that from Ana in a context outside the gym, outside of their standard training, made her feel ten feet tall.

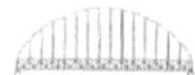

Soon Ana was ready for her big swing. Dutiful student as always, Ana took Ivy's direction and adjusted her posture accordingly. "You can do this," Ivy assured her. "I'll be right here to help."

"What if I kick you in the face when I flip?"

"It wouldn't be the first time," Ivy said. "This nose? Not my original one, let me tell you."

"All right. Here goes," Ana said. As promised, Ivy held her to help her flip, but she didn't have to do much. Ana's momentum did most of the work. She was a little clumsy wrapping her other ankle around the silk, but she got there easily enough. Then she settled into the pose. "Whoa. It's a little weird trying to figure out where to put my hands right now," she said. "I feel like the Hanged Man tarot card, but less graceful."

"How does that feel on your back?"

"I feel so ... long!" Ana said.

"And the silk, is it pinching your hips at all?"

"No, I feel pretty comfortable. The stretch feels so good on my spine." She moved her hands on the floor one way, then the other, so her back was arched. "I shouldn't have done this in shorts," Ana said.

"I disagree," Ivy said. "What would you do if I licked your pussy in this position?"

Ana hadn't thought she could feel more of a head rush.

"Probably fall out of the hammock. Or pass out from being upside down. Or both."

"I bet you can hold it there for longer than you think," Ivy said.

"Well now that you've dared me," Ana said, her voice strained, "go ahead."

One thing about dating someone older was that Ana felt more aware than usual of her sexual inexperience. She'd had sex, sure, but she never really had a serious relationship. She'd lived at home to save money for her bakery until she was 23, and she hated the idea of bringing a girl home to sleep with and have to keep it down so her parents didn't hear, like she was a high schooler. It was embarrassing. So a lot of her early sexual experiences had been rushed hookups on first dates, ill-advised workplace flings when she'd worked in other people's establishments, and a couple of very confusing sexual relationships with "straight" girls.

Ivy had experience. And she was about to give Ana one. She hoped her giddiness didn't give her lack of sexual worldliness away.

Ivy knelt down next to Ana, sitting on her heels so her head was hip-height with Ana. "Hold on to me," Ivy instructed.

Ana reached one of her hands in the wrong direction and then corrected herself, and was wrapping her arms around Ivy's thighs soon after. Then Ivy put her left hand around the small of Ana's back, and pulled her sleep shorts — borrowed from Ivy, and tight on Ana's fuller bottom — aside with her right.

Ivy had licked her pussy three ways to Sunday — literally — the night before. And now Ana was reminded of why they'd gone to sleep so late. This woman loved to take her time.

"Your cunt," Ivy said, taking a long, slow lick that sent a shiver through her bound hips, "is the best thing I've ever tasted."

"Tastier than my buttercream?" Ana gasped out, remembering an old innuendo between them. Ivy teased Ana's opening, eliciting a moan from below as she twirled her fingers in the wetness and spread it across her clit. Then she pressed a kiss to the swollen button, letting the kiss turn into slow upward strokes of her tongue. Ana let her hands wander anywhere she could reach, their bodies drawn closer together easily despite the awkwardness of Ana being upside down. "You still good?" Ivy asked.

"I'll let you know when I get dizzy," Ana said. "Don't stop. Not yet."

Ivy responded by circling her tongue, alternating between flattening it against Ana and pointing it, changing the pressure until she found a pattern that made Ana clutch her Ivy's ass hard enough she might have left a bruise.

Ana came with a cry muffled against Ivy's thigh. She felt her body, rigid with building pleasure moments ago, soften again. Ivy eased her hands down Ana's back, helping to right her, and eased her out of the silk.

"You good?" Ivy asked, helping Ana sit on the ground. "Put your chin to your chest and hold the back of your head to reset your blood pressure."

In a daze, Ana nodded and did as she asked. "Now I'm starving," she said, then added with a laugh, "Take your pants off."

Ivy kissed her and playfully bit her lip. "You need actual sustenance. Want me to make the croque madames?"

"No," Ana said, sitting up. "No offense, I'm sure you'd do great. My croque madames are just legendary."

"All right, then. No need to twist my arm."

Ana stood up and rolled out her neck. "I definitely feel taller," she said. "All right, I cook, you clean."

eighteen

W inter arrived like an icicle to the face. Ivy felt it in her joints first, the stiffness in the wrist she broke a decade ago while filming a snowboarding scene. Sig was perched on top of her dresser, looking out the window and at Ivy in bed as if it were her fault the city was now encased in snow.

"Don't look at me that way, Sigourney," Ivy said, groggy. "I don't like it any more than you do."

She grabbed her phone and pulled it under the covers with her, blocking out the bright white sunlight reflecting off the snow outside. "Let's see what the damage is." She opened the weather app and gasped at the feel-like temperature: 14 below.

"Motherfucking shit bag god damn," she said. Not only was it cold enough for the wind chill to slice off your nipple, but there were 5 inches of snow on the ground. No way was Ivy going anywhere in this, and she wasn't about to make some DoorDash driver risk their life and their vehicle to bring her some egg rolls that would be popsicles by the time they arrived.

She thought of just calling it a day and staying in bed, but her growling stomach said, *bitch, you thought.*

Taking her duvet cover with her as a cloak, she dragged herself to the kitchen. Everything in her fridge required prep, and she was not in the mood. What would take the least time?

She trudged to the pantry and decided: oatmeal, raisins, protein powder. Done. It was filling, nutrient-dense, took almost no effort to prepare, and it would warm her up.

While microwaving her breakfast, she texted Ana. They must have sent thousands of text messages over the past few days that they hadn't seen each other. Ana had begged off training all week to pull some late nights at the bakery.

IVY

Please tell me you're closed today

ANA

Ha ha ha ha

Oh you're serious

No, way too much to do

IVY

But it's apocalyptic outside

ANA

Believe it or not we're really busy

I gave everyone the option to take the day off

One person took me up on it, so I definitely
need to be here

IVY

Ugh

I'd ask you to come over after work, but I don't
want you driving more than you need to

ANA

But if I do, I might get snowed in with you
smirking emoji

IVY

Intriguing idea. Sig would be happy to see you.
She's acting like I made it snow

ANA

Tell her I said I love her and she's the prettiest
kitty in the whole wide world

After she'd eaten her oatmeal, she settled back in bed with her laptop. Era had sent her the access code to play a demo of her new game. She said she specifically wanted feedback from non-gamers, because she wanted to know it was accessible and had a compelling story.

The game, as Era had described it, was a dating sim set at a bookshop, but it had a supernatural element. The shop owner was a witch, and the other people she'd meet throughout the storyline would also have magical powers that would later be revealed.

The purpose of the game was to explore relationship skills. There were options to romance no characters, one character, or several characters. Before she'd realized it, she'd been playing for three hours and her bladder was screaming at her. This game was addictive. The art style was adorable, the dialogue felt realistic but heightened enough to keep her on the edge of her seat, and the story branching was impressive. Even though Ivy didn't know a lot about video games, she could tell that a lot went into this to make the story so responsive to the player's choices, without one character contradicting a decision made with another character.

As she played, she kept imagining what this would be like as a movie, or maybe a series. Would she add the meta element of branching storylines, have it be a sort of *Sliding Doors* scenario? Maybe each episode could show how one relationship would play out, then everything would rewind for the next episode with a new love interest, with little Easter eggs calling back to the previous episodes. Or ...

would a choose your own adventure format work? If something like this were released as a web series, each episode could have links in the show description leading the viewer to whatever their next choice was. That would be complex to put together but easy enough to present. Would audiences respond to it? Would it be possible to do something similar in a streaming service?

IVY

OK I know that you're working and very busy so please ignore me if you're currently pulling something out of an oven or operating some big slicer thing

But I'm playing a demo of Era's new game, and it's incredible. I wish I could see it adapted into a series. It's such an interesting story

ANA

Ooh! I want to play!

IVY

Do you play video games?

ANA

Every once in a while I play Super Smash Bros. with Tony

IVY

Next time you come over I'll show it to you

ANA

Is that something you'd be interested in?

Adapting a video game, I mean

IVY

I mean

It sounds like a fun idea, but I wouldn't know the first thing about producing something

I'd have to get the money for it, maybe some investors

Buy the rights from Era

Hire a screenwriter

A casting director

Then actually do the casting

Then do all the filming

Would we put together a pilot and try to shop it to a network or a streamer? Or would we just produce it independently and put it on YouTube or something?

ANA

It sounds like you *do* know the first thing about this

And anything you don't know, you know people who would

Or who would know the right people

IVY

You're not wrong

ANA

Is that something you want to do? Get back into filmmaking but not stunts?

IVY

I don't know

Maybe?

Or maybe it's just fun to think about

ANA

I have one of those things

I think about opening another location

But do I want to? Or do I just want the prestige of being big enough to expand?

IVY

It's hard to tell sometimes

By that afternoon, the snow had stopped and salt trucks had made conditions navigable, so Ivy decided to go to the bakery. She was impressed by the whimsical holiday decorations. At Double Dare, there wasn't a ton of floor space that Ivy could devote to holiday decorations, but she felt like she should acknowledge the winter festivities in some way. She'd ordered some red and white battle ropes and striped bo staffs that looked like candy canes, and swapped out the images in the digital poster frames behind the front desk from Ivy's favorite action movies to Ivy's favorite action movies in which snow was prominent, like *Alien vs. Predator*.

With how busy the bakery was from people trying to avoid the cold but likely stir crazy in their homes, Ivy realized she wouldn't be able to linger lest she distract Ana.

Regardless, Ana did come by with a coffee pot, looking flustered and covered in flour, but still the most gorgeous woman Ivy had ever seen.

"Top you off?" Ana asked, trying her best to keep a serious face.

"Sure, you can top me," Ivy said.

"Oh my god, stop," Ana said, laughing. "How is it out there?"

"Not so bad now."

"Good. I wasn't looking forward to driving home if it was as bad as this morning. Or sleeping in my office." She shuddered.

"Hey," Ivy said, feeling something off about Ana aside from the stress of a busy snow day. "What's up? Your energy is like ... I don't know, like you've had too many energy drinks or something."

"I could use an energy drink right now, actually. I'm exhausted." She paused to look around the store, then motioned Ivy to scoot over so she could sit next to her in the booth. "So, yeah, you know how I take anxiety meds? I think they've pooped out on me, which happens sometimes. They're just not having the same effect as usual."

"Oh, wow. That's rough. Can you increase the dosage? Or try something else?"

Ana sighed. "I mean, I can, but it's always such a rollercoaster. I never know if I'm going to have an annoying side effect pop up that had never been an issue before. And, I don't know, I'd really wanted to decrease the dosage or get off them completely at some point." She scoffed. "But, I'll probably have to be on them the rest of my damn life."

If they were in private, Ivy would have stroked her hair, but she held back. "Hey. There's no shame in that. If you need medication to be OK, then you should take your medication."

"I know that," Ana said. "I'm not ashamed of being on meds. I believe in science and vaccines and following the doctor's orders. I know anxiety isn't, like, a moral failing. It's fine if I can't taper off them. That shouldn't be my goal so much as feeling better."

"But?"

"Even though I know all that, I still wish I didn't need to take medication. It's just another thing to manage."

Ivy nodded, wishing so badly that she could squeeze her tight. "Is there anything I can do to help?"

Ana shook her head. "Just this. Talking about it is good. And it'll be fine," she told Ivy. "I just need to get through this next week."

nineteen

Nine of Wands — *The hits just keep coming. It's like the universe is saying, "Whack her again!"*
Ingredient — *Cardamom. Blackthorn's Botanical Magic says it's good for strength, focus and creativity, which I need to survive this week. Can lean into the heat with some black pepper and cinnamon for protection, too.*

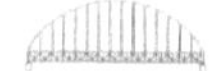

Ana had been floating. Of course she was going to crash.

It had been two weeks since the earth had shifted with their first kiss, and Ana had been bending time and space to be with Ivy as much as possible. That had decreased the already pitiful amount of sleep she was used to. If Ana could give up the need for sleep, she would. She'd become a Cullen if she had to. Anything to be able to claw back the few hours she absolutely had to be horizontal and unconscious.

Her exhaustion didn't match her surroundings. Besos was decked out in Ana's idea of winter splendor. She had chosen a white artificial Christmas tree, like the ones that were popular when she was a little girl. Her mom had thought they were fancy at the time. Now, Ana found them tacky in the best way. She and her team had decorated it with strands of pink and white fairy lights and ceramic ornaments shaped like cookies and cupcakes. At a local thrift shop, she'd found the tree topper, a pinup girl in a Santa-inspired negligee riding a candy cane like it was a witch's broom. Ana had screamed when she saw it because it was so perfect, and had to explain to the terrified proprietor that she was just excited. "Oh," the old woman said with a smile and a pat on Ana's shoulder, "that's not the first time that's happened, but you never know when there's a situation and I have to grab my base-ball bat."

After much pleading and promises that she'd make them coffee cake, Ana enlisted papi and tio to install LED strip lights where each wall met the ceiling, and it bathed the entire bakery in a peachy glow. She wondered if she should just keep them up year round, or if people would eventually get tired of the mood lighting. At least for now, it counteracted the fluorescence that could give her a headache some-times, especially if she was already having a stressful day.

There were just never enough hours in the day. One project snow-balled into the next and the next, until half her to-do list got moved to the next day and everything else she'd started was only half done. She lived life in constant cycles of "I just need to get through this week and things will be less crazy." Rinse and repeat, the same lie over and over until the inevitable collapse. The cake that cut it too close to deadline, the mistaken order quantities she caught too late because she was exhausted while doing inventory. The banquets she catered that told her day-of that they'd have 30 more people than they'd previously anticipated, as if she could just throw some crackers on a platter and call it a day.

Ana had been dealing with the anxiety of everything pretty well until recently. Sure, the couple of hours she spent a week training with Ivy helped. The couple of hours she spent with Ivy doing exer-cises of the naked variety were also helpful. Exercise was great for stress relief. Who knew? No one knew, it was a brand new discovery.

But those sessions added to her anxiety, too. She became obsessed with scrutinizing her workout leggings from every angle. Did they pass the squat test, or were they even the slightest bit see-through? Was there camel toe? Where would the sweat patterns form? Not to mention her anxiety about her workout tops. Did they ride up too much in an unflattering way? Were they too tight? Was she too bouncy? Too nipply?

Of course, Ivy had already seen her nipples and anything that camel toe would put on display. But anxiety wasn't rational.

She just needed to adjust her medication. She'd been resisting it for months, but the truth was inevitable.

She told herself this every week, but this was genuinely going to be a big week. Ana was going to be a guest on a local morning show, 'Burgh Breakfast. It would be a short segment about holiday baking, the type of segment in which she'd run through some techniques while chatting with the host, then bring out the pre-prepared finished version, all while drumming up some promo for the bakery.

That wouldn't have been that stressful during a normal week — if there was such a thing as a normal week in a professional kitchen — if not for the frantic call she got from the bride of a 300-person wedding about how her husband-to-be had developed a sudden allergy to almonds when they had ordered a five-tier almond cake. For this weekend. That was almost done.

"Don't worry," she told the bride, while booking it to the walk-in freezer to scream as soon as she hung up, "I can switch to the vanilla and we'll get it done. What hospital is he staying at, if you don't mind me asking? Oh, he's not … allergic to any flowers that you know of, is he?"

The decor for the cake she had to redo was intricate. Piped flowers with edible pearl centers, spiraling up the five tiers of the cake. The flowers started out white, to match the fondant covering the cake, but gradually, pops of color were incorporated into the parts of the flowers in a gradient ascending to the top, starting out with a gentle pastel color palette at the bottom tier and exploding into neon flowers for the top tier.

Looking at her to-do list, there was no way Ana could get this done without help, and she was more short-staffed than usual this week.

Her best decorator was going on vacation, and Ana refused to accept her offer to stay late one night to help.

"You working overtime before your vacation completely negates your vacation time. No. Thank you, but I'm not letting you do it. Go have fun and don't worry. I'll figure it out."

"Figuring it out" meant begging her sister for help.

Aracely agreed, but she wanted something in return. She wanted the gossip.

So on Wednesday, the night before her big morning show appearance, Ana and Aracely were in the bakery until 2 a.m., piping tiny flowers onto a massive cake while Ari asked her annoying questions about what was happening with Ivy and if she was her girlfriend and whether she thought there'd be any famous people invited to their wedding.

"Just because I'm … sleeping … with someone doesn't mean I'm going to marry them," Ana said, whispering the word "sleeping" because it didn't matter that Ari was all grown up, she was still her baby sister and she felt super weird discussing this with her.

"Well, she's a lot older than you, right?" Ari asked. "So like, she probably does want to get married to someone."

"She's not that much older," Ana said, though inside she felt unsure. Though it wasn't the first time she'd done the math, it was really striking her that a 14-year age difference was not nothing. Ana's career was just getting going. Ivy had already retired from one career and was thriving in another. She'd gotten to travel and work in different places. Ana had never even left the United States. And while she didn't know much about Ivy's previous relationships, and wasn't in any hurry to ask, she assumed she'd had some long-term girlfriends.

Ana hadn't.

She had one completely chaste relationship with a boy in high school. He had also later come out as gay, and part of her felt they'd both always known that about each other. Then there was the frustrating, painful friendship she'd had with the hostess at one of the first restaurants at which she'd been a line cook. The girl would make out with her whenever she was drunk and fighting with her boyfriend, then pretend it hadn't happened and repeat the cycle the next weekend. Even though it hurt, Ana did cut her off eventually.

She'd dated a few other women, but never for more than a few months. There wasn't much drama to it. One of them got bored, or Ana just worked way too much until women broke it off with her, because what good was having a girlfriend you never actually saw?

Marriage wasn't even something that had crossed her mind. Yeah, Ivy said she'd been looking to eventually get into something serious, but she seemed too … cool? … to get married.

Ana thought about her parents, her aunts, some of her cousins. There were plenty of cool married people she knew. But she just couldn't picture Ivy wanting a little wife. Ivy, married? The two of them married, maybe? In some old church that had been refurbished into a nightclub, with her favorite taco truck catering? Living in a suburb with some kids they'd conceived with a sperm donor and becoming really invested in making their own organic baby food? And going on vacations to historic cities, staying at adorable family-owned bed and breakfasts, and then being able to have dinner parties with all their fabulous friends and tell them they learned this incredible roast recipe from a little old grandma they stayed with in Prague?

"Hey, you still here?" Ari said, waving a hand in front of her face.

"Yeah, sorry. Can you please mix more of the turquoise buttercream? No, that's the teal. I need the turquoise. Thank you so much."

"Gotcha." Ari turned to look at her halfway between work stations. She had that look on her face that she'd had as a kid when Ana was babysitting her and Ari was about to tell her she'd microwaved something for too long and now the microwave was covered in an explosion of cheese.

"What is it?" Ana said. Her heart immediately started racing.

"So I got an email about one of my scholarships. The one I have to re-up every year with volunteer hours?"

"Yeah," Ana said, scared of what would come next. "Did you not do your hours?"

"Of course I did my hours," Ari said, offended. "But the organization that funds the scholarship decided they're canceling it for next year."

"What? They can do that?"

"Apparently."

"Those fucking assholes. So how much are you going to lose?"

Ari told her the amount, and while it wasn't insurmountable, it was still a hardship. Without those funds chipping away at Ari's tuition, the portion that Ana was paying was going to have to go up. And while she'd have a semester to prepare for that, if there were any other unforeseen expenses, like her landlord raising the rent or some unexpected medical bill, that could be a big problem.

"I can look for some part-time work," Ari said, sounding helpless. "I'm so sorry."

"You can do that, but how many hours can you actually work before your schoolwork suffers?" Ana said. "Those are hours you could put toward an internship. We'll figure it out, OK? I really need that turquoise, OK, Aracely? Get back to it."

twenty

I want someone who will confide in me.

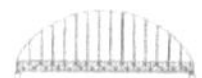

"It was fine. You looked great and I'm sure no one thought anything of it."

Ana was curled up on Ivy's couch with her legs tucked into her chest, and Ivy was doing her very best to calm her down after her appearance on 'Burgh Breakfast. Ivy had cringed through watching it — not because she thought Ana had done a bad job, but because she knew Ana would think that.

"I just can't believe I broke a basic sauce on live television," Ana said, grateful to accept the glass of wine Ivy was handing her.

"But you fixed the sauce, right?"

"I did."

"So that's awesome!" Ivy said. "You probably ended up teaching someone that skill who really wants to be a better cook but does things like break sauces."

"I just wish I hadn't gotten so flustered when doing it. I dropped the freaking bottle of oil and had to crawl on my hands and knees to get it. The camera guy followed me under the counter to watch me. It was humiliating."

"Maybe for you," Ivy said, wrapping her arms around Ana. "But to viewers, it was probably charming. It was for me."

"Well, you're carnally biased in my favor," Ana said.

"That may be so, but look!" She pulled out her phone and opened Instagram. "Look how many new followers Besos has. Look at these comments. People thought you were adorable and are talking about how good the food looked. Savory bechamel and chorizo galettes are going to be on every winter holiday table in the city."

"I'm going to vomit," Ana said.

"Hey. Hey." Ivy snapped her fingers in Ana's face. "Don't make me make you run laps around my living room until your attitude improves." She was desperate to make her cheer up, because she had news she wanted to share and she hoped for a good reaction.

"It's not just the show," Ana said, sitting up. "I got some really bad news from my sister."

Ivy stiffened. "What's wrong with Ari? Is she OK?"

"She is, but my wallet won't be real soon." She wrung her hands together and sighed heavily. "I don't want to talk about this. I really don't. But I haven't talked to anyone about this and it's starting to wear me down."

Ivy rubbed small circles on her back. "It's OK. You don't have to tell me if you don't want. But if you do tell me, maybe I can help?"

"Ugh. OK. So, I've been paying a big chunk of her school costs, and one of her scholarships was just canceled, which means I'll have to come up with the difference. And this last quarter has been pretty tight at the bakery because the fucking inflation has been driving food costs up, so it's just a lot to deal with. I think it'll be fine, but it's stressing me out. I wanted the morning show appearance to drum up new business, but even if it does, it's a double edged sword because I can't afford to hire more staff that I desperately need to keep up with it."

"I wish I knew more about the food industry so I could give you any kind of advice. Or maybe I could come knead some dough for you?"

"Oh hon, that's a 2 a.m. shift and I would never ask you to do that. No, don't worry about it. Maybe you could give me an accountant recommendation? I can't afford to hire someone full time right now, but I could use some help looking at my budget."

"Yeah, of course. I'll text you her contact info."

"That'll be good. OK. Attitude is adjusted." Ana straightened her back and tugged the corners of her mouth up with her index fingers into a fake smile.

"I have something that might cheer you up. Let me show you something." Feeling giddy, Ivy ran to her front door mail tray and back, and handed Ana a navy and gold embossed envelope.

"Is this a wedding invitation?" Ana asked. She looked a little green.

"No, it's for a critics awards show in New York. My friend Vanessa is getting an award for her directorial debut, and then the production company is hosting an afterparty. I get a plus one. So." She didn't know why she was so nervous. If Ana said no, she would understand. Ivy would just invite Rahul if she couldn't or didn't want to go. "Would you like to be my plus one?"

Ana looked a little confused. "When is this?" She read the date on the invitation. It was a week before Christmas. "Oh shit, I don't know. I need to go into the bakery to check the schedule and make sure there aren't some huge deliveries I have to be there for. But I think that weekend could work? Should we look at flights now? I need to know how much to budget. Maybe I can find some last-minute deal."

"No need," Ivy said. "It's taken care of."

"Ivy." Ana was scowling.

"It's OK, Vanessa's paying for it," Ivy lied. She knew it wasn't the *best* move, but she didn't need Ana to worry about one more thing when she could easily cover the cost of their trip, and knew that if she said she'd pay for it, Ana would insist on going halfsies. "Just see if you can take off running a baking empire that weekend, and I'll take care of everything else. Zero stress, OK?"

"OK," Ana said. "Zero stress, huh? Sounds fake."

"Come on. Let's watch a movie. Take your mind off things."

They cuddled up and watched *Bound*, which Ana had never seen, and then a few episodes of *The Great British Baking Show*. At some point they both fell asleep, and Sig nestled herself between them. Ana yawned in her sleep, rubbed her cold feet against Ivy's and gave Sigourney a little kiss on the head.

Ivy didn't want to go back to sleep. Taking her phone off the night-stand charger and then ducking under the blanket to hide the light, she looked up Aracely's university and started digging through its website. Once she found the page for the bursar's office, she started typing up an email.

twenty-one

I want someone who can vibe with my friends. Cue the Spice Girls.

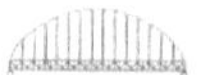

RAHUL

You wanna climb today?

I'm dragging Liam

IVY

Oh, so he's alive, then?

I feel like I haven't seen him in weeks.

RAHUL

He says he's just been busy, but I mean

I went over to his place to play Tears of the Kingdom, and it was musty in there.

IVY

Isn't Tears of the Kingdom a single-player game?

RAHUL

Yup. I just watched him while cracking
windows surreptitiously

IVY

I'm sure you were very subtle

RAHUL

Fuck you. See you at 2

I vy sent a quick text to Ana.

IVY

Hey, you're off today, right? Do you want to go
climb rocks with me, Rahul, and one of our
friends?

ANA

I was off, but apparently we were supposed to
make 100 sandwiches for a catering thing and
I completely spaced it until Nino texted me that
we didn't have enough ham

So now I'm making sandwiches

IVY

Shit.

Well … maybe later you could meet us for
drinks?

ANA

Maybe. I'll have to play it by ear. I gotta let you
go though

IVY

Oh, sorry. Good luck!

Every time Ivy went bouldering, she wanted to renovate the gym again to add a climbing wall. She loved the jutting geometric structures and the neon handholds, the way a climbing gym sparked this spirit of childlike playfulness.

But damn, why did it have to be so painful? An hour of this, and she wouldn't be able to hold a fork, let alone a barbell. The grip strength that was required to hoist your full body weight from one side of a wall to another by a couple of fingers was significant.

Rahul climbed more often than she did, so he was able to do more of the advanced routes, the ones with less surface area in the handholds that required more strategic use of momentum and foot placement.

Liam never climbed, so he was having a miserable time. He was keeping up just fine for a novice, but he was complaining about it the whole time.

"Why is this fun for you?" she asked Rahul.

"I don't know, why is World War I fun for you?" Rahul retorted.

Liam was a history teacher and originally from England. He went to college in Pittsburgh, where his parents both worked as professors, and met, fell in love with, married, and then divorced Ivy's friend Camila. The two were still very good friends, though that hadn't always been the case based on Ivy's understanding of the early days of their separation. And while Ivy didn't believe Liam was still in love with his ex-wife, she had a feeling that watching her move on with a new partner while he was still decidedly single might have felt weird for Liam.

"You're doing great," Ivy said. "Learn to love it. Nothing feels as good as working up a sweat when it's cold outside."

"I can think of a few things that feel better," Liam said. "Drinking a beer, taking a nap, watching a ten-part World War I documentary."

"See, this is exactly why you need to get out more," Rahul said. "You need hobbies."

"World War I is my hobby," Liam said. "And!" He paused dramatically. "I am writing a thriller."

Rahul raised an eyebrow at Ivy.

"When was the last time you went on a date?" Ivy asked.

Liam scowled at her. He'd taken a date to Era and Seth's wedding in late summer, but as far as she'd heard, that situationship had fizzled out.

"OK, forget I asked," Ivy said.

"I got him to make a dating app profile," Rahul said.

"And studying war is far less painful and humiliating," Liam said.

Ivy felt for him. The women-loving-women dating apps were stressful to be on, but nowhere near the level of what she saw her straight female clients complaining about when they talked about their app experiences.

The latest thing was AI profile pictures. Men would use readily available software to make themselves look younger, buffer, taller.

"One time," her client Erica told her in hushed tones, still in disbelief, "I saw a guy who had one of those 'holding a fish you just caught' photos, but the fish was clearly AI. It looked like a mutant. The eyes were weirdly human and it was as long as a preteen is tall. I matched with him just to tell him it was obviously fake, because I felt so bad for the poor guy embarrassing himself like that, and he called me a dumb ugly bitch and blocked me."

She'd also heard horror stories about "are we dating the same guy" Facebook groups, where women would post images of the men they were dating, and women who recognized the potential love interests told them all the dirt.

"Look, let me show you," another client said. "This is just from this morning," she said after a quick scroll. It was a photo of a relatively bland looking man, with the caption: "Met this guy last night and we texted for hours. Any red flags?"

There were 27 comments. "That's my boyfriend. This was last night? Where did you meet him?"

"I'm currently talking to this guy. He just texted me five minutes ago," another woman said.

"Um, I have a kid with this guy. We split up a year ago, while I was pregnant. All the red flags."

"WHAT THE FUCK? A YEAR AGO? WE WERE TOGETHER A YEAR AGO!" the first commenter said.

"Jesus," Ivy said. "What even ARE men?"

"That's an unsolved mystery," her client had replied.

So in one sense, she felt for Liam, but also, there was no way a straight guy had it as bad as a straight woman on a dating app. But she wasn't about to invalidate her sad sack friend's experience.

Thankfully, Rahul did it for her.

"You know who has it the worst on dating apps? Trans people. For you, you're risking humiliation and rejection. For me? I have to calculate how to disclose something about myself that could turn a hookup into a hate crime. It's fucked that the first question someone has for me isn't what I like to do for fun, but what's in my pants."

"That's fucked," Liam said. "I hate that for you, man."

"Who the fuck opens with 'Have you had *the surgery?*'" Rahul said. "Um, have you had a lobotomy? Headass."

"Headass indeed," Liam said gravely, and both Ivy and Rahul chortled.

When they were done climbing, Ivy and the guys went to a sports bar for a couple of beers. Well, they had beers — Guinness for Liam, a craft IPA from the pub's own brewery for Rahul — while Ivy got a chocolate old fashioned.

"You and your sweet tooth," Rahul said warmly. "I'm never going to make a beer drinker out of you, am I?"

"Not if other options are available. My sweet tooth just won't allow it."

Liam said, "What a loss," and took a swig of the Guinness, fully aware of the rich foam on his mustache but making no effort to wipe it clean.

She enjoyed that about Liam. He had this dry and ever present sense of humor, even when he would get into funks like this.

Her phone vibrated.

ANA

I'm free! Where are you?

She frantically started typing back and dropped her a pin.

"Analeigh's going to join us. She'll be here in fifteen minutes."

"Who's that?" Liam asked.

"Ivy's girlfriend," Rahul said.

"She's not … yeah. Yeah, she's my girlfriend."

"What's that all about?" Liam asked.

"What's what?"

"That," he said, waving at her face. "Whatever that reaction you just had was."

"Ana's 25," Rahul whispered loudly.

"Ivy! You dirty dog!" Liam said.

"Fuck you, dude," she said with a laugh.

The conversation shifted away from Ivy's dating life, and she was only half listening as she watched the clock. Twenty minutes in, she started to feel anxious and wonder whether she should text Ana again, when she showed up.

"Hey, sorry I'm late," Ana said. She leaned in like she wanted to give Ivy a kiss but held herself back. Ivy put her arm around her and kissed her on the cheek.

"Ana, you know Rahul," he said.

"Hey, nice to see you again," she said, waving.

"And this is Liam. Liam, Ana."

"Have we met? Why do I know that name?" Ana asked the second question to Ivy.

"I'm Camila's ex-husband."

"Oh, yeah," Ana said. "Um, she's … nice?" Ana looked helplessly at Ivy, who shook her head. She'd have to explain to Ana the complicated history there, later.

Rahul nodded at the bartender and asked Ana, "Whatcha drinking?"

"Um, how about a vodka cran?"

The TV right behind the bar switched to commercials. The first was for a chain restaurant opening in the city, and then one for some all-natural shower cleaner. Then there was one for a documentary series about the royal family, and Liam slapped his hand on the bar with a groan when King Charles's somber mug flashed on the screen.

"I will never understand," he said, in his posh British accent that had failed to get twinged with Pittsburghese (nary a "jeetjet" or "yinz" or "jagoff" in earshot), "the American fascination with these imperialist fops."

"Coming from someone you could argue is an imperialist fop," Rahul said with a meaningful sip of his beer, "that's ironic."

"Listen," Liam said, and it startled Ivy because although he didn't say words the way a Pittsburgher would, the way he said "Listen" reminded her so much of Camila, "I know. I fucking now. I teach European history to American teenagers, for fuck's sake. The way history has been sanitized and decontextualized, and I'm expected to just go along with euphemisms about atrocities that could fill a whole library of books, versus getting a throwaway paragraph? Maybe I'd be interested in the royals, too, if I hadn't been steeped in learning everything terrible about them."

"I don't think it really has anything to do with the politics of it," Ivy said. "It's just celebrity culture."

Liam grinned, a teacher eager to hear a student's take on the discussion at hand. "Go on."

The years she spent working in movies and television disillusioned Ivy from any lofty ideas about celebrities. She still admired many people in the industry who she had gotten to know, for their talent and love of their craft. But she made no assumptions and held no unconditional ideas of someone's goodness or good intentions. She knew celebrities could be like anyone else in this world, ignorant at best and callous and bigoted at worst.

"I think that we have these ideas about meritocracy and that if someone is famous or successful in any way, they are totally deserving of it. That they 'worked' for it. And the idea of royalty, of someone being born into that worthiness, is a different type of celebrity that we don't really have in the states. We're starting to see it a little bit now with the trend of nepo babies, but royals are the ultimate 'famous for being famous' and so we fixate on them because we're trying to find out how we can fit them into our 'they deserve to be that beloved' programming."

"And do you think anyone deserves to be that beloved, on a global scale? Should we divest from the idea of celebrity because it reinforces the ideas of meritocracy?"

"Maybe we should," Ivy said. "Like, do celebrities really need to hold honorary doctorates? Do we really need to treat people like they're groundbreaking activists for hosting $10,000 a plate political fundraisers?"

"Or their perfectly curated red, white and blue feeds when it's time to remind people to vote?" Ana chimed in.

"Exactly. Some of the people with these impeccable public images are the worst people you're glad you don't know. Or they're not terrible people, but they're miserable human beings. Oh, the stories I could tell if I ever decide to write a memoir." Like the singer who did a cameo on a Western movie that Ivy worked on, who had a panic attack in her trailer and had to have her makeup redone after crying it off, setting back their start time two hours for what amounted to two lines of dialogue. Or the actor she trained who was known as a perpetual bachelor but confided in her that he had a longtime girl-friend from his hometown. Because his team had decided to capitalize on the idea of an unobtainable heartthrob, they'd been unable to be seen in public for the past three years. He had started needing to drink in order to cope with the pain it was causing them both, but more so the way she was wounded by it. He got his fame, while she stayed in their hometown, getting pitying stares from the locals who assumed he left her for the greener pastures of lingerie models and K-pop idols.

"Maybe it's bigger than just celebrities," Rahul said. "Do you know how often I think of deleting every trace of myself from the Internet? Or switch back to a flip phone because I'm tired of reading terrible comments and seeing how awful people are? Sometimes I think we really do need to know less about each other."

"I wish I didn't have to use social media for work," Ana said. "I wish I could take it away from some of the brides I work with, actu-ally. Like why are you trying to have a wedding fit for a Russian oligarch when you're a real estate agent in Pittsburgh? Be so fucking for real right now."

"And that's back to the royals," Liam said. "From ol' Lizzie on down, it's all wall to wall coverage of the gowns and the crowns and the fucking hats."

"Ooh, I love the hats," Ana said.

"The hats are pretty fun," Rahul admitted.

They were all quiet, contemplating their drinks. Eventually Rahul broke the silence by talking about his sister Saanvi, who lived in New York but was currently job hunting to come to Pittsburgh. She was also in the online dating trenches, so they got back to where they started. Liam suddenly wanted to call it a night, so he bailed.

The remaining three had a couple of drinks after that, and Ivy called a Lyft home.

It had started to snow, and she lured Ana into staying with the secret weapon she'd dug out of her linen closet — an electric blanket.

Too tired to fool around, they snuggled under the warm blanket until Ana was snoring. As Ivy drifted off, she realized she hadn't deleted the dating apps off her phone, though she hadn't opened them in weeks.

Maybe she never would again.

twenty-two

Eight of Wands — *Swift travels, good luck*
Nine of Pentacles — *Enjoy the abundance around you. Comfort, luxury*
King of Pentacles reversed — *This trip is going to be expensive, huh?*
Ingredient — *So Cunningham's* Wicca in the Kitchen *actually has a section on junk food! That's how I learned that french fries are good for grounding and that Fig Newtons are good for sex magic? Fig Newmans would make more sense, since Paul Newman was such a sex symbol. Anyway, definitely going to be grabbing fries at some point while traveling.*

Ana had never flown first class. She'd been to New York only once, when she'd graduated high school and took a bus there on a weekend trip with a couple of friends who were going to NYU in the fall. That bus had smelled like boiled peanuts and mothballs, and then the rental they stayed at had a leaky ceiling in the kitchen and a rat problem. Ana blacked out with rage when she went back to the listing to complain — something she also never did — and saw they'd agreed to a $150 cleaning fee.

This was about as far from that experience as one could get. She struggled with her bulky carry-on, feeling sloppy in her sweatpants next to Ivy. Ivy was wearing an expensive-looking and perfectly tailored version of Ana's outfit, with slim joggers, bright red sneakers, and a raglan top that looked like the softest cotton in the world. Ana wanted to reach out and pinch the fabric between her fingers.

It was just a long weekend trip. She could pretend to feel comfortable with cutting to the front of the line, extra legroom and expensive cotton for one trip. She could act like a girl who was used to all of this.

On Saturday morning, she'd gotten green tea instead of coffee at the airport, to try to avoid exacerbating her anxiety. It didn't work. She was still anxious but now sleepy and cranky on top of that.

"You OK?" Ivy had asked her, noticing her wringing her hands together and fidgeting with her howlite necklace. She'd worn it for its alleged calming effects.

"I'm a little scared of flying," Ana admitted. Ivy reached around between the plush first class seat and Ana's back and rubbed it like you would for someone who was sick and needed comforting. It kind of worked, but not enough.

"You know what Camila told me helps with anxiety?" Ivy asked.

"What's that?"

"Stimulating your vagus nerve. I've seen her putting an ice cube in her bra, like on her sternum, and she says that it helps regulate your nervous system."

"Sometimes I put ice on my inner wrists," Ana said. "I think it's the same thing."

"Want to ask the flight attendant for a cup of ice?"

"Yes," Ana said. "With some vodka in it."

"I'll have what you're having," Ivy said.

A few swigs of a vodka soda and a couple of bra cubes later, Ana was feeling less anxious and even managed to doze off for a few minutes. She worried she'd snored or drooled, but if she had, Ivy either wouldn't have noticed with the movie she was watching on her iPad (*Gunpowder Milkshake*, Ivy told her) or she would have said nothing and pretended she hadn't noticed.

When she woke up from her quick snooze, Ana reached into her bag for Ivy's copy of *Circe*. She'd read a few chapters already, though she hadn't been able to carve out a big chunk of time to dig into it.

They landed and took a cab to where they were staying. Ana was used to spending the rare trips she took in cheap motels and Holiday Inns she secured with a promo code. She was not used to staying in boutique hotels with penthouses and rooftop pool bars near the High Line, supposedly a stone's throw from Ariana Grande's place.

It wasn't that Ivy seemed blasé about the luxury. She was excited and appreciative of the comfort of their surroundings. But she wasn't awestruck by them. What must it be like, to have access to this kind of wealth more than once in a lifetime, more than for a weekend being whisked away into a fantasy?

"I was thinking," Ivy said, "that we could maybe take a nap, because that flight was exhausting, and then get ready, figure out the subway and go to Momofuku Milk Bar."

Ana's eyes went wide. "I've always wanted to go there!"

"Me too," Ivy said. "Did you know my first birthday back in Pittsburgh, I ordered their birthday cake? It was still frozen solid when it arrived. Took all day to thaw but it was delicious once it was soft enough to not crack my tooth on." She looked down and peered at her through her lashes, looking shy. "But that was before I'd gone to Besos and tried your Dominican cake, of course. Which I then got for the next birthday."

Ana's heart warmed with pride. "I'm going to have to step things up for your 40th birthday cake, then."

They stripped down to their underwear and got under the covers, planning out the rest of their day until they passed out. Ivy took charge of setting their alarm so their cat nap didn't turn into an overnighter. Ana almost wished it had become an overnighter. When they woke up an hour later, she was groggy and fussy, but quickly changed into a chunky sweater, jeans, and her comfiest shoes that weren't nonskid work shoes.

Ivy said the nearest subway stop wasn't far, but in the December chill, the five blocks it took to get there felt like miles and miles.

Ana had taken the T all over Pittsburgh, of course, but the city's light rail system felt very different from the cavernous tunnels and behemoth trains of the New York subway system. After they made it down the steps, hazardous with the day's drizzle people had trudged in on their shoes, they were promptly informed by someone exiting the subway that their train wasn't coming. Someone had gotten hit at the previous stop, and they were still sorting everything out.

Ana's stomach soured. She thought of videos she'd seen shared on social media before she could scroll away, of confrontations that ended with someone getting pushed onto the tracks. How often did that happen? Were there statistics on it, documentation? She pulled out her phone but she had shitty reception down here.

"Hey," Ivy said, bringing her back with one of those soothing back touches. "It's OK. We'll just go down a couple of blocks and take a different route. We'll still make it to Milk Bar."

Ana had forgotten all about why they were here in the first place. "Right," she said, trying to smile. She wrapped herself around Ivy's arm, and Ivy pulled her close. She didn't want to see Ivy as her protector around the unpredictable streets of the city, as her bodyguard, but she did.

She went on autopilot while they walked to the backup subway stop, not quite letting Ivy drag her, but not too far from that, either. She wasn't in her body when they scanned their phones at the turnstile to pay, or when they descended the steps, or when the train on the far tracks rumbled past. She jumped back into herself when their train got there. The pit in her stomach grew as they went through the doors behind the crowd, worried she'd get left behind on the other side of the doors and have no idea where she was, or worse, trip and fall in the gap.

The train was standing room only. Ana was grateful for the gloves she wore, the same ones from her Halloween costume, so she wouldn't have to think about all the germs on the pole. She closed her eyes, but it made things worse because she couldn't keep her balance as the train lurched forward.

"Hey," Ivy said, "what's happening right now?"

"I think I'm going to be sick," Ana whispered.

"Are you physically sick? Is it anxiety?"

Ana nodded, hoping Ivy would figure out she meant both.

"OK. You're safe," Ivy whispered back, pulling closer to her. Their fingers touched on the subway pole. "What helps you? Does that sensory thing help, with describing things?"

"Sometimes," Ana said.

"All right. I don't remember exactly how it works."

"It's five things you can see, four things you can touch, three things you can hear, two things you can smell, and one thing you can taste," Ana recited.

"Describe five people to me," Ivy said.

"OK. There's a woman with a leopard print fur hat. A boy with an instrument case. Maybe a guitar? No, it's bigger. Like a cello."

"Good, keep going."

"A woman reading a novel with a cartoon couple on the cover. A man changing his shoes?" They laughed. "And a guy just bobbing his head to whatever is on his headphones."

"Four things you can touch?"

"The pole. The inside of my gloves. My sweater," she said, reaching for her hem. "Your hand," she said, tentatively tapping Ivy's knuckles. Ivy undid her grip on the pole and wrapped her hand around Ana's, as if helping her hold it, lending her strength.

"Three things you can hear?"

"The sound of your voice," Ana said. "The rattle of the subway on the tracks. A girl telling a story about a date."

"Was it a good one or a bad one?" Ivy asked.

"Terrible. God. It sucks out there," Ana said.

"Two things you can smell?"

"My perfume," Ana said. "And something … sour," she said, wrinkling her nose. "Gross."

"That's the subway for you. What's one thing you can taste?"

"I can tell you one thing I want to taste," Ana said. "Your lip balm."

"It's supposed to taste like cherries," Ivy said. "Does it taste like that to you, chef?"

Ana wondered how anxious she should be about being Visibly Queer on a crowded subway car. It was New York, sure, but it was also

America. She decided they could take anyone who hassled them, and gave Ivy the quickest kiss.

She licked her lips. "It's sweeter than any cherry I ever tasted," she said.

By the time they made it to Milk Bar, Ana's anxiety attack felt like a distant memory. She was delighted by the surroundings — the Art Deco floor tiles, the glossy black tiles of the walls and counters, and the Barbie pink accents under the tables.

They got a dozen Apple Cider Doughnut truffles to share, and Cereal Milk soft serve. Ivy went back after they finished eating and got a tin of assorted cookies for later, and since they were lingering, Ana got the *All About Cake* and *All About Cookies* cookbooks (she already had the shop's first cookbook at home, and used it constantly for at-home stress baking).

Ivy asked where she wanted to go next, so she Googled a metaphysical shop that was within walking distance (though walking distance in New York, she was learning, was subjective).

INT. METAPHYSICAL SHOP — LATER

Ivy had been in a witchy shop or two. To her, going to one of those shops was like going to a movie you felt meh about seeing, but at least it gave you something to do to kill an afternoon. She liked the oddities, liked looking at the pretty rocks, but she didn't buy into any of it.

Ana, however, was enthralled by this shop. She had to look at every crystal, from the enormous towers to the small palm stones. She sniffed incense and showed Ivy the labels on pre-spelled candles, noting what ingredients were good for the stated intentions. She read book titles out loud to Ivy, telling her which of them she'd read and which ones she'd heard good things about, and which ones were by witchy influencers that had been exposed for being secretly racist

("It's a real problem in pagan circles," Ana said, looking over her shoulder as she did).

But where she lingered the longest was with the tarot decks. Out of her friends, Era was the one who had a couple of decks and would whip one out every once in a while when they were over at her place. She didn't realize just how many permutations of tarot decks existed. There were watercolor decks and Art Nouveau decks. Collage-style, two-color. There were decks for *Buffy the Vampire Slayer* and *Golden Girls* and the works of Edgar Allan Poe.

"This is one of my favorites," Ana said, showing Ivy the Modern Witch Tarot. "It's close enough to the original Rider Waite Smith deck everyone learns on that it makes it really easy to pick up on the card meaning, but it's not just a bunch of white people. And a lot of the male cards have been changed to be gender neutral or androgynous. The art is so beautiful. Ugh, I just love it."

"So do you have decks that you use all the time and decks you have just to collect?" Ivy asked.

"That's about it, yeah," Ana said. "This is one I use a lot, except the paper is really thick so it's hard to shuffle. This one," she said, grabbing another deck, "is plastic and shuffles like a dream. One of my friends has it, but it's too expensive."

"I'll get it for you," Ivy said.

"Ivy. Come on."

"You're on vacation. You deserve a little treat. Plus, I saw you eyeing that big ass obsidian. You go get the crystals you want, and I'll just get you this deck."

"Fine," Ana said. "That's sweet of you. Thank you."

At the checkout, Ivy cut in front of Ana and handed the clerk her card. "I'm paying for everything she's getting," Ivy said. Ana made an affronted sound, and after arguing for a while she succumbed.

"I'm so mad at you right now," Ana said.

"It's not a big deal," Ivy said. "Let me treat you." She winked.

"I'm buying your drinks at the awards show."

Grimacing, Ivy told her, "It's an open bar."

"Maldita sea," Ana swore in Spanish.

twenty-three

The subway was less eventful on day 2, and they had a few hours to get to and explore the MoMA before needing to get ready for the awards show.

"OK, so I normally don't take photos in a museum because I think it's tacky, but we need to get a picture in front of Starry Night. Camila will kill me if I don't," Ivy said.

"I'm so excited to see it," Ana said. "I don't know anything about art, though. It's just really famous."

"I know enough to get by at a dinner party," Ivy said. "Camila and her boyfriend are the art hoes of the group. Camila says she takes a notebook to museums to journal her feelings on the artwork."

"Sounds like a therapist thing to do," Ana said with a laugh.

"Right? She said she got the idea when she saw someone sketching, but she can't draw, so she started journaling instead."

The featured exhibit was on dolls. The entry room was fashioned to resemble the Barbie Dreamhouse, but the artist had turned the dreamhouse concept into a post-apocalyptic bunker. There was a faux hydroponic garden of survival crops, a wall of hot pink hunting weapons, a sequined hazmat suit in a decontamination chamber, and bags of freeze-dried food rations with technicolor labels and cursive writing.

"The thing is, if I could afford a doomsday bunker, this is exactly what I would want it to look like," Ana said. "What does that say about me?"

"That you have taste," Ivy said. "Plus if you're going to endure a zombie apocalypse, you should at least get to have a pink velvet sectional in your quarantine zone." The placard describing the exhibit said it was a commentary on overconsumption and aesthetics as a bandaid to the grief of late-stage capitalism. Point taken.

In the next room, photographers had displayed their interpretations of the theme by photographing dolls in different scenarios, from American Girl dolls at national landmarks to the doll from the Annabel movie placed into re-enactments of scenes from romantic comedies. In the last room of the exhibit, there was a physical timeline of dolls throughout the years, starting with ancient poppets and ending at modern day handpainted fashion dolls, displayed next to a looping timelapse video of the artist painstakingly adding a cut crease eyeshadow look with a paintbrush thin as a pushpin.

They spent less time on the rest of the exhibits until they got to the holy grail Van Gogh. They both took turns posing with the painting, which was behind thick glass and a velvet rope, after waiting in line for 20 minutes to see it.

"It's beautiful," Ana said. "I thought it would be bigger," she whispered.

"I did too," Ivy whispered back.

Ana wanted to sit on her hands at the gift shop, because she feared a repeat of the night before. She didn't want Ivy to swoop in and spend a bunch of money on her.

"You're not getting anything?" Ivy said, with her hands filled with art history coffee table books.

"How are you going to fit everything you're getting in your carry on?" Ana asked.

Ivy shrugged. "I'll just ship anything that doesn't fit. Or buy another suitcase and check it. Not my favorite thing to do. I hate waiting for bags and I've had more than a couple get lost."

"That's what happens when you don't fly private," Ana drawled in what she thought sounded like a new money affected accent.

"You're so fucking cute," Ivy said. "I've never been on a private jet, by the way. They're terrible for the environment."

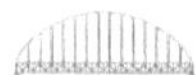

They'd had plenty of time to get ready until they didn't. Now Ana was frantically curling her hair, cursing when she burned her temple with the iron and popped off one of her press-on nails.

After that was done, she walked out of the hotel bathroom, nervous about whether Ivy would like her dress.

"OK," she said, uncertain, "what do you think? Is it too prom?"

She'd been smoothing the gown's skirt down and looked up to find Ivy sitting in the wingback chair, mouth open in shock, looking at her with naked desire. Ana didn't need a mirror to know she was looking at Ivy with her version of the same expression.

She had not been mentally, emotionally, physically or spiritually prepared to see Ivy in a tuxedo.

Ivy was all angles in a tailored cobalt suit. The smooth fabric looked touchable and luxurious, too luxurious to actually touch because looking at it made Ana feel like her fingers were covered in caramel and she needed to wash her hands before approaching. Underneath a crisp blue suit jacket, Ivy wore a plunging white shirt, unbuttoned down to the sternum. The gentle slope of Ivy's small breasts, caressed by the open shirt, scandalized her, because how close was the shirt to revealing all of her?

Ana's eyes trailed down the rest of her outfit, the equally sharp pants, slim at the ankles and ending above the strap of aquamarine platforms with a thick high heel. She didn't wear any earrings or a necklace, but had beautiful ornate gold rings on most of her fingers. Scanning back up Ivy's body, Ana realized the shirt was actually the palest robin's egg, and that Ivy was clad in blue from head to toe.

"You look unreal," Ivy said, and Ana had to shake her head a bit because she'd taken the words from her mouth and it sounded so strange hearing her exact thoughts in Ivy's husky voice.

"*You* look unreal," Ana said, unable to think of anything better.

"Can I see the back?" Ivy asked. She was leaning back in the chair, legs open, fingers on her lips. She looked so commanding and powerful and hot, like a very bad woman with a very naughty secret room in her mansion.

Attempting to make it look effortless and sexy, Ana spinned for Ivy. Her gown was from Rent the Runway. Ana had paid $60 to have it for the long weekend. It was an A-line metallic lavender gown with a high tie neck. It was backless (Ana was shocked how low it plunged on her — the model on the website must have been six feet tall) and the slinky fabric flowed over her curves like water, the skirt swishing around her legs when she twirled. "So, not too prom?"

"No, darling, that is a red carpet gown. You're stunning. You're an ingenue. Jesus, I hope Kristen Stewart isn't there tonight. Let me see if she's winning something." Ivy started tapping on her phone. Ana laughed.

"I don't think you have to worry about Kristen stealing me, if that's what you're getting at. If anything, she's going to try to steal that suit off your body."

Ivy lifted one shoulder in response. "I have a favor to ask. Do you know how to do a French braid? Or some kind of a quick updo?"

Ana cracked her knuckles. "You've seen my challah, right? Give me your hair brush."

She started to brush Ivy's hair, letting the platinum strands slip through her fingers on each downstroke. "Are you sure you don't want to leave it down? I kind of like this tousled-on-top, sharp-on-the-bottom look. Like lace cookies drizzled in white chocolate ganache."

Looking over her shoulder back at her, blue eyes dreamy, Ivy teased, "Does that mean you want to eat me up?"

Ana gave Ivy's hair, wound around her fist, a gentle tug. "I'm not going to be late for my first ever red carpet."

"Then we might need to leave early from your first ever afterparty," Ivy said.

Starting the braid, Ana replied, "I've been to an afterparty before. I baked a cake for the wedding of one of the Steelers and got an invite to the reception. That counts, right?"

Ivy's friend Vanessa, who was being honored for her directorial debut, had sent a car to pick them up. Ivy held Ana's hand as she slipped into the backseat, and helped her smooth out her skirt around the ankles before closing the door and moving to the other side. Ana's mind was racing at double the pace of New York traffic, her nerves and her fears of staining this rented dress or of tripping in front of a Getty camera backdropped by Beyoncé's "Partition" stuck in her head.

Then she started arguing with herself about the ethics of having sex in the back of a car, because it's not like the driver consented to be a pane of glass away from people getting it on. And whether or not they knew what they were getting into when they signed the NDA, NDAs were exploitative and there was the power imbalance to think about. The driver just needed the paycheck and to provide for their family, right? So of course they'd sign the NDA. It didn't mean they wanted to overhear anything. Then she had the absurd thought that she better lock down her thoughts, because what if a nearby Beyhive member had telepathy and could hear her?

This train of thought continued until they arrived in the car line for the awards. It wasn't the way it looked in the movies, being on the other side of it. They were ushered opposite one photographer who got their arrival shot, before they were escorted to a longer press line.

"Should I go off to the side and let them shoot just you?" Ana whispered.

Ivy gave her a funny look. "No one here has any idea who I am. That's why we handed the invitation in at the start of the line, so they would have a name to put on the captions. Besides," Ivy said, pulling her close with a possessive arm, "I want the record to show I had the most beautiful woman here as my date."

The awards themselves were also unlike anything Ana had seen on

TV. The ballroom was small, the décor subdued. This was a ceremony that only presented awards to previously announced winners, instead of listing off nominees with a dramatic pause for an envelope opening. As a result, the speeches introducing the winners and the acceptance speeches themselves were longer, less rushed. White and red wine flowed.

More time was given for technical awards than at something like the Golden Globes or the Oscars, and Ana thought that was nice. But then again, she had to admit how enthralled she was with the acting awards, when she got to see celebrities she'd watched for years in real life. No one was the height she'd imagined. Everyone had fantastic skin. Actors she'd only seen in dark, intense dramas were alarmingly funny in their speeches, and she wondered how much was off the cuff and how much had been written for them by a professional, another performance.

She was used to thinking of herself as a behind-the-scenes person, but didn't everyone perform all the time? Customer service was itself a performance, the way she wooed potential clients during a tasting or chatted with the regulars at the bakery when she did her coffee rounds. She performed for Ivy, didn't she? Acted more together and grown-up than she felt?

Except not anymore, not lately. Ana felt less and less like she needed to project anything with Ivy. She tried to remember the last time she felt anxious around her, that "Is there something stuck in my teeth?" feeling she'd always had when Ivy was present. She couldn't remember. Ivy made her feel … calm. One-drink-in calm. New-lavender-pillow-spray calm. Scent-of-bread-just-out-of-the-oven calm.

Huh. That was an interesting thing to think about while in the same room as Cate freaking Blanchett.

After the ceremony, they went to an afterparty hosted by the studio that produced Vanessa's film. Ana was glad Ivy was there to lead the small talk, and to whisper bits of industry gossip in her ear. The event was catered by a local husband-and-wife food truck company. The cuisine was Asian and Latin American fusion, inspired by the wife's Japanese heritage and the husband's Puerto Rican origins.

"I can't believe my life right now," Ana said between bites. "I'm at an afterparty crawling with celebrities, in a rented designer gown, eating a California roll topped with plantains." She could feel her eyes get misty and blamed it on the eyelash glue. "And I'm looking at you."

Ivy put her chopsticks down and leaned over to kiss Ana's bare shoulder. She sighed at the warm touch of her lips on her skin. "I was just thinking the same thing," Ivy said.

Back in the hotel room, Ana pounced.

She pushed Ivy against the door and claimed her mouth in a kiss that vanquished the last traces of her lipstick. Ivy pulled her body firmly against hers, but Ana wasn't going to be maneuvered right now. She had a clear vision, and she was going to manifest it.

She kissed her way down Ivy's neck and chest and eased a few more buttons of her blouse open, revealing pale blue pasties with a touch of shimmer. Ana growled, "Wear just those and some trousers for me sometime, hmm?" Ivy gave a rough nod, hands tangling in Ana's hair as she circled around her nipples and nibbled her breasts.

Ana watched with lewd satisfaction the way Ivy stared at her as she unbuckled her pants and tugged them down to her ankles before biting off the press-ons on her index and middle fingers.

"I've been starving for this cunt all night," Ana said. She gave herself a little thrill — she wasn't usually a big dirty talker! What had gotten into her? From her knees, she started licking Ivy in long, hard strokes of her tongue, using the fingers of one hand to spread her labia apart. She craned her neck up to look at her woman, so blissed out she was barely keeping it together. It was like looking up at Everest after she'd climbed it.

"Whose pussy is this?" Ana asked, again shocking herself.

"Yours!" Ivy gasped out. "It's all yours."

"That's right, baby," Ana said, pushing her digits into Ivy's slickness. "You're all mine."

Her knees were starting to sting from the hotel carpet on her knees, but it was too cinematic of a moment to yell cut. She knew how she must look to Ivy right now, like she was an ingenue defiled — or was it Ivy who was being defiled, being brought metaphorically to her knees when Ana was the one kneeling? And what a pretty picture it was for Ana, too, looking at her Amazon's immaculately tailored suit disheveled along with the rest of her.

Even with the pain, she couldn't stop herself. The taste of Ivy was a drug to her, a fucking sugar rush going straight to her head. She wanted to devour her for every meal, lick past both their fills.

"Baby, that mouth of yours is deadly," Ivy said. "You're going to put me through the door."

"Can't. Have. That," Ana said between licks. "Then everyone who walks through the hallway will see the state of that needy pussy."

"Fuck. Keep going. Oh god!"

"Uh uh," Ana said, drawing out her fingers, taunting her. "Don't give any of them the credit. What did we say?"

"It's yours! Ana, I'm yours! Oh, fuck, I'm coming!" Ivy was grabbing wherever she could, at the doorknob and the do-not-disturb sign they'd forgotten to put outside, at the nape of Ana's neck, tangling in her waves.

Ivy writhed against her face as orgasm took her, her pretty mouth only being able to form primal syllables interrupted by her name.

Ana's skin buzzed in the stillness after. She wiped her lips with the back of her hand and looked up at Ivy, who reached down and tilted her chin with the gentlest of touches.

"You did so well," Ivy said.

"Hey!" Ana retorted. "That should have been my line!"

"Let's get out of the rest of these clothes and I'll fight you for it," Ivy said.

"OK, but I'm going to need help, because if I rip this zipper, they're going to charge me the full price of the dress," Ana said, already making a beeline for the bed and thinking of all the other games they could play before the sunrise.

twenty-four

I want someone down for choosing our own adventure.

The next morning, Ivy was deep into her first cup of hotel room coffee and scrolling TikTok on mute when Ana stirred.

"Mmm. What time is it?"

"7," Ivy said.

"Shit," Ana said. "I haven't slept in past 5 in … six years?" she said in a hoarse whisper. "It feels…" she yawned, "… incredible."

"You can go back to sleep if you want," Ivy said.

Ana tried to open her eyes wide, but she only managed a goofy squint that scrunched up her forehead. It was adorable. "Really?" she said.

"Really. We've got nowhere to be except wherever we want to be. We can stay here all day if we want."

"But what about touristy things?" Ana asked, half the words mumbled into the pillow.

"Fuck touristy things," Ivy said. "This is our vacation. We can do whatever we want with it. New York is still going to be here if we want to come back one day."

She saw Ana smile at her and knew what she was thinking, because she was thinking about it too. The implication of a future, that they'd be together long enough to take another trip like this. It was loaded.

"Just let me sleep, like, 30 more minutes," Ana said.

Two hours later, Ivy had showered, had a second cup of coffee, ordered room service, and caught up on the group text. Ana stretched like a cat in the sun.

"Is that coffee I smell?" she asked.

"Yup. It's single-cup. Let me make you one."

"Thanks, baby," Ana said, grabbing her phone and bundling back under the covers. Ivy heated at the casual endearment. How strange to be "baby," to imagine herself precious and lovable.

Ana was full of surprises, like her sexy show of dominance the night before. Ivy thought she'd lived through enough to know what she wanted, but she had never thought to want all of this. And now, she couldn't un-want it.

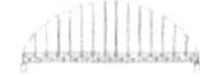

Ana felt fantastic after sleeping in. She showered and washed her hair with the hotel's lavender and oud complementary minis, and felt so relaxed that she almost wanted to go back to sleep. She instead dressed in leggings, ankle boots and an oversized T-shirt, and a camel coat Ivy had just bought the day before at a department store.

"It looks good on you," Ivy said, admiring her. "Maybe you should keep it."

"No way," Ana said, but it did look really good on her.

While she was sleeping, Ivy booked them a bus tour that looked so cute on the website. It was a pink double decker bus that served tea, champagne and pastries while taking passengers to all the touristy spots. Ana could have cried in elation that most of today would be spent sedentary, not testing the soles of her Target boots she bought on clearance, when her feet were already sore from wearing heels to the event the previous night.

The performers who worked on the tour wore pink suit vests and toile neckties over crisp white blouses, pink pinstripe pants and shiny black oxfords. Ana and Ivy were cozied up on the second floor of the bus. They drank lavender earl grey tea — Ana with milk, Ivy with lemon and honey — and ate orange scones, lacy caramel tuiles and fudgy brownies with perfectly crisp edges and soft, gooey centers. They gulped down their champagne flutes when they stopped at the NY Public Library, and Ana watched with awe as Ivy walked through the building like it was a church. She was reverent and hushed as she told her about movies that had been filmed here, then panicked that she wouldn't have enough time to walk through and see some of the shelves. She wanted to find her favorite books and "visit" them, even though she could do the same at any bookstore or at the Carnegie libraries back home. But no, she wanted to see the NY Public Library copies, because those were different, somehow.

After the bus tour, they Googled a burger place and walked there for a quick lunch. It was two storefronts down from a sex shop. Ana wasn't sure why the thought hadn't occurred to her until just now how much fun it would be to take Ivy toy shopping. It was probably because she hadn't been in one in a while — her Old Reliable was less reliable by the day, so she was due for a replacement.

"This is ... tiny," Ivy whispered when they got in. "Like, I've had shoeboxes full of vibrators bigger than this shoebox full of vibrators."

"Real estate is expensive, honey," the bored-looking cashier said. Ana watched Ivy apologetically bow her head at him, and the cashier nodded. "Let me know if you need help finding anything," he said with a satisfied smile.

They looked at the clit suction toys and the Rabbit-style vibrators before approaching a shelf of partner toys, including strap-ons. Ana felt Ivy's intense focus on her as she tentatively picked up one of the harnesses.

"Do you enjoy using them?" Ivy asked.

"I never have," Ana said. "Giving or receiving."

Raising a perfectly laminated eyebrow, Ivy asked, "Want to?"

Ana nodded enthusiastically.

"Pick one out," Ivy said.

Ana glared. "I'm going to pick it out, and I'm going to pay for it. OK?"

"OK."

"I'm serious," Ana said, pointing a blue dildo with ridges and a protruding nub at her like it was a loaded gun. "If you pull out your wallet, I will cause you bodily harm. I've been training. I can throw a punch now."

"Easy, slugger," Ivy said. "Message received." She wrapped her arm around Ana, and she leaned into the embrace. "OK, so. Which one looks good?"

"How about this one?" Ana said, picking up a purple one with a slot to insert a bullet vibrator. It was shaped like a checkmark, with one long shaft forming an angle with a shorter one. "Looks like this one goes inside the giver and the receiver."

"No strap?"

"That one is strapless," the cashier said, not looking up from his phone. "Customers enjoy the added closeness that it provides and the fact they don't have to worry about adjusting the straps beforehand, but it takes some practice and a strong pelvic floor to be able to keep it in."

"You up for the athletic challenge?" Ana asked.

Ivy gave the toy a hard look. "Yes. What have I been training for if not this?"

"We have a 20 percent off lube sale going on right now, and some people like to use it with our realistic white lube."

"I feel like that's messier than I want to get," Ana said. "Clear is good."

"This one," Ivy said, grabbing an ornate glass bottle. Ana looked at her quizzically. "Camila says she's a convert. Don't worry, you can pay for it."

twenty-five

Knight of Swords — *Charge! Head empty, no thoughts, just go go go!*

"I'm a little intimidated, if I'm being honest."

Ivy was looking at Ana's new toy, wondering aloud if her kegel game was really as good as she thought it was.

"I am so confident in your abilities, but if it gets too hard, it's fine! It's just an experiment."

"Well, if it doesn't work for us," Ivy offered, "I would still love to fuck you with a strap-on. I have one with actual straps we could try."

"And you've been holding out on me?" Ana asked, faux-affronted. She was so excited to try something she'd never done before, and to get to do it with Ivy.

"OK, let's see if this is even going to work," Ivy said. She poured some of the fancy lube on her hand and started rubbing it on her clit. Ana groaned watching her stroke herself, and planted herself between Ivy's spread legs.

"Let me help," Ana whined, and teased Ivy's entrance with her fingers. She watched Ivy bite her lip. "Let me take over. Pinch your nipples for me."

She watched Ivy twist and pinch the peaks of her small breasts, watched her gasp as she slowly, so slowly, pushed two fingers inside.

"I can feel you squeezing," Ana joked. "Practicing?"

"I want to be able to fuck you long and hard, baby," Ivy said. To pay her back for her cockiness — no pun intended — she curled her fingers firmly and watched Ivy squirm. "OK. I think I'm wet enough," she said with a laugh. "Let me see if I can grip this toy."

Ana lubed up the dildo and pushed the shorter end into Ivy's pussy. When it was fully in, and Ivy got on her knees to face her, she felt dizzy at the atypical, wholly erotic sight of Ivy sporting a long, thick purple boner.

"I feel so powerful with a cock," Ivy said. "Is this gender euphoria, or just what unearned privilege feels like?"

"I'll let you know my thoughts on it next time, when it's my turn," Ana said. "For now ..." Feeling a little self-conscious, like Ivy might laugh at her, she opened her mouth for the dildo and sucked it. She made eye contact with Ivy, who groaned at the sight. "Remember I said I've never given a blow job?" she asked. "Now you're my first." *My only*, she thought, taking the toy as far into her mouth as she could, digging her fingers into Ivy's firm ass cheeks as Ivy dug her fingers into Ana's hair.

"You should see how you look right now sucking my cock," Ivy said. "You're so goddamn beautiful."

Ana grasped the base of the dildo and pushed up, watching Ivy's hips shake at the penetration. "I need you inside me right now," Ana said.

"Get on your hands and knees," Ivy said.

Ana was hit with a sudden wave of self-consciousness. She'd long since gotten past any insecurity about what her pussy looked like. Never, not once, had she seen someone else's and not just been stoked to be there.

But she'd never been fucked the way she was about to be, which meant she'd never been perceived from this exact angle. What if Ivy didn't like what she saw?

Ivy was lubing up her entrance. "Wait," Ana said, and Ivy pulled her fingers away. "I just need a second. I'm kind of in my head right now."

"Talk to me," Ivy said. "What's going on?"

"I'm just feeling … insecure? Like, I don't know? About this angle? About how I look?"

"You look fucking incredible," Ivy said. "What, you think I'm going to do anything but worship this ass?" She grabbed a handful, and Ana felt like hiding her face even though Ivy already couldn't see it. "Baby, do you know how much time I've spent staring at this ass while you're at work?" Ivy squeezed both of her cheeks. "I've been lusting after this ass. Do you know how lucky I am to have this view?" She moved her hands from Ana's ass down the back of her thighs and back up, palming her pussy. She squeezed her labia while planting kisses on Ana's left cheek. "Do you know how lucky I am to be back here watching you drip for me?" she said, putting one finger into her pussy very slowly.

"More," Ana whimpered. "I need more."

"I can give you more," Ivy said. Ana felt her maneuver the thick head of the dildo past her entrance and let herself sink into the sensation of fullness. When Ivy was in her to the hilt, Ana felt her hips against her butt and sighed. She loved being this close to her.

As Ivy started to thrust into her, she wrapped a hand below her to stroke her clit. "Harder," Ana said. Surprising her not at all, Ivy understood that "harder" wasn't the same as "faster," and the slow, agonizing, delicious pounding was sending Ana into orbit. "How does it feel for you?" she asked.

"Unreal," Ivy said. "I wasn't sure it would feel good for me, honestly, but each thrust feels fantastic for me, too." She stroked Ana's back tenderly. "You're taking me so well, baby."

"Do you think I could get on top?"

Without warning, Ivy grabbed Ana by the hips, planted one foot next to her in a lunge, then shifted their weight back until Ana was in reverse cowgirl.

"Ivy!" Ana shrieked, collapsing into laughter. "Are you trying to throw out both our backs, or is it your knees you have a vendetta against?"

"Hey! Less talking about my creaky knees, more bouncing on me, please."

Ana tried going up and down, letting the dildo slide in and out, until she found that a hip grinding motion felt much better.

Ivy said many words that weren't in the Bible, with the exception of "Jesus Christ."

She rotated so they were facing each other. Ivy looked stunning — her face was flushed, making the freckles on her cheeks more obvious. Her blonde hair framed her face like a halo, the humidity making it revert to its wavy state. And she was looking at her like she had walked directly out of her wildest fantasies.

In that moment, Ana actually understood how magic worked. She hadn't called any corners, but the circle was cast, a dome of stone and flame, ocean waves and mountain winds. And all those elemental forces weren't going to be enough to contain this. She could see the panorama and every pixel within it, could feel reality rearranging itself around their bodies.

"Woah," Ana said.

"Yeah," Ivy said. "Woah."

"I touch you, you touch me," Ana said, pressing her fingers to Ivy's clit and guiding Ivy's hand to her.

They rocked against each other, precise fingers and unruly, rocking hips and mouths desperate for any surface they could kiss. Their gazes linked and Ana knew Ivy needed more, so she gave her more pressure, made the circles she was stroking faster and wider the way she knew Ivy preferred when she was close. Her heart was beating faster than it did during the lunch rush when she was running on four cups of coffee, and Ivy's ragged breaths kept pace with the pounding in her chest.

"Oh god, Ana!" Ivy cried as her hips bucked uncontrollably. Her fingers jerked on Ana's clit, losing their rhythm, but Ana was already on the verge regardless, and there was no going back. She could feel Ivy's orgasm, the aftershocks of the quake that rocked through her affecting

Ana as well through the toy connecting them. And Ivy's gasps and moans and fervent cries about Ana being perfect, beautiful, incredible, a goddess, were enough to push her over the edge, and she rode the silicone cock in a frenzy as her own climax kept coming, and coming, and *coming*.

She swore she must have blacked out, because she had no recollection of rolling off Ivy onto her back. Ivy was draped against her, kissing her neck and whispering endearments.

They lay there catching their breath for what felt like a long time before Ivy spoke.

"Shit. We forgot to use the vibrating function," Ivy said.

"That's … probably for the best," Ana said. "Am I … am I dead?"

"Maybe," Ivy said, and they burst into hysterical laughter. "We fucked each other to death."

"You deserve some kind of medal."

"A medal?" Ivy said. "Maybe a world record for longest kegel exercise. I might need a doctor after this."

Ana rolled on top of Ivy, somehow getting a second wind after that near death experience, because she was ready to go again. "Poor baby," Ana said, moving herself down Ivy's body and spreading her legs. "Let me kiss it better."

twenty-six

```
INT. AIRPLANE — DAY
Ana leans over to Ivy, pulling up the arm rest
that separates them. She brushes hair behind
Ivy's ear to whisper.
```

"I just know the FBI has a file on both of us now with a big red 'lesbian' stamp," Ana said. "Suitcase full of crystals and dildos. I can't think of anything gayer."

"Maybe carabiners?" Ivy asked, settling back in her first class seat. She and Ana both had on hydrating undereye patches for the flight. There was something very cute about her girlfriend raiding her skincare stash.

"Carabiners are just useful," Ana said. "Do straight people not use them?"

"I don't know what straight people use," Ivy said, sighing.

"There are books about them. Speaking of," Ana said. "I'm really loving *Circe*. I'm going to try to zone out of the, you know, physical improbability of air travel."

"I knew you'd like it," Ivy said. "OK, those patches just look adorable on you. We have to get a selfie."

"If you're hard launching me, it better not be with an undereye patch picture," Ana said, grinning for the camera.

As Ivy finished snapping the picture and reviewing it, a notification popped up from her dating app. "COME MEET YOUR MATCHES."

The bottom fell out of Ivy's stomach. Ana glared at her. "Um, excuse me bitch? Are you joking?"

"No no no no no," Ivy said, desperate to find some way to prove her innocence. "I haven't been on it in forever. That's probably why it's sending me push notifications all of a sudden."

"OK but why didn't you delete it?"

"Forgetfulness! I swear."

"Well, consider this a reminder, then?"

"Look, see, it's deleted," Ivy said, wishing she could set the corporate headquarters on fire with her mind.

"Good," Ana said. She glared at Ivy then softened, likely seeing the contrition and panic there. "I'm going to just sit quietly now and read this book and hope there are instructions for how to turn my girlfriend into a pig."

Ivy scowled, but Ana was true to her word and ignored her, speeding through the book. Ivy searched through her photos and picked one from the awards show afterparty that Vanessa had taken. Ana was holding the skirt of her dress off to the side with a flourish while Ivy dipped her back at the waist, their noses touching and huge, cheesy grins on their faces. She wrote a caption, tagged Ana and posted it to her Instagram feed.

Ana's phone buzzed with the notification and she checked it. Turning the phone to Ivy, she read the caption to her. "'Hard launch'?"

Ivy gave her a "yeah, duh," expression. "Harder than Bezos' dick rocket's launch."

Ana tried and failed to hide a smile. "You chose a very good picture of me."

"There are no bad ones, honey."

They sat in silence for a bit, Ana returning to her book and Ivy scrolling through her phone. She pulled up Steam and scrolled through reviews for Era's dating sim game. The demo was getting positive feedback, and lots of it. She typed the title into YouTube and saw lots of "let's-plays" of the demo. It looked like Era was about to have a hit on her hands.

She looked at the reviews and then at the paperback in Ana's hands. She remembered how much she loved reading film scripts, how she'd study them from cover to cover and annotate them like she would one of her favorite novels.

"You know when you asked me if I'd ever want to go back into film?" Ivy asked Ana.

She bookmarked her spot. "Yeah. Are you thinking more about it? Like, producing Era's game?"

"Maybe. But, I don't think I want to produce," Ivy said. "Maybe I could, I don't know, get into screenwriting."

Ana made the cutest little surprised expression. "I have just had this flash of you in a café — wait, what am I talking about, in *my* café — with your laptop, papers everywhere, chewing on a pencil, mouthing words to yourself then frowning and deleting them. Then taking a big angry bite of something — a bear claw. Crumbs everywhere."

"That's ... specific?"

"I don't know if it's manifesting or if I have The Sight, but I see it. I love this for you."

Ivy felt a surge of excitement. "Yeah. I love it for me, too. Maybe I'll start writing some spec scripts for practice. Dust off that Ao3 account."

Ana looked at her quizzically. "What's Ao3?"

She blinked at her. "Oh. I'm about to spam you many, many links."

"I can't wait," Ana said, grinning. "Oh, you know what you should do? You should practice with how you'd write *Circe*!"

"You really want me to aim high, huh?" Ivy said, laughing.

"I'm serious. You love this book, and I want to know what you'd do with it. Like ... maybe I'd need to see a screenplay to see how this looks when written, but I know when I see movie adaptations of books, they have to show a lot of stuff through the acting that we might get as inner monologue in a book. And Circe is such an inner monologue book, it would be great practice. Like when she met Penelope, how she was feeling versus how she presented herself, how would you approach it when you don't have access to that inner monologue?"

"That relationship was one of my favorite parts of the book," Ivy said. "How they were both so intrigued by each other."

"Bad bitches recognize other bad bitches," Ana said.

Ivy thought about it more. "Something I've liked in other scripts I've read is how the dialogue gets longer when characters get closer. They aren't holding their tongues as much. But there's also a lot more action in between the dialogue. The scripts start focusing in on really minute cues because the characters are seeing each other more clearly. So that's what I would do."

"I love it," Ana said. "I can't wait to read whatever you write."

"Well then," Ivy said, digging her iPad out of her bag, "better not keep you waiting. I've been thinking more about Era's game, so maybe I'll toy around with that."

"I'll try really hard not to read over your shoulder," Ana said.

Thinking back to the game's premise and tutorial, she started from the moment the player arrives at the magical bookstore they inherited.

BOOKED AND BUSY

```
    Episode 101 — Pilot/"The Dropout"
     Written for television by Ivy Lowell


EXT. ABANDONED BOOKSTORE — DAY


The afternoon California sun casts the shadow of
MADDIE, a 20-something grad school dropout, on
the dusty glass door of a stone cottage.


Maddie looks down at the rusty key in her hand,
then back at the door, then sighs.
```

                    MADDIE
          OK, Aunt Bunny, let's see what
             kind of mess you left me.

Walking into her dusty inheritance from her great
aunt, she's greeted by the sight of a cobweb-
covered cash register, tackily upholstered
armchairs, and rows and rows of wooden shelves
crammed with books.

A cat runs in through the open door and perches
by the cash register, as if guarding against the
intruder.

                    MADDIE
          Oh. Hey. You come here often?

The cat purrs in response.

                    MADDIE
          Do you know where Bunny kept the broom?

The cat leaps off the counter and runs to the
back. Shrugging, Maddie follows it to a broom
closet.

Now armed with miscellaneous cleaning supplies,
Maddie returns to the cash register and starts
dusting off the cobwebs. The cash drawer pops
open. We zoom in on Maddie's hand pulling a note
out of the cash register.

                    MADDIE
        "Look under the candelabra"? Bunny, I swear to
                     goddess...

She looks around until she finds the item.
Removing it and coughing at dust, she finds a
book with an attached note that reads *For Maddie*.

*"To my darling grandniece Maddie — You know more
than most how the best laid plans don't always
pan out. So here's something that'll help. I've
enchanted this planner with an old family spell.
Anything you write in this planner will have a
greater chance of success. Now be careful — you
know our family's magic packs a punch. But you'll
need it! You've got a big project ahead of you
with fixing up this bookstore, so start writing.*

All my love from the beyond,
  Bunny.

*P.S. I've left you the number for a carpenter,
Logan. He's a very good boy, and easy on the
eyes, too. I know, I know, you hate me trying to
set you up, but what else am I supposed to do
with my time? I'm dead. I'm sure it's boring. I
know you've had some big setbacks lately. But I
know you, and I know how powerful you are. Soon,
you'll know that, too."*

Maddie puts the note down and strokes the cover
of the planner. She looks around somberly. She

hears the sound of cracking wood and books
tumbling to the floor. She closes her eyes in
silent resignation, gathering herself.

                    MADDIE
OK then, I guess the first item of business is to
                hire a carpenter.

Pen in hand, she opens the planner.

When Ivy got to a lull in her typing, Ana put her book down.

"So? What do you think?"

Ivy grinned and leaned over to steal a kiss.

"I'm wondering if streaming services are ready for a magical poly romance?"

twenty-seven

I want someone who keeps me on my toes and calls me on my shit.

Every Christmas Eve since she'd moved back to Pittsburgh, Ivy had taken part in a White Elephant gift exchange with her friends.

This year, Rahul was hosting. He'd recently bought a house in Mount Lebanon. It was an older home with tons of space, taking up two stories plus an attic and unfinished basement. "I want to host this year," he'd said at one of their standing karaoke nights. "It'll give me an excuse to finish decorating."

"You're never going to 'finish' decorating," Era said. "I've rearranged my living room furniture three times this year."

Ivy invited Ana, and she seemed a little hesitant, maybe nervous, to come. Was it because she didn't know her friends as well as she knew Ivy? She shouldn't be nervous about that. The people she hadn't met yet were going to love her.

Ivy was nervous, but not so much about introducing her girlfriend to the friend group. She was nervous about two big gifts she was going to give tonight, not including her contribution to the gift exchange. For that, she'd chosen the Hot Ones "Truth or Dab" card game, which turned the YouTube interview series into a truth or dare-style party game, hot sauce included.

"You ready?" Ivy said to Ana. It wasn't snowing, but it was bitterly cold, and her down coat was just barely keeping out the sharp chill.

"I am," Ana said, squeezing Ivy's arm. "I hope people like the gift I brought. No one is gonna be offended by witchy stuff, right?"

"Please. I would be shocked if by the end of tonight, they don't have you lead a seance to talk to Mr. Rogers or some shit."

"I would love to talk to Mr. Rogers," Ana said dreamily. "OK, let's do this."

Ivy rang the doorbell but let herself in. "Hey hey, where's my eggnog?"

Rahul rounded the corner, a rocks glass in hand. He'd said on the invite to "dress to impress," and he'd followed his own instructions, wearing a green velvet smoking jacket and metallic green trousers with golden ikat embroidery. "One nog coming right up. It's really good to see you, Ana! Coat closet is right over there —" he gestured. "Ana, can I get you something to drink? I've got … um, everything?"

"That eggnog sounds good."

"Do you want the white people version, or my special chai version?"

"*My* special chai version," said an absolutely stunning woman who appeared next to Rahul, wrapping an arm around him. "I won't have my little brother taking credit for my recipe."

Rahul rolled his eyes. "May I introduce you to my incredibly arrogant older sister, Saanvi?"

"You mean your sophisticated award-winning bartender sister, Saanvi," she said, extending a hand for both of them to shake. She had glossy black stiletto nails, outshined only by her equally glossy, pin-straight black hair. Her dark brown skin was clear and glowy, and her full lips were painted a matte crimson.

The lesbians were too stunned to speak.

"Oh, definitely that one," Ana said. "The special chai. Do you need any help in the kitchen?"

"No, but you're so sweet to ask," Saanvi said. "Just make yourselves at home!"

Rahul pointed at his sister as if to say, *Can you believe the nerve of this chick?*

Ivy took both their coats while Ana added their gifts to the pile. The way the exchange worked was that everyone in attendance would draw a random number, and the person who picked No. 1 would choose a wrapped gift first. The next person had the option of opening a gift or stealing the gift from the first person, and so it would go with every subsequent person who would have the option to open a new gift or steal one that was already unwrapped. Then it went back to the beginning, with anyone who had been stolen from getting the option to swap gifts with someone else.

She introduced Ana to everyone she didn't know yet, and they sat close together on the couch while people refilled their drinks and nibbled on snacks.

"All right, everyone! Let's get started. The rules are as follows," Rahul said, recapping the exchange for the participants. He passed around an acacia bowl with wrapped pieces of paper.

"What number did you get?" Ivy asked, showing Ana her "3."

"Lucky number 13," Ana whispered. "I might have hit the jackpot on this."

"So lucky."

Seth had drawn No. 1, and he went straight for the smallest box. "The biggest box is always the silliest gift," he reasoned. He unwrapped the tiny parcel and found an AirTag. "Ah, this is actually useful. Thank you, whoever that was!"

"It was me," said Jason, Era's preppy executive assistant.

Camila was next, and she got the Hot Ones game. She was not at all a spicy food person, so when her boyfriend Zach's turn came around, Ivy wasn't surprised he stole it from her.

"I would have given it to you anyway," she whispered to him, giving him a giddy little kiss.

"I guess I'm not good at this game, then," Zach said, pulling her onto his lap.

Camila then chose a new gift. Even if Ivy hadn't seen the wrapping paper earlier, she could tell it was Analeigh's by the way she stiffened next to her.

"Ooh!" Camila said, unwrapping a red satin cloth printed with black text, and a palm-sized organza drawstring bag full of clinking metal charms. "Is this a game? Or…"

"It's for casting charms," Ana said, her voice shy and strained. "You roll out the mat and ask a question, then you toss the charms and use where they land to interpret the answer. I can show you how later, if you want."

"That's so cool!" Camila said. She was already sorting through the charms. "There's a little monstera leaf. This one's a lollipop. Ooh, a little handbag! This one, I know what this one means," she said, holding up a piece that looked like a stack of bills with angel wings. "This one means, RIP my wallet."

"See, you've got it already!" Ana said, laughing.

When it was Era's turn, Camila stared daggers at her, dissuading her from stealing her precious charms. Era ended up going for the biggest gift, against her husband's logic, and was rewarded with a very soft-looking burrito blanket.

In the end, Ivy ended up with a wooden serving board that had the words "Shark Coochie" and a Great White burned into it (from Camila), and Ana stole Liam's Chia Pet Sophia from *The Golden Girls*. Liam ended up with an embroidered kitchen towel that said "Thou May Ingest a Satchel of Richards" he stole from Rahul, commenting, "I will cherish this all my days."

They chatted more with Saanvi, who was currently living in New York but was in the middle of packing everything up to come to Pittsburgh.

"I thought I'd get a head start scoping out places I could apply," Saanvi said. "Not that it would be hard to get a job at a bar with my experience, but it would be nice to get a vibe for different places before I try to spend most of my time there."

"My friend Maggie and her wife own a great bar that just opened recently," Ana said.

"Oh yeah," Ivy added. "It's so cute."

"Here, I'll show you pictures," Ana said, Googling it and scrolling through images while Saanvi watched, admiring them.

"Oh this is gorgeous," Saanvi said. "Think I could persuade you to introduce me to the owner?"

"Of course!" Ana said. "I can vouch for your skills. This chai nog is, whew. Something else."

"I'm so glad I met you both," Saanvi said. "It'll be nice to have someone else I know when I move here. Other than my brother, I mean." Ivy noticed Saanvi's eyes darting just then to Liam, who was drilling holes into Saanvi's head with his eyes until the moment she looked at him. He became enthralled by a conversation with Jason.

What the hell was *that* about?

Once everyone dispersed back to snacking and drinking, Ivy told Ana she'd be right back and followed Rahul into the kitchen, hiding a manila envelope behind her back.

"Hey," she said to Rahul, who was mixing up another chai eggnog.

"Hey yourself. Are you having fun? Is Ana having a good time?"

"I think so," Ivy said. "I want to give you your Christmas present."

He raised a full eyebrow as the manila envelope came into view. "Am I being served?" he asked, grinning.

"In a way. Open it."

Rahul reached for the envelope and pulled out the stack of papers. He immediately opened his mouth to protest, but Ivy cut him off.

"Just look through them, show them to your lawyer," Ivy said, knowing full well Rahul could dissect the contract himself three drinks deep, "and think about it."

"You know I don't believe in going into business with friends," Rahul said.

"But we're already in business together," Ivy said. "This just gives you a fair partnership stake in Double Dare Fitness, paid for with the time you've already put into the business. It gives you a salary commensurate with a partnership stake, not a part-timer stake, but gives you all the freedom you need to keep working the same hours and keep practicing law. I think you'll find the dissolution terms, should you one day decide you want out, to be very reasonable."

Rahul was giving the papers a hard stare. When he looked up at Ivy, he was shaking his head, but he was smiling.

Ivy walked across the kitchen island and put her hand on his arm. "This business wouldn't exist without you. You are my partner in this even without the title. This just gives you your due, officially."

"I'll look it over with my lawyer and get back to you," Rahul said, formal. "Then you and your lawyer can review any proposed amendments."

"Sounds more than fair," Ivy said.

Rahul wrapped her in a fierce hug. "You're the worst, you know that?" he whispered, voice thick with emotion.

"Yeah," Ivy said, trying not to tear up herself. "It's a problem."

Now, on to Ana. She was going to wait until they got back to Ivy's place to hand over her gift. She was really nervous. She hoped she loved it — or at least didn't kill her.

At any rate, it wasn't the kind of gift she could return to the store. She had one of those, too, but it wasn't the real gift.

When she walked back to Ana, she looked at her curiously. "What was that about?" she asked quietly. "You and Rahul. Looked intense."

"I gave him his Christmas present," Ivy said. Giggling at Ana's raised eyebrows and her "go on" expression, Ivy said, "I drew up partnership papers for the gym. He's said before he doesn't want to have a stake in the business, but … he deserves it. No one has put in as much effort into the place other than me, even though he's part time."

"Huh," Ana said. "Do you think he's going to agree to it?"

"I hope so," Ivy said. "The terms are excellent for him, and I'm happy to make any changes he wants to the agreement." She was confused by Ana's neutral expression. "What? What are you thinking about?" she asked nervously, looking around to see if any of her friends were watching the exchange that suddenly felt tense.

"Nothing, it's just a big thing to spring on someone. Financial stuff, it's touchy."

"I mean, yeah, but, I've never really understood that."

"Well. Have you always had money?"

Ivy's cheeks warmed. "I didn't grow up rich or anything. My parents did fine, I suppose. And I didn't start making any real money until a few years ago."

"I might be overthinking it," Ana said with a shrug, taking a sip of her drink. "I know you'll both sort it out. It'll be a good thing, in the end. As long as he feels like it's his decision as much as it is yours."

Was she right? Had she overstepped somehow?

twenty-eight

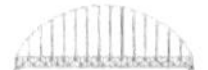

Despite her social anxiety, Ana had a great time at the Christmas party. Ivy's friends were fun, and she hadn't made a fool of herself, so that was good.

Now she was just excited to give Ivy her gift, drink some cocoa, and pass out. Maybe fool around a little and then pass out.

"You've gotta open mine first," Ana said, handing Ivy the neatly wrapped box. She was so proud of herself, and Ivy's reaction didn't disappoint.

"Oh my god!" she said, pulling the thick hardbound book out of the box. "The annotated script of *Everything Everywhere All At Once?* This is incredible. This has been sold out everywhere."

"You're not the only one who can call in a favor," Ana said. When

Ivy looked at her curiously, Ana laughed and said, "No, I'm just kidding, I just got lucky right when the preorder opened."

Ivy was surprised. "So you've been planning this for a while?"

Ana shrugged. "It just seemed like something you'd like. I didn't expect the context I'd be giving it to you in. I thought it would just be a thank you, you know? For training me."

"This is the best gift anyone has ever given me," Ivy said, and Ana could tell she meant it.

"All right, don't get sappy on me. Give me my present! Give me my present!"

Ivy laughed and slid over a small box and an envelope.

Ana shook the box and smirked. "I think I know what this is," she said, hearing the telltale thud of a tarot deck.

"Now, I don't think you have this one based on my snooping of your shelves," Ivy said, as Ana unwrapped the deck featuring artwork from famous movies.

"I love it! I'm excited to work with it. Pop culture decks give you interesting perspectives. Is this a card?" she asked, holding up the envelope.

"No, that's part of your gift," Ivy said.

"Hmm, interesting. Is it a gift card? Is it Taylor Swift tickets to some as-yet unannounced concert your connections hooked you up with? Is it an autograph from Meryl Streep?" She screeched. "Is it an autograph from Pedro Pascal?"

"Just open it!" Ivy said.

Ana was gentle with the envelope's seam, and took out the plain printer paper and opened it.

She read it, and read it again. "I don't understand," she said. She understood the words printed on the paper, saw the dollars and cents listed, but she didn't understand how this was possible. "You paid Aracely's tuition?"

Ivy's grin was so big it hurt Ana physically. "This should cover anything not paid for by her grants and scholarships through the end of her junior year. Or at least it should be pretty close. Some of that information is confidential, so I kind of had to play a game of over-under with the bursar to come up with a figure. It's set aside as a gift fund, so she can use anything extra for books or toward housing."

Ana looked at the paper in her hands, which were shaking, then looked at the book she'd gotten Ivy. Here she was thinking she'd done something, gotten her this cool, grown-up gift. Instead she looked like a silly little girl, while Ivy was here dropping thousands of dollars on her sister. Doing what Ana herself couldn't afford to do.

Rescuing her.

"Take it back," Ana said, sliding the paper over like it was crawling with spiders. "Or let me pay you back."

Ivy just looked sheepish. "I thought you'd maybe react that way, but it's really not that big of a deal. I had plenty in savings, and I can tell you've been really stressed over this. Now you have one less thing to worry about."

"This is too much," Ana said, but the words sounded strangled. "I have to pay you back. I'm going to pay you back."

"Ana," Ivy said, finally catching on that Ana was not just choked up, but possibly actually choking. "Was this ... did I do the wrong thing?"

"Yes," Ana said, almost yelling. "I'm sorry. I mean, thank you. I appreciate it, I really do. But this is just — I can't — this just illustrates it perfectly, you know? I couldn't even imagine just giving something this big to someone, not at this stage in my life." Her stomach felt like it was being ripped apart from the inside. "You're just on this other level that I'm not. And this isn't a 'girlfriend' gift. This is, like, an engagement gift. This is something you give a wife. Not something you give someone you just started sleeping with. It's too fast, Ivy. I don't know if I'm there yet. I don't know if I'll ever be there, with anyone."

Ivy was standing now, and Ana realized she'd been pacing. She put her hands on her arms, warm where Ana had gone cold. "Take a breath, Ana. I'm not saying all that. I'm not expecting all that. I'm not expecting anything."

"How could you expect anything?" Ana said. "I'm just ... I'm like this nobody. I'm this stray cat you're trying to rescue."

"Whoa. Absolutely not. Ana. You're the most incredible girl I've ever met."

"Girl," Ana repeated.

Ivy shook her head viciously. "Woman. You're the most incredible woman I've ever met. Please stop twisting this into something it isn't. Ana. Please."

"You said you didn't want someone you had to rescue."

Ivy looked at her with confusion. "Rescue? What are you talking about."

"Your list," Ana said. "Your Wife List. Here you are, rescuing me. Being my sugarmama. Doing all these things you said you didn't want to do in a relationship. To me, because of me."

Breathing deeply, Ana looked at Ivy. Really looked at her. Her kind blue eyes, filled with such worry for her. The freckles showing through her makeup. The lips she'd kissed so many times she'd lost count, sweet as candy even now, because they were kissing her now. Because nothing and no one calmed her down the way that Ivy did, and it didn't matter to her body that Ivy was the one who had caused her so much distress. It was what she read in every herbalism book. Ivy was bane and blessing growing from the same stalk.

Ivy was on her knees, kissing her stomach under her shirt, her thighs over her jeans.

"No, no, no," Ivy was whispering between kisses. "It's not like that, I swear."

"I'll just be another name between the lines of your list," Ana whispered.

"Never," Ivy said.

It was all playing out like images rendered into slow motion by a strobe light. A blink, and they were kissing. Another, and they were in the bed. One more, and clothes were off and mouths and hands were frantically searching for comfort, to give it, to take it.

"Forget the list," Ivy said, burying her face between Ana's legs. She gasped at the pleasure that didn't fit with the terrible pain building in her chest. The gasp turned into a sob as she dug her hands into Ivy's hair. "I'll print it just to burn it," Ivy said.

Helpless against her own body, betrayed by it and how much she wanted to feel anything but what she was feeling inside, she tugged Ivy's hair to pull her mouth off her cunt.

"You paid for the trip, didn't you?" Ana asked. "Not Vanessa."

"Yes," Ivy said, guilty as sin. Ana shook her head then moaned as Ivy pushed her fingers inside her. It wasn't sweet or tender. It was desperate.

"Harder," Ana cried out. Now she wanted it to hurt. The pleasure didn't make sense, and she needed something to.

Ivy lapped at her ferociously, and Ana came just as sloppily, not sure whether she wanted to pull her closer or push her away. She chose the former, wrapping her exposed legs around Ivy's waist and rolling to straddle her.

They kissed for a long time. Ana broke the kiss first.

"I think I want to sleep in my own bed tonight," she said.

"Ana, please. We should talk."

"Yeah," Ana said. "We should. You should have talked to me, about a lot of things."

She found her underwear on the floor and scooped it up, jumped back into her jeans.

"Ana —" Ivy started. Ana held her hand up and silenced her.

"We'll talk when I want to," Ana said.

She gathered her things as elegantly as she could, trying to project confident, embodied woman who took no shit, and not some helpless little girl whose partner could lie to her while hiding big financial decisions. "Don't follow me," Ana said when she heard Ivy stirring. Ivy stopped as if Ana had cast a binding spell on her.

Maybe she had.

As she walked into the living room, she found Sigourney, who was staring up at her with big, pondering eyes. She meowed once and tilted her head.

Ana knelt in front of the cat. "Bye, Sig," she said, kissing the cat on her head. She looked back at Ivy's room, where she could hear soft sniffles. "Go hug your mommy, OK?"

This is what was going through Ana's head, through her dark red thoughts that were getting muddled with the pleasure Ivy had given her and the screaming banshee in her head telling her to turn around, to not leave it like this.

First: She was never going to live down the reaction she'd just had.

Second: She was furious, both at the gift and at her reaction to it.

Third: She loved Ivy so much, it was always going to blow up in her face.

twenty-nine

I want someone to put me out of my misery.

It was Christmas morning and Ivy was alone.

Well, not completely alone. Sig was doing what could only be described as an angry nuzzle. She was cuddling Ivy while hissing.

"Listen," Ivy said. "I'm going to die all alone, and when I do, you get to eat my corpse. So you'll get your revenge, OK?"

Sigourney purred, satisfied.

IVY

Hey. Can you just let me know that you're OK?

She knew she was once again crossing a boundary, but if she didn't confirm that Ana had made it home last night and not careened off a snowy bridge, she would die. She must have seen that in a movie or commercial at some point — the lover fleeing a fight only to meet their end.

Ana responded right away, which filled Ivy with an embarrassing amount of relief.

Ana responded by liking her text.

That felt like a hate crime.

Ana really was hungover. Rahul and Saanvi had heavy pours.

But mostly, she was stewing in a sludge of anxiety.

She had texted Ari this morning. Ari had gotten an email from the school confirming that her tuition had been paid off and she had additional funds in her account for expenses, and texted Analeigh to ask her how she managed that.

When she told her she hadn't, that Ivy had, Ari called her.

"She did what?"

"I know."

"Did you know she was going to do that?"

"Nope."

Aracely was quiet. "You OK?"

Ana thought about it. "No. I don't know if I'm angry or embarrassed or what. Actually. It's all of the above."

"Well," Ari said, "I feel like shit that I'm in the middle of this. Can I pay her back or something?"

"I'm pretty sure she would refuse your money."

"So you already asked her if you could pay her back."

"Yup."

Ari sighed. "I'm bringing laundry over."

When Ari showed up, hamper in hand, Ana threw her arms around her.

"You smell like rum," Ari said. "Have you taken a shower?"

"I've been in the fetal position all day," Ana said.

"You do realize that you're having a panic attack because your girlfriend did a really nice thing for your sister, right?"

"I know it's fucking crazy!" Ana said. "I completely shut down, Aracely. She must think I'm insane. But!" she said, sticking her finger up in the air. Ari lowered it. "She crossed a huge boundary, and she kept secrets, and she lied. She treated me like a child and like she knows better, and the worst part is I doubt she realizes what she did wrong."

Ari was already putting her clothes in the washer. "I doubt it. I'm sure she's thought it through and seen it your way, and is now going crazy, because she's clearly in love with you."

"I think that's the problem," Ana said. "You were right when you said that she's definitely looking to settle down. And I don't know if I can live up to those expectations. I don't want to disappoint someone or waste their time."

"And would you be?" Ari asked.

"Would I be what?"

"Wasting her time. Would Ivy be wasting her time on you, or are you as in love with her and invested in her as she is in you?"

Ana stared at her. Then she went into her kitchen and poured two shots of rum.

"Um, it's a little early for me, thanks."

"This one isn't for you," Ana said, holding one shot aloft and downing the other. She put the second shot on her altar and pulled out her tarot deck.

She shuffled and shuffled and shuffled, trying to get the questions clear in her head. Cards started flying out, and she kept shuffling.

"Is this spiritual psychosis? Because I read about that. Well, no, I saw a TikTok about it. Should I call someone?"

"Shh, Ari," Ana said. She put the deck down and collected the cards that had flown out.

"Which one says you're being a little bitch?" Ari asked.

"This one," Ana said, picking up the Knight of Wands reversed. "And this one," she said, grabbing Strength reversed. "And this bitch right here," she said, signaling the Eight of Swords, the card that was always stalking her. Fear, fear, and more fear.

She was afraid of going broke and afraid of succeeding. Afraid of crowds and afraid of being alone. Afraid of being in love and afraid of falling out of it. None of this was new information. Fear was Ana's oldest friend. Fear was her girlfriend.

What she didn't know was how to break up with her now that she'd fallen for someone else.

"All right. Let's put the cards away and get you in some clean clothes. Mom's going to be expecting us in a few hours."

"Damn it," Ana said. "Can I call out sick?"

"You cannot call out sick from Christmas dinner. Get it together. Go shower, now."

"Jesus," Ana said. "When did you get so bossy?"

thirty

Ivy had gone over to Camila's boyfriend's house for a few hours, because she knew that if she was by herself she was going to spiral.

"Just give her a minute," Camila said after Ivy had told her the whole story. "And when she reaches out to you again, which I'm sure she will, actually really listen to what she says and internalize it. Understand where she's coming from. And then learn from this in the future before you swing your financial dick around all willy nilly." She made a flapping motion with her hands.

Ivy had glared at her, then looked over at Camila's boyfriend, Zach, hoping she'd get some kind of support from a fellow queer. He shrugged.

"You can give me that look all you want, but you know I'm right. You're in a position of being financially secure enough to not have things like this be a big deal. But that's not Ana's reality. So you made a decision for her about her life that's only based on your lived experience."

"And that probably made her feel like you don't see her experiences as valid," Zach chimed in. "Or like you think she needs charity when she's worked really hard and is just as capable as you are. Imagine how easy it would be to then think your partner sees you as beneath them in some way."

Ivy blinked at him then looked at Camila. "Look at what you've done to this man. Are you proud of yourself?"

"Yeah," Camila said dreamily. "That's mine."

Ivy didn't want to overstay her welcome, because it was Christmas after all, and she knew she was bringing the vibe down.

She decided she was going to text Ana one more time today, then leave it alone. Just to check on her hangover and make sure Ivy hadn't totally ruined her Christmas.

She shot off a quick text as she got in her car.

Then she called Rahul over her car speakers.

"I haven't even read the whole contract yet," Rahul answered grumpily.

"Oh, I wasn't expecting that you had. I was actually calling to, um, apologize?"

Rahul didn't say anything for a second. "Huh?"

"I want to apologize if I railroaded you with this. But like, you know that I had good intentions, right? I'm not just, like, swinging my financial dick around?"

"You sound like Camila right now. What is this about?"

"I did something maybe kind of stupid. But well intentioned! But maybe stupid."

"OK, lay it on me."

She gave him the lowlights of what had happened and he let out a whistle. "Jesus, Ivy. The thing with me is one thing, because even though you did railroad me against my expressed opinions against friends working together at that level —"

"I'm *sorry*," she groaned. "I still have a whole apology about that to get through."

"But for her, you haven't been together that long. You crossed a big boundary that I think any reasonable person would have known was a boundary. And I think you're a reasonable person, so on some level, you had to know it was kind of fucked up."

Had she? She maybe thought that Ana would be annoyed at first, then grateful. She just wanted to help her. But yes, on some level, she knew Ana wouldn't accept help, and she felt like she should make that decision for her, for her own good.

"I guess I can admit that, yeah. But like, I have so much. And I love to share it. People shared with me what little they had when I was starting out in my career, so why can't I do that now?"

"Because that was community care, Ivy! That was people in similar positions sharing resources, and communicating about what they need. This is you being in a position above her financially and making that painfully obvious to her. It probably felt like charity."

"Shit."

"Yeah, you're in it deep," Rahul said. "And also … did you maybe do this big thing as a way to accelerate your relationship?"

"Oh god," Ivy said. "Maybe? I think maybe I did, yeah."

"Deep shit," Rahul said.

"How do I fix this?" Ivy asked.

"That's just it," he said. "You got into this fight because you wanted to just fix things. I think you need to ask her how you fix this, not me."

"You're trying to use logic on me."

"That's how I passed the bar on the first try."

There was a pause. "So, about you and me," Ivy said.

"In the future, I want us to brainstorm business decisions together before we draw up official papers for things. I'm going to want us to be really clear on that — what needs to be a partner decision and what can be individual decisions."

"Are you saying you're going to sign?"

"I'll certainly have some amendments I'll want to make, but yes. Probably."

"I don't deserve you," Ivy said.

"Yes you do. Just because you can be kind of pushy doesn't mean your heart isn't in the right place."

"All right, man, I've gotta go think of some stuff."

"Good luck. My lawyers will be in touch."

A few minutes later, as the snow was starting to come down, Ana's name lit up the vehicle's display.

"So you're really not going to let me try to pay you back," Ana said when she picked up the call.

She was so relieved to hear her voice, but she was annoyed despite herself.

"Ana, no. That defeats the purpose of what I was trying to do. I'm sorry that I overstepped, and I want to ... *hold space* for whatever you're feeling." She was trying to talk like Camila. "But you have to know that I didn't have bad intentions. I was trying to help."

"Well. Thank you. For trying to help, and for 'holding space.' Where are you right now? It sounds like you're in your car."

"I am. I just left Camila and Zach's place. Well. Zach's place. Camila is still telling herself she doesn't live there." They both laughed. "Where are you?"

"I'm at my parents' house. Locked in the bathroom. I'm sure you can still hear the rager going on."

"Your family knows how to party," Ivy said. She was coming up on the big hill, and the snow was starting to come down thick enough that her windshield wipers weren't doing the trick. "Hey, hold on a second," Ivy said. "I'm driving uphill in the snow."

"Be careful," Ana said.

"It should be fine, I mean the tread on my tires is still pretty good. I just need to not ... lose ... momentum."

The sedan kept slipping to the right, and Ivy had to remind herself to try to drive into it and then gently correct, instead of yanking the wheel all the way to the left. But in the process of gently maneuvering it, she started to lose that earlier momentum. She tried to press on the accelerator, felt her wheels spin, and ... stopped.

"Shit," Ivy said, turning on her hazards. "Shit shit shit."

"What's wrong?" Ana asked.

"Um, I think I'm stuck."

"Oh no. Do you have AAA?"

"No, damn it, I ignored my renewal notice. I guess I could call them and reinstate it over the phone?"

"Nah, that's going to take too long and the temperatures are going to drop into the teens tonight. Drop me a pin. I'm going to come get you."

"No, don't worry about me. I don't want to interrupt your family evening. Plus, I don't want you to drive if you've been drinking."

"I had one of my mom's way too strong coquitos earlier in the evening, hours ago. I'm good. Let me come get you. I'll borrow my uncle's Subaru."

"I knew I should have gotten a car with all-wheel drive," Ivy groaned. "OK. Fine. I'll owe you big time."

"I think after this, if you find yourself feeling you owe me, we'll just call it even. Because that's a ridiculous thought."

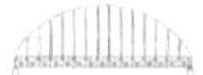

The Star — *After catastrophe comes peace.*
Ingredient — *This card means "healing" to me. The list of herbs associated with healing is extensive, and there are some you can't cook with. For example: ivy. But there are some you can cook with, like lime. I remember having a key lime pie on the menu last summer that Ivy loved. Makes me think of warmer days to come.*

Of course asking her uncle if she could borrow his SUV couldn't be as easy as letting him know what for and grabbing the keys. He had to ask a million questions, and then her mother overheard and she had a million questions, and then Aracely said she wanted to come, and her uncle said he might as well come too because he didn't want her denting his SUV. But really, they all just wanted to snoop on her reunion with Ivy.

Well, at least she'd have a lot of people to help push Ivy out of the snow if the van didn't do the trick.

Ana insisted on driving because her uncle had not stopped at one coquito, but he rode shotgun. Aracely and their mom sat in the back. Ana had tried to persuade her it would be rude to leave all her guests, but she insisted her father could handle them and complained that no one would miss her anyway, because she'd been slaving away in the kitchen over a hot stove all night, and who was going to do the dishes anyway? Her, probably. At least if she wasn't there, there was a hope of Ana's lazy father deciding to do them instead of passing out on the couch watching reruns of *King of the Hill* after everyone left.

"Yeah, OK, mami, sure, whatever," Ana had said.

"Do you think she's really stuck in the snow, or is this some ploy to make you talk to her?" Ari asked.

"I think she's really stuck. I don't think Ivy is that manipulative. We're adults. We can talk things out like adults."

"Which is why you ran out like a little bitch after she paid my tuition?" Aracely asked.

"What did you say?" their mom asked.

"Aracely is drunk," Ana said. "You shouldn't have even let her drink all those coquitos, she's not 21."

"The drinking age in Cuba is 16," Ari said.

"And 18 in Puerto Rico," Judi chimed in. "Don't change the subject, girls! What's this about your tuition? I thought it was already paid for."

The girls were silent for a moment, during which their uncle decided to have a coughing fit.

"Cover your mouth!" Ana said.

"Este es mi maldito carro, coño."

"I don't care if it's your car, I don't want your germs. I can't take time off work right now."

"ANA!" her mom shouted. "What is Aracely talking about?"

"Well," Ari said, "Ana has been helping me pay for school, and one of my scholarships was just dissolved, so she was going to have to pay more to help me cover costs."

"And you didn't ask us to help?" their mom said, affronted. "How much was it?"

"We don't have to talk about the number," Ana said, sending Ari mental daggers and ordering her to shut the fuck up.

"You didn't have to do that by yourself, Analeigh," their mother chastised. "It is our responsibility, not yours. At least you could have respected us enough to ask us to contribute."

"You already contribute so much," Ari said.

"Not just to Aracely," Ana agreed. "The amount of time you and papi put into Besos, all those trips to the hardware store, letting me live at home rent free as long as you did. You've done enough."

"I am your mother," she said. "I will always be willing to do more."

"But you didn't have to this time," Ana said. "I had it handled."

"Sounds like your little novia had it handled," she muttered — if a mutter could be as loud as a shout, which was quite a feat — and their uncle laughed before trying to hide it behind a coughing fit.

"Mami, I'm sorry," Ana said. "In hindsight, I should have let you know what was going on."

"I'm sorry too," Ari said quickly. "But look, after I graduate, you're going to have Tony to worry about. You have enough on your plate, financially."

"And we all know he ain't getting no scholarships," their uncle said. Their mother yanked his ear from the backseat and he swore.

"So Ivy paid the tuition and what? You're angry at her?"

"Yeah," Ana said. "I wish she'd asked me first."

"Oh, the irony," Judi said. "And pobrecita, you have a rich girlfriend who wants to take care of your family and support you. Que pesadilla."

"OK, mami, that's enough," Ana said, losing her patience.

GPS let them know they were nearing their destination, just as she saw the hazard lights of Ivy's sedan.

"There she is," Ana said. She had to catch her breath just seeing Ivy's car. Anything associated with her knocked her off her feet.

"Be careful getting out," mami warned as Ana put it in park. "It's slippery."

"Yes, thank you, mami, voy a tener cuidado."

She exited the van and found her footing on the slick snow, holding on to the side of the vehicle for support. She inched her way toward Ivy's car and saw her get out. She looked happy, stressed, terri-fied. Her hair glowed in the snow and streetlights like a halo.

"Hey," Ivy said, catching herself as she slipped a little. Ana caught her, too, grabbing on to her elbows.

"Hey," Ana said. "Um, you should know I'm not alone."

"Who is with you?"

"My uncle. And Aracely. And my mom."

"And the neighbor's cat? And your childhood pediatrician?" Ivy joked. Her uncle honked the horn a couple of times. Ana's mom stuck her head out the window and waved.

"Hola Ivy, cariño. Merry Christmas."

"Merry Christmas, Mrs. Fonseca," Ivy called back. "Thanks for coming to help me."

Mami nodded and kept her head out, watching. Ana cleared her throat.

"Mami."

"Si si, right. You need some privacy. To ... plan how to get the car up the hill."

"Exactly. Thank you. So," Ana said.

She was interrupted by Ari sticking her head out. "Thanks for paying my tuition even though it gave my sister a panic attack," she shouted.

"Um, you're welcome," Ivy called back.

Ana pinched the bridge of her nose before continuing. "I figure we can shovel a clearing in front of your front tires to get them unstuck, and I can get in the SUV and push your car with it while you have it in neutral."

"That's a good plan. I already did some shoveling, so we're good if you want to push."

"Oh, good. I hope it wasn't too long. You're not dressed warm enough."

"I'm OK," Ivy said. "You know, once you get moving, the exertion warms you up."

They looked at each other, not knowing what to say. As Ana was about to turn to get back in the car, Ivy spoke.

"Look, I'm sorry again about paying the tuition without consulting you."

"We can talk about this later. Let's get you unstuck first."

She got back in the van and told her family the plan. Her uncle got out of the van and walked in front of Ivy's car, to spot her in case she started to veer.

"Maybe it would be better if you got on the side of my car," Ivy said. "For safety, and also because since it's in neutral, you might be able to give it a shove in the right direction if necessary?"

"Good plan," he said.

"You ready?" Ana called through her window. Ivy gave her the thumbs up.

"OK, here goes." Ana put it in drive and eased up to Ivy's bumper until she felt the tap, and then slowly accelerated. Her uncle watched and then gave her the thumbs up and a "keep going" gesture, and Ana accelerated a bit more. They paused to check their progress.

"If you get me a few more feet, it's downhill from there and I can make it the rest of the way."

"OK," Ana called out. "Tio, I think you should get back in the car."

"You've got it," he said.

"Entonces que when we get her to her place?" Mami asked.

"Entonces we get the fuck out and leave them be," Ari said, and their mom pinched her arm.

"Don't swear in front of your mother, coño!"

"I guess it would be good for us to talk. Is it weird, if I just assume I'm staying the night?"

"I think it's probably what she's hoping for," Ari said. "I'm still not convinced this wasn't a stunt."

"Typical of a liar to assume everyone else is one," mami huffed.

"Enough," Ana said. "I don't want Ivy to feel like she caused a fight between us."

"She didn't cause any fight, you two did, you pair of mentirosas."

"OK, OK, yes mami. Please, let's drop it for tonight? It's Christmas."

Mami huffed.

Ivy's car was pulling away now, traction recovered.

"I'm good now. Thank you!"

"Wait!" Ana called out. She shut off the ignition and got out of the van, then walked up to Ivy's car. "Can I get a ride?"

thirty-one

"So, looks like I rescued you, for once," Ana said, hanging her coat by the door. Sigourney perked up at her voice and leapt off the top of the cat tree, then sauntered right up to Ana. It made Ivy's heart too full. "Hi, sweet girl," Ana said, bending down to pet her.

Sigourney gave Ivy a sidelong glance that she swore was meant to convey "Don't fuck this up, mother."

"About that," Ivy said. "You never needed me to rescue you, and I never thought you did. When I wrote that list, I was specifically thinking of situations with girls who did not have their shit even a little together. I'm talking being in the middle of a Miami club and Googling 'how to bail someone out of jail' because the girl I'd been dating was in the back of a cop car. I'm talking staying with someone who I'd been broken up with for months because she couldn't afford her rent by herself, but every audition she was going on was going to be The One. But you? I don't ever feel like you need my help or I have to help you. I just want to, OK? Because I want to take care of you like you take care of me, of everyone. Because we all deserve a little help. You do so much and it makes me worry for you."

Ana chewed her lip. "OK. Well. You can start by making me some coffee or something, because I'm fucking freezing."

"Isn't it a little late for coffee?"

Ana raised an eyebrow.

"Obviously that was a stupid question. In a second," Ivy said. She put her arms around Ana's lower back. "I just … I think I'm going to die if I go another second without you in my arms."

"Ivy," Ana said, cupping her cheek. Ivy put both her hands around Ana's face. "I'm sorry about the way I left. It's not how I want to handle things with someone I love."

Ivy blinked rapidly. "You love me?"

"Yeah. I think I do."

Their lips met, a glancing, tentative touch, and they held each other, swaying in place. "I love you, too. OK," Ivy finally said. She wiped at her eyes, not even embarrassed that she was tearing up. "Let's get some coffee to warm you up. And then we can talk."

She let Ana get settled on her couch with a blanket, Sigourney quickly making herself at home on her lap. Ivy brought out coffee for Ana and a hot chocolate for her.

"I was so scared we'd never speak again," Ivy said. "I felt like I'd said all the wrong things, done all the wrong things. Like I hadn't explained well enough how I felt about you, how everything I thought I wanted changed because of you."

"That sounds like … I don't know," Ana said, staring into her coffee like she was trying to divine her next words. "Like you had this plan and I ruined it."

Ivy shook her head vigorously. "Trying to dream up the woman who would make me happy was like trying to draw a sketch based on a game of telephone. Like trying to film an action scene in pitch dark. Any list I made was based on what had gone wrong. I didn't know until I met you how right it could go.

"I don't need a list, Ana. But I can give you one if you need one to measure yourself against. I want someone who makes the life of everyone in her orbit better, who doesn't trample anyone for her goals. Someone who loves her family while being her own person apart from them. I want someone who can see an empty fridge and turn what's there into an exquisite dish, who inspires me to be more creative and resourceful, too."

Ana had been petting Sigourney, but she had stopped, hands and face so still, except for a tiny quiver in her lips.

"I want someone who makes the time she has with people meaningful, even if it isn't as much as she wants. I want someone who is learning how to rest. Someone who can roll with the punches and who has a mean right hook."

"Someone who's been practicing," Ana interrupted.

"When she kisses me, it feels like nothing I've ever felt, better than any climactic kiss at the end of any movie I've seen, better than the first time I did a harness stunt, better than the feeling of getting the keys to the gym."

"That's a big ask," Ana said in a whisper. "Who could possibly be all that?"

"Oh, I'm not done," Ivy said. "I have one more precondition. It's a dealbreaker."

"Let's hear it."

"She's Analeigh. That's where I won't budge. You are my only nonnegotiable."

Ana placed a palm over her heart and took a deep breath. "I have my own list," she said, setting Sig down on the floor.

Ivy braced herself. Whatever Ana had to say, she would listen. Really listen. She wouldn't read between the lines and guess that what Ana really needed was something she wasn't saying, that Ivy could just fix whatever was bothering her.

"I need someone who treats me like an equal partner," Ana said. "Someone who can make big decisions with me and not for me."

Ivy nodded, rightfully chastised.

"I want someone who sees when I'm getting anxious and can help me feel safe enough to keep going, and you do that so well."

"I'm happy I make you feel safe," Ivy said quietly.

"I want a partner who tells me her goals and lets me be part of them."

"I can do that, Ana. I promise I can. I will."

"I want to be with someone who loves her friends and wants them to know how much they mean to her. Someone who can jump head-first into a dinner with my ridiculous family and take it in stride when everyone wants to dance with her. Someone who is curious and open-minded, who reads good books and can't watch horror movies without spoilers and who will have a tea party with me on a tourist bus. I want — I want you. I want only you. But it scares me. I think you're my first love. It's impractical, right? To try for forever with your first love?"

"I love you, too. And maybe," Ivy said. "But I'm not asking you for forever, not right now, anyway. I might, one day. I mean, I'm going to start letting you in on my goals more, so if I'm honest, I am definitely going to ask you for forever at a yet to be determined date if everything goes according to plan."

Ana smiled, then closed her eyes. "You know how I told you about how ingredients have magical properties? Correspondences?"

"Yes," Ivy said. "When we went to Maggie's bar."

Nodding, Ana said, "I looked up ivy the other day."

"Yeah? What's ivy for?"

Breathing deep, Ana said, "It's associated with Saturn, the planet of discipline. But also Dionysus, the god of wine."

Ivy smiled. "Work hard, play hard."

"Women carry it for luck. Brides, specifically. It's said to prevent negativity. And it's used in love charms." She looked at Ivy with desperate, earnest intensity. "I feel completely bewitched by you, Ivy. When you're around, you're like an antidote to everything that makes me anxious. But what if the spell breaks? What if you fall out of love with me? Or I might fall out of love with you. Is that a risk we're willing to take? If you want to find your future wife, is that a risk *you're* willing to take?"

It was a good question, and a few months ago Ivy would have had a completely different answer. But she was different on every level now, like a spring bloom erupting from the dirt where the past her had been frozen. "Everything has risks, Ana. We do what we can to prevent injury, but nothing is guaranteed. I don't have a script for this. I don't know how this story is going to end even if I know how I might like it to end. I just know I want you for as long as you want me back. The only question left is whether you're in, or you're out."

Ana squeezed her hand and held her gaze. "I'm in."

thirty-two

INT. AT THE GATES OF PARADISE

"Come on, just one more set."

"We're not in the gym, and you said that the last time!" Ana whined, using the very last of her strength to prop herself up on her elbows and look at Ivy.

"But it's my New Year's present," Ivy said, sounding like a petulant brat.

"People don't give presents for New Year's," Ana teased.

"Then it's my New Year's Resolution to make you come one more time. Now come on! I know you're strong and you've got this."

Ana met Ivy's intense gaze and saw the challenge there, and yeah, she liked a challenge. "Fine! But you're not going to get my best performance. I can't remember the last time I went four in a row."

"Perfectionist Virgo," Ivy chided.

"Bossy Capricorn!" Ana said, but the last syllable was drowned out by a gasp as Ivy sucked on her clit.

They'd been practically intertwined from the moment they were both off work, every day since Christmas. When they weren't pawing at each other, they were cooking together, watching movies, and having long talks in bed before Ana drifted off to the most restful sleep she'd had in years. The closer they got, the more convinced Ana felt that this could work, for real. Yeah, they were both stubborn, goal-oriented to the point of ridiculous (though Ivy was in recovery from that, to an extent), and pathological fixers who wanted to solve everyone's problems. But they were also devoted to the people they loved, passionate, creative, and idealistic. She was finding that Ivy had her own brand of anxiety, and they were learning what they needed from each other to move past the obstacles their brains would create for them.

Like the mental block Ana had about coming again, which was crumbling brick by brick, lick by lick.

"Just like that, baby," Ana said. "Twirl your fingers. Mmm, fuck, that's incredible. Keep going."

She felt Ivy's moan reverberate through her, and her hips involuntarily rocked forward, seeking more pressure. In response, Ivy licked her in big, slow circles, grounding Ana in her body, making her slow down her breathing and focus.

With one long, intense stroke of her finger inside her, Ivy undid her. The climax knocked her out, left her panting and grasping, desperate, at sheets, at Ivy's hair, at her own thighs (wow, where did that muscle definition come from?). She dug in her nails like she was trying to hold on to a ledge. The pleasure subsided enough for her to catch her breath, but the motion of Ivy pulling her fingers out of her brought another wave of sensation, her body too conditioned to arousal now. Another rush of heat and wetness and she was tugging Ivy back to her, another few licks sending her back over the edge.

"Fuck!" she cried out, the sweet relief so overwhelming that she wanted to actually cry. "Oh my god, baby. I love you. I love you so much."

"I love you too," Ivy said, finally leaving her post from between her legs and ending her torture. She curled up against Ana, not seeming to care that she was a wet, sweaty mess. She kissed her lips and her neck, nuzzling her sweetly. "I love you so much. And I'm so damn proud — that was a personal best!"

"I need a minute," Ana said. Ivy left and came back with a warm towel for Ana to clean up — a towel warmer, how had she ever lived without one? — then draped the blankets over her. "But just a minute," Ana said, opening one eye. "I have to work on your birthday cake."

"Oh baby, you don't need to put in all that work for me."

Giving her a dirty look, Ana said, "It's your 40th birthday. You're letting me make you a fantastic cake. OK?"

"OK, OK. But I still think we should take a nap first. We were out late last night."

"All right, mi viejita," Ana said, screaming when Ivy pinched her butt for calling her a little old lady.

The day before, they'd watched movies in bed and ate Little Debbies and caramel popcorn. There was something so sinful about slumming it with grocery store snack cakes when Ana could have whipped up a gourmet version or raided Besos for leftovers. But that would just mean less time in bed, so she said she was happy to slum it just this once.

Then they had attended Seth and Era's New Year's Eve bash and hadn't left each other's sides the whole night. It made Ana feel more comfortable while she met new people to have Ivy holding her hand or putting a possessive arm around her. The Times Square live stream played in the home movie theater, and at midnight, they'd kissed under the glow of the projector.

A new year, like a birthday, was a portal. Ana couldn't wait to see what was on the other side.

thirty-three

I want the sparks. The butterflies. The magic. ~~*And I deserve that.*~~ *And I have that.*

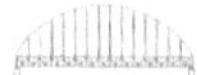

"This is 40! Swipe for a sweet treat."

Ivy had posted the photo Ana took of her stirring batter and sticking her tongue out at the camera. She'd been making them chocolate chip pancakes. The next slide was a photo of Ana eating them and giving an enthusiastic thumbs up.

They had needed that fuel for the day ahead. For Ivy's party, she was initiating her girlfriend into her friend group with their own sacred ritual — karaoke night.

Instead of their usual spot, they were trying out a new Korean-style karaoke bar where you and your group could book a private room.

Ana had clung to her arm like a koala. "I'm not going to have to sing, am I?"

"It's *Fight Club* rules," Liam said, greeting Ana with a friendly hug and Ivy with a hug and kiss on the cheek. "Happy birthday, love."

"*Fight Club* rules?" Ana asked.

"If it's your first night," Ivy said, "you have to sing."

"Don't let her give you a hard time," Era said, handing them both drinks. "Ivy almost never sings."

"Oh yeah?" Ivy asked. "Give me that song book."

Camila clapped her hands giddily. Rahul stood between Ivy and Ana, slinging an arm around each one. As Ivy reviewed songs, Rahul and Ana both chimed in with their requests and vetoes.

"OK OK, I've got it," Ivy said. "I'm not going to tell you until I'm up there. Now you have to pick," she said, passing the book across Rahul to Ana.

"What are you going to sing?" Ana asked Rahul.

"It's always Hozier or Beyoncé," he said.

"You know what? That makes sense for you," Ana said.

The drinks were flowing and the laughs were booming. Camila and Rahul sang a duet of Beyoncé and Lady Gaga's "Telephone," and then Rahul joined Liam, Seth, and Zach on "Everybody (Backstreet's Back)."

Her beautiful beloved Ana gave a haunting rendition of Olivia Rodrigo's song "Lacy," ("I just like the line about puff pastry" she confided over her cocktail when she was done), and then it was Ivy's turn.

"This one goes out to all of my wonderful friends who still take this old crone out on the town," Ivy said into the microphone as the first cheery notes of the song that opened and closed *Legally Blonde* played. "Thank you for making this a 'Perfect Day.'"

As she sang through Hoku's infectious summery pop bop in a karaoke bar with her friends, insulated from the January chill, and watching the woman she loved sing along, she'd never felt more like a star.

ONE YEAR LATER

The World — And they all lived happily ever after.

The grind of the holidays was winding down, but Ana was busier than ever.

After Aracely's college expenses were no longer an issue, she took a long, hard look at her budget. She realized that with some strategic cost-saving measures, she could make room for hiring a full-time accountant. That way, she could stop spending time on payroll and invoicing. She was also able to promote a part-timer to full time. And with Sharon back from maternity leave, things eased up a lot. Just those staffing changes changed everything. She was able to get back to the part of the job she actually enjoyed, which was the craft of baking. And she didn't have to cut benefits or hours or lay anyone off. She knew it was possible, she just needed help figuring out the details to make it work for her and her employees.

It was liberating. She was still so busy, still spent way too many hours at work, but the work was more rewarding. She was less stressed, and she slept so much better. Had she really wanted to open a second location? Wow, that would have been way too much. That dream didn't resonate with her anymore. Maybe someday she would, but for now, she was happy with one store that was causing her a lot less heartache these days.

Ana had moved into Ivy's condo six months ago. It was a tight squeeze for both of them — it took moving all the furniture in the living room twice to find a good location for her ancestor altar, and then they had to move it again because Ivy decided she wanted to honor her ancestors, too, and Ana was happy to oblige. They were going to make it work while they saved up for a place they could buy together. Another great reason for Ana to put a pause on getting more commercial real estate tying up her finances.

Priorities.

She was off today, and making use of their now correctly organized kitchen decorating Ivy's birthday cake. Ivy didn't agree that 41 was a big one, but Ana thought Ivy's existence was worth a parade if she could have swung it.

They were having the party in Seth and Era's backyard, where they were setting up a projector and screening the Keira Knightley *Pride and Prejudice* movie. Ana and Rahul had gone halfsies on paying Jason's sister's roommate to DJ, and she would be playing orchestral covers of Megan Thee Stallion and Carly Rae Jepsen all night. They had tiny champagne bottles with sparkly straws for all the guests (and little bottles of sparkling cider for the nondrinkers), plus a signature cocktail Saanvi and Maggie had put on the seasonal menu at Lost Marbles. There would be outdoor heaters and a bonfire to keep things cozy, and an incredible spread of Ivy's favorites from Besos.

But the cake was going to be the star of the show. It was a triple layer chocolate cake with Italian meringue filling, covered in white buttercream and a hot pink white chocolate ganache drip. The cake would then be topped with candies — spiral black and white lollipops, marshmallows, peppermint bark, marzipan shaped like old fashioned hard candies, chocolate covered ice cream cones, even doughnut holes. Ana couldn't wait to watch Ivy beg people to hurry up and eat all the stuff blocking her from cutting into the cake itself. What could she say? She'd been watching so many movies with her girl that she'd developed a flair for the dramatic.

She was in the middle of skewering some doughnut holes when the front door opened.

"You're not supposed to be here!" Ana shouted. "You're supposed to be working!"

Ivy walked toward the kitchen with her hand covering her eyes. "I'm not looking! I'm not looking! My personal training client canceled and Rahul told me to clock out. I'm going into the bedroom to work on that first kiss scene again. Just let me know when it's safe to come back out." Ivy had been practicing her screenwriting skills by writing spec scripts, adaptations of her favorite books, and hypothetical remakes of movies she loved. She was currently imagining a remake of *Imagine Me & You*. The sapphic rom-com couldn't be topped, in Ivy's opinion, but paying it homage was still good practice for when she eventually wrote something she wanted to try to sell.

Ana moved the cake parts in progress back into the extra freezer they'd bought. "OK, you can come out now!"

Ivy came back to the kitchen and gave her a big smooch. "I'm really excited about tonight," she said. "I can't wait to see this cake. You've been so secretive!"

"I've got a whole movie screening extravaganza planned for you, and all you can think about is cake?" Ana teased.

"You knew what you were getting yourself into when you started dating me," Ivy said. "Nothing but movie marathons and an insatiable lust for baked goods." She pretended to nibble on Ana's neck. "And for you."

"Oh my gosh, not in front of the baby," Ana said, breaking the kiss to scoop up Sigourney. "Who is the most beautiful kitty princess in the whole world? You are! You are!"

"We should get another cat," Ivy said. Ana lit up. "Since you've stolen mine."

"She's so jealous of our love," Ana whispered to Sigourney. The cat purred smugly.

Ivy wrapped her arms around Ana, kissing Sig's head and then Ana's cheek.

"Happy birthday, babe," Ana said.

"The happiest," Ivy agreed.

224

The End

acknowledgments

I'm sitting here still in disbelief that I wrote another full-length novel. It took me so long to write and release *How That Makes You Feel*, but the support from everyone who has read it so far encouraged me to keep going. So my first thank-you is to those debut readers and to you, for giving my first sapphic novel a chance.

Thank you to Meg Kennedy and Courtney Clark Michaels for always cheering me on and reading my messy unfinished drafts. My eternal gratitude to Jen Prokop, who knows exactly what I'm trying to accomplish with those messy drafts and points me in the right direction.

Special thanks to Jonlyn Scrogham and the team at A Novel Romance for curating a welcoming space for romance readers and writers. By extension, thanks to all indie booksellers who give indie authors shelf space.

Many miscellaneous thanks to Molly, Deanna, Brittany and Elizabeth. Whether it was sharing dating app horror stories or letting me talk through the yoga swing scene during brainstorming, you had a small and crucial role in developing this story.

Finally, to my beautiful love. Eric, your support of my dreams keeps me going. Raising a toddler with you is a wonderful adventure. Thank you for all the times you wrangled our kid for hours at a time so I could write. At some point I'll take a break. Maybe.

witchy recs

If you had as much fun exploring Ana's witchy side as I did, here are some of my recommendations as a real-life pagan for further exploration.

Tarot

The best straightforward resource for learning tarot is *Tarot: No Questions Asked* by Theresa Reed, also known as the Tarot Lady. I was lucky enough to get a couple of readings from her before she stopped reading for the public, and she's phenomenal. She's very active on social media and has an excellent Patreon. If you're interested in politics and astrology, her political astrology posts are well worth the cost of subscribing. Reed has written several other books, and co-created a deck called *Tarot for Kids*.

Spellwork

If you're on witchy YouTube, you know who The Witch of Wonderlust is. Olivia Graves has educational and entertaining videos on anything a beginner practitioner would want to know. She's also a prolific reader with excellent recommendations. I'm pretty sure I've heard about most of the below books from her videos.

The Elements of Spellcrafting by Jason Miller is a masterclass in how to think about magic.

The Book of Candle Magic by Madame Pamita teaches you all about carving and dressing candles, how to work with different colors and shapes, spell layouts, and more.

Sigil Witchery by Laura Tempest Zakroff takes an in-depth and artistic look at the kind of magical symbols Ana worked with in the book.

Ancestor Veneration

Honoring Your Ancestors by Mallory Vaudoise rocked my world. This book is just beautiful and vital if you have any interest in working with your ancestors or anyone long gone who you feel a connection to.

Herbs

Ana's go-to is *Cunningham's Encyclopedia of Magical Herbs* by Scott Cunningham. Cunningham wrote a lot of reference books, but this one seems to be the most popular, and it's easy to flip through and find what you need.

A newer title that also teaches you about making spell oils is *Blackthorn's Botanical Magic* by Amy Blackthorn. And Maggie, the owner of the bar Ivy and Ana visit, definitely has a copy of *Blackthorn's Botanical Brews* to reference the magical correspondences of her cocktails.

A word of caution: Because we live under late-stage capitalism and everything is commercialized and curated to an aesthetic, you might think you need to go broke to buy witchcraft supplies. You don't. You can check out pagan books on Libby or find most of them on Everand with the monthly subscription, and you can cast a spell with stuff that's in your pantry right now.

The pagan space online has some bad actors. Use discernment, maintain healthy skepticism, and touch grass regularly. Good luck!

about the author

Elle Diaz once received a well-meaning critique from a fiction professor about how she tied stories up too neatly and with a little bow. She decided to double down on that trait. Her work features messy, funny characters, and love stories that are equal parts sweet and salacious — with an HEA guaranteed. You can listen to her on Make Out Already wherever you get your podcasts.

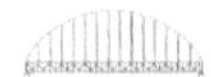

Thank you for reading! If you enjoyed this book, please consider leaving a review and recommending it to your friends. Follow the author for updates on upcoming projects, including the next book in *Seducing Steel City*.

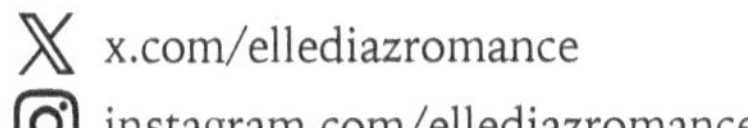

X x.com/ellediazromance

instagram.com/ellediazromance

How That Makes You Feel (Seducing Steel City #1)

And They Were Roommates – An MMF Short Story

www.ingramcontent.com/pod-product-compliance
Lightning Source LLC
Chambersburg PA
CBHW051423130726
47987CB00005B/1886